——————— TH

BLOOD IS

CW00725256

THE BLOOD IS STRONG

Richenda Francis

British Cataloguing in Publication Data
A catalogue record for this book is available from the British Library

ISBN 1 899863 22 2

First published 1989
First paperback edition by House of Lochar 1997

© Richenda Francis, 1989

All rights reserved. No part of this publication
may be reproduced, sorted in a retrieval system,
or transmitted, in any form or by any means,
electronic, mechanical, photocopying,
recording or otherwise, without the
prior permission of the publisher.

Printed in Great Britain by SRP Ltd, Exeter
for House of Lochar, Isle of Colonsay, Argyll PA61 7YR

for
Mary Kate, with love

From the lone shieling on the misty island
Mountains divide us, and a waste of seas;
Yet still the blood is strong, the heart is Highland,
And we, in dreams, behold the Hebrides

(Canadian Boat Song)

CONTENTS

CHAPTER 1

I

Kat leaned over the rail of the steamer and gazed across Oban harbour towards the open sea. Moored yachts lined the jetties; motor boats trailed blue smoke across the water; a trawler, its decks strewn with piles of nets, came chugging in from the south channel, mobbed by gulls. Oblivious of the press and chatter of her fellow passengers lining the rails and staking claim to the rows of seats above the car-deck, she concentrated all her attention towards the islands that lay out of sight beyond the western horizon.

The engines of the steamer throbbed into life: on the quay behind her, the crew prepared to cast off. She crossed the deck to watch. Massive ropes were lifted from bollards and winched inboard. The men called to each other in Gaelic. Tourists on the quay stood back and waved up at the passengers. The steamer began to move.

Excitement gave way to a curious yearning. '*A throwback, that's what you are, miss.*' She could hear her grandmother's voice as if she was standing beside her now. '*Celtic to the eyeballs, with that pale skin of yours, and that dark, dark hair. Kat indeed! Catriona Macdonald you are, and don't you forget it.*' And that was just how she felt: an exiled Celt, returning home. Catriona, Katherine: named after one of her ancestors, and as fiercely proud of her roots as any other expatriate islander.

'*Cia mar tha thu?*' She turned, startled. A man stood beside her: a priest in a black suit that was shiny with age. He was thin and stooped, with a hawk-beak of a nose, white hair and piercing blue eyes.

'I'm sorry?' His look of recognition changed to one of uncertainty as he scrutinised her.

'Well, well, what a strange thing.' He smiled, shaking his head. 'You have a look of the islands on you and I thought

1

I was greeting one of my flock.' Delighted, she held out her hand.

'That's the nicest thing that has happened to me today,' she said. 'My name is Catriona Macdonald and . . . '

' . . . you are returning to the land of your ancestors,' he finished. His grip was firm. She laughed and nodded, tucking her hair back behind her ears, and he laughed with her.

'Oh dear, is my accent so obvious? I guess you must get hundreds of Canadians all the time, disturbing your peace and claiming your ruins as their heritage.'

'A few, but they don't disturb our peace at all and they're welcome to our ruins. I'm Father John Campbell.' He leaned on the rail beside her.

'Was that Gaelic you were speaking?' He nodded.

'Yes. I'm sorry. It is still the first language for many of us in the islands, and as I told you, I thought you were a local girl!'

'My grandmother always tells me I'm a throwback. My ancestors were victims of the clearances.'

'Indeed? Poor souls. They were hard times.'

Two women in headscarves and quilted nylon anoraks came towards them, calling out a greeting to the priest: *'Athair Eoin: cia mar tha thu?'*

'Excuse me,' he said, turning to acknowledge them. 'Will you come and talk, later? It's a long crossing.'

'I certainly shall,' she told him. She listened happily to the unintelligible syllables of their conversation behind her as she resumed her vigil at the rail; it all seemed so right; so strangely familiar in spite of her inability to translate their words.

The steamer slid out of the harbour past Kerrera Island into the Firth of Lorn. On the tannoy, the skipper addressed his passengers, welcoming them aboard and telling them that the crossing would take six and a half hours. It would be choppy in the middle, he said.

She spread her map on the rail and tried to identify the coast line: Benderloch, Lismore, Kingairloch, Morvern, Mull – names she remembered from her preliminary research which now took on new substance.

The wind freshened as the steamer headed up into the Sound of Mull, plucking at the edges of the map; she folded it down to a manageable size. The sun touched off blinding sparks on the deep blue-green water; the hills on either side blazed with early-flowering bell heather among rock and turf – a patchwork of magenta, slate-grey, cobalt and emerald. And this was only the beginning; the outer isles would surely surpass even this. . . .

'Would it not be easier to start on the mainland? Sutherland, for instance, where the evictions were particularly harsh?' She could hear the voice of Stan MacIntosh, her tutor, and she remembered how she had pleaded with him to give her a completely free hand in planning her itinerary. 'You see, Mr MacIntosh, my own family emigrated from South Uist. I know I shall find it much easier to understand how it was, if I start there, because I shall feel more involved.' And she remembered his dry comment: 'All right, but don't make the mistake of getting too involved. I want this thesis to be totally objective.' Objective! How could anyone expect her to be objective in this, the most personal pilgrimage of her life.

An expensive looking yacht towing an inflatable dinghy came slicing through the water towards them on a collision course; at the last moment it turned smartly up into the wind and veered off on the opposite tack, heeled over at a sharp angle. A group of men in oilskins waved to the steamer. Kat waved back. That would be the best way to cross the Minch; better by far than in a car ferry whose cafeteria lounge carried an uneasy smell of yesterday's fried fish and chips and whose saloon bar had no portholes and smelled of beer and stale cigarette smoke. She had looked in there, when she explored the boat. Even before they sailed, the seats had been occupied by recumbent figures in various stages of anticipated misery. She was not looking forward to the moment when it became too chilly to stay on deck.

The last time she had sailed had been with Johnny . . . she waited for the usual stab of pain. . . . it didn't come. On this last leg of her long journey, something had changed. That dull ache of unhappiness that had been her constant companion for the last few weeks had gone. Was she free? Cured? Tentatively, like a finger probing a half-healed wound, she let her mind range back over the recent past. Back to the times before she'd heard the whispers of his infidelity, to when she had lived only for him. She remembered the tears, the anguish, the emphatic certainty that her heart was broken. She remembered that last, painful attempt to rekindle the flames of their earlier passion, and the humiliation of knowing that his lovemaking had been an appeasement. She tried to summon his face in her imagination. Nothing came. Johnny, the man whom she had sworn she couldn't live without, had stepped down from her heart and all she could think of now was the ugliness of his hands and the loudness of his laugh which had always embarrassed her in public and his incredible meanness with money.

She sat on a slatted wooden bench, facing aft. Release from the crushing burden of misery that had slid unnoticed from her shoulders left her almost euphoric, as if she had just been relieved of a migraine. She turned her face towards the sun and took a deep breath. A few gulls kept station alongside, swooping to grab at scraps thrown from the steamer. A flock of sheep huddled in a pen on the car deck below her. Unbelievably, in spite of her conviction only a week ago that she could never, ever be happy again, she was now so choked with happiness that she knew she was beaming like an idiot.

Most of the other passengers on deck looked like tourists; presumably the islanders were too used to the magnificent scenery to brave the freshening wind. Again she felt that curious yearning; it was a feeling of belonging, of going home. She looked no different from her fellow tourists: jeans, loose sweater, denim jacket, trainers: her knapsack was indistinguishable from the others piled in the rack outside the saloon. Her accent revealed her as a foreigner, just as did the accents of the French couple beside her, and the German family in sprayed-on bicycling shorts and the two men in green, oiled cotton jackets with brown corduroy collars, who exchanged fishing stories at the rail, in loud, stage-toff voices.

Yet somehow she had this overpowering sense of being part of her surroundings, not an outsider.

'That's Tobermory in there on the left,' said a bearded man in front of her to his companion, 'and that's Ardnamurchan Point ahead.' Kat scrabbled in the capacious, suede shoulder bag that had been her parents' going-away present, and pulled out a guide book she had bought in Oban. Ardnamurchan, she read, was the most westerly point of mainland Britain, further west than Belfast. Ardnamurchan means *the point of the pounding waves*. She stared at the rugged headland: what can it have been like before the days of steamers with stabilisers, when the islanders crossed the Minch in open coracles? How had it been when her ancestors had lived beyond this turbulent stretch of water? She dug a notebook out of her bag and wrote: Boats – what sort? Sails? Oars? Size?

The islands of Coll, Muck, Eigg, Rhum and Canna slipped astern, more familiar names from her preliminary research, and ahead lay the open sea with nothing on the horizon. The Minch: a notoriously capricious sea which had claimed so many lives over the centuries. As if to emphasise this the steamer began to pitch and roll and the waves, which until now had been gentle undulations, swelled up into an undisciplined cauldron of movement. If she was going to get anything to eat, she knew that she should do so at once, before the saloons became uninhabitable for a poor sailor like herself.

Reeling like a drunk, she clawed her way along the rails and into the cafeteria. Her stomach gave a lurch in protest as the smells of cooking engulfed her. An apple might be the safest thing, she thought, and a cold, sharp drink – fresh orange maybe. She stood in line at a counter, peering into a glass showcase full of crisps and stodgy buns and peanuts. There were no apples and the fruit juices, when she enquired, were served at room-temperature. She settled for a disposable mug of tea and carried it to an empty table under a porthole. Taking out one of her books, she tried to concentrate. The rather pedantic prose was no match for her churning stomach however and she had to give up. Looking round the lounge, she caught the eye of Father Campbell. He left his seat and came across to hers, making sideways lunges from table to table.

'May I join you for a while?' he said in his soft, lilting voice. 'I find the motion of the boat makes it difficult to read my office.' He indicated a well-worn breviary in his hand. Ruefully, she held up her own book.

'*The History of the Highland Clearances*,' he read. 'Ah! So you are taking your holiday seriously.' He thumbed through the book, pausing now and then to read. It was difficult to put an age to him; his alert attention was that of a man in his prime, but his body was old and his hands were mottled with age-spots, the fingers crooked with arthritis. 'This version was rather biased,' he told her, 'in favour of the dispossessed.'

She forgot her nausea, firing questions at him, scribbling his answers in her notebook. He chuckled at her enthusiasm.

'It is difficult for us, now, to judge impartially. You see, although there were, indubitably, many many injustices committed during those dark years, it is indisputable that a great many families finished up in considerably improved conditions.' She started to protest, to cite the cruelty of uprooting people from the only homes they had ever known, but he held up his hand. 'It is easy to be romantic now; to sing laments for the empty straths and glens, but you know, many people were starving, barely existing. It wasn't only in Ireland that the potato crops were failing. The only black houses you'll see now are folk museums, cosy as dolls' houses. They are equipped authentically enough I grant you, but they lack the damp, the stench from the beasts, the vermin and disease, the choking smoke from the fire. The waxwork model of the mother, in shawls, rocking the cradle and stirring the broth is not tormented with anxiety in case she can't supply their annual rent and must sacrifice their only cow or the meagre harvest to appease the landlord.'

'But the landlords had so much already, in comparison. Were they all so greedy?'

'Not all of them. But you have to realise how things had

changed. Before the clan system was crushed out of existence, at Culloden, the chief was the father of the clan and his clan family gave him their allegiance in return for his protection. It worked well enough, in the days when each chief could call on the men of his clan to follow him into battle. But when the need for loyal warriors was past, the chiefs, deprived of their authority, went south to London.' Father Campbell tapped her book. 'It's all in here. Men whose material needs had been modest enough, suddenly found themselves running up huge debts in extravagant living and gambling. The pathetic rents they drew from their lands in the north didn't begin to meet their new standard of living. And along came the southern sheep farmers prepared to pay thousands for sheep-walks, as they called them, on condition that the land was cleared of tenants.' He picked up the book and flipped through it, pausing here and there to read a sentence.

'When people talk about the Highland Clearances, and the evictions, they tend to see only one side of the story, and of course it is a very emotive subject. What a lot of people don't realise is that vast numbers of their ancestors emigrated entirely voluntarily for various reasons, long before their landlords started evicting them.'

'Why, for instance?'

'Religious persecution, for one thing. Many Catholics believed that they would never have freedom if they stayed. Also, after Culloden, all the Highland culture was being supressed, stamped out, discouraged. Gaelic, highland dress, all the things that set highlanders apart. That is why you find areas in your country and in the United States, where the people still cling fiercely to their old customs, the customs they brought with them. And then, of course, there was the poverty and starvation that drove them overseas. You'll have read about the kelp, I've no doubt?' She had, but she wasn't going to miss the chance of hearing local opinion.

'The seaweed, you mean?'

'Kelp was what they made from burning seaweed; it was used for many things, especially for making glass and soap I believe. It was a valuable industry until the end of the Napoleonic Wars. The landlords brought in as many people as they possibly could, paying them a pittance, to work the seaweed. It was what I think they call a . . . *Catch 22* situation.' He nodded, looking inordinately pleased with his modern idiom. 'The people had to work to pay their rents, and because they worked so hard there was not time or incentive to till the land, what little land they were allowed. So when the kelp market failed, there were all these people crowded on to tiny, sour plots, unable to pay the rent, living on potatoes. And then the potatoes failed. Many of the landlords were bankrupt by then, having sunk fortunes in the kelp industry. They had little alternative but to look elsewhere for their revenue.

'Well, I'm glad no one is allowed to go round evicting people today, just because they can make more money with different tenants in their property.' He looked at her, his head on one side – an elderly bird of prey, inspecting an offered tit–bit.

'Oh come! What about the property developers we are always reading about today. Granted, we don't hear of houses being burnt down, but there are plenty of stories of intimidation, of offers for alternative housing, of "inducements".'

She leaned forward, her elbows on the table, chin on hands. 'At least, these days there are allowances for people who are destitute, like, what do you call it, social security? Human rights, and all that. Somehow it doesn't seem quite the same.'

'But it is, if you think about it.'

'I suppose so. God, it seems so unfair!' If he noticed her expletive, he showed no sign of offence.

'Life is unfair.' He pushed the book back across the table towards her and settled back on the uncomfortable upright seat. 'It's a long time since I was talking to any visitor with such a keen interest in our history,' he said. 'Is it a book you are writing?'

'Not exactly. I'm writing a post-graduate thesis on the origins of Scottish Canadians. I've been given a grant, well, it's a sort of scholarship, to tour Scotland for a year . . . '

' . . . and you decided to start in the land of your ancestors?'

Once again he had anticipated her. She felt a warm bond between them, as if in some way she had known him all her life.

'Yes.' She hesitated, looking at him. 'Do you know, Father, I've got this odd feeling that I'm going home – not just going back to discover my roots, but actually going home.' She shook her head. 'It really is bizarre and I guess it sounds corny, but that's what I feel. I almost know what it will be like, as if I've been there before.'

'It isn't so very strange. It can't be all that many generations ago that your ancestors emigrated.'

'It was my great-grandfather.'

'There you are! You have grown up with the old stories in your ears and probably many of the old ways and customs. Of course you feel you are coming home. Indeed, you *are* coming home.' She shook her head.

'No, it's stronger than that. Almost *dejá vu*.' He shrugged indulgently, reached across and patted her hand.

'With your looks, you couldn't have come from anywhere else,' he told her. 'Your colouring and the bone structure of your face belong to the islands and that's for sure.' She knew he was right for she had seen photographs of her ancestors: her high, wide cheek bones, her thick dark hair and pale complexion that neither tanned nor burned, had set her apart from her Canadian peers with their open-air faces and blonde and golden colouring.

'Do you hold the parish records, Father? Births, deaths and marriages, and all that sort of information.'

'The Catholic ones, yes. Do you want to look up your forebears?'

'Yes.' Excitement made her clasp her hands together as if in prayer. 'If I can find the entries of their births, I shall know where they lived. It'll make it so much easier to trace what happened to them.'

'Of course. Drop by the presbytery some time and we can look them up.'

'I certainly shall, thank you. Do you come from South Uist yourself, Father?'

'Indeed I do. It is an island that always draws its people back to it, however far they stray. I go to the mainland for my holidays, now and again, to visit relatives in Glasgow, and I'm always thankful to get home again.'

'I've read that it's mostly Catholic, even now.'

'The islands to the south of Benbecula are almost entirely Catholic: somehow the Reformation never quite caught up with us. The people in the islands to the north, however, are probably the strictest Presbyterians in Scotland.' He fingered his breviary. 'But there's no animosity,' he added; 'not yet at any rate, though the media would dearly love to turn us into another Ireland.' His eyes were disconcertingly shrewd. 'And you? Did your family keep the faith?'

'Yes.' She hesitated and then gave him a rueful smile. 'Well, up to a point. My parents are very religious. I'm afraid I lapsed when I grew up.' She glanced at him, expecting to see the same shocked condemnation that her mother displayed whenever the question of religion arose. But all she saw was a kindly nod of understanding.

'It is difficult, these days,' he said, 'surrounded by so many worldly temptations.' Her mind slid involuntarily to Johnny and the days of her abandonment to his demanding body.

'These days?' she ventured. 'I would have thought that worldly temptations were around right from the start.' His laugh surprised her.

'It depends what you mean by worldly temptations,' he said. 'If, as I suspect, you mean the temptations of the flesh, then yes, of course they have been in the world since flesh was created. I'm talking of the temptations that rise from the dazzle of modern life.' The boat tilted alarmingly to one side, causing people to clutch at objects sliding about the tables. Behind her, Kat heard a moan of misery from a white-faced woman who had been lying prone on her seat since they started. 'Perhaps we are being too serious for a rough voyage.' Father Campbell pointed to her notebook. 'Who knows: when you've been about the island for a while, and observed how the people there live, you may rediscover your own faith. The modern world hasn't made much impression on our way of life – yet.'

II

It was dark when the boat arrived alongside the pier in Lochboisdale. Kat leaned over the rail, watching, while men in boiler suits and knitted woollen hats, with features so strong they almost seemed like caricatures, hoisted the gangplank up from the quay on ropes. Lamps lit the tarmac which glistened under a light drizzle, crowded with people, cars, trailers and container lorries. She listened to the babble of Gaelic as friends called out greetings and news. As she stepped ashore, shouldering her knapsack she could smell peat smoke. Walking up the path to the hotel above the quay, she passed a bedraggled sheep rubbing itself against a post. The strong feeling of familiarity with her surroundings persisted.

Her last thoughts before she fell asleep in her hotel bedroom overlooking the loch were of her ancestors. Very little was known about them and she was determined to use her free time here to unearth some record of them: of where they had lived and how, and why they had emigrated.

What little she knew had been passed down on her father's side of the family and so embroidered and embellished by nostalgia that it was hard to uncover the bare bones of fact. Her great-grandfather, Francis Macdonald had sailed from here, from this very harbour, though there had been no harbour then, just a deep-water anchorage, in August 1851. And his twin sister, Catriona, her namesake, had sailed with him. They had been twenty-three years old, the same age as herself. That was the last that was known about Catriona. From the moment when Francis disembarked in Quebec there was no further record of her. Francis had been a wild young man, so the story went, and this was where the embellishments had begun to obscure the facts. To repay his fare, he had been indentured to a farmer, but his reckless nature had led him into so many scraps that he had been released from his obligation and took to the road.

Like a stray animal, he had roamed the country, picking up casual jobs on the land and dropping them whenever he had earned enough to move on. Further embellishments gave him such a handsome face and such charm that many a Canadian lass had been willing to comfort his loneliness and many a family even now could boast a member who bore his wide-set eyes and beguiling smile. In his early fifties, he returned to Quebec and married a woman called Lucy, who had emigrated on the same boat as himself. Marriage tamed him for a while. He consented to settle down and with what money he had managed to scrape together, he bought land and built up a farm while Lucy bore him three children in quick succession, of whom Thomas, Catriona's grandfather, was the youngest. The birth of Thomas was a hard one and Lucy in her late forties, was too old to to survive it. Her death left Francis with three babies and, apparently, a broken heart from which he never recovered. The wild rover had become silent and withdrawn. Instead of learning the stories of their heritage at their mother's knee, his children grew up without any knowledge of their forebears at all. At the turn of the century, now in his seventies, Francis announced his intention of returning to his homeland. He was secretive about his purpose and was away for three months. When he returned to Canada that second time, he had been different, changed. He had shut himself away and refused to say anything about his trip. He had died, soon after, and his secrets had died with him, including the fate of his twin sister. Family tradition held that she must have died of a fever on the voyage, a not uncommon event, though a thorough search of documents had failed to produce any evidence of this.

It was not a remarkable story, what there was of it, unless it was remarkable for its lack of detail. Kat, lying in her hotel bed, staring out of the open window into a star-bright sky, thought, not for the first time, that it must be easy enough to trace the origins of people who had still been alive in this century. Her great-grandmother had died before her children were old enough to ask her questions. Her great-grandfather had chosen not to talk about his past. But she was here, on the island they had both come from, with access to parish registers and with the possibility of meeting people who might remember stories.

All her life, she had been haunted by a passionate desire to know more about her ancestors, as if that knowledge would somehow make her complete. Neither her parents nor her five brothers showed the faintest interest in the past. Her grandfather, Thomas, who had grown up speaking Gaelic had married the daughter of another Hebridean exile, Flora, and it was she who had stoked up Kat's burning need to investigate.

Sometimes, when her restless spirit came up against the solid wall of indifference presented by her immediate family, whose only interests lay in material assets and sport, she felt a great longing for the twin brother she had never known, who had died at birth without even a name to identify him.

Sleep crept up on her. As she gave way to it, she heard the sound of a sheep, rubbing its back on the bumper of a vehicle in the carpark below her window.

III

The next day, directed by a friendly waitress, Kat found a house offering bed and breakfast in the south of the island. Her landlady was Flora Kate Macdonald.

'There's a lot of Macdonalds about, my dear; as you'll soon discover.' She was a plump woman in her sixties, with toothless gums, and clumsy with rheumatism. Humour erupted from her like a ceaseless flow of lava.

The house was only two years old, built beside the family's previous dwelling which now served as the byre – a dry-stone bothy with tiny windows, rounded corners and the remains of a reed-thatched roof anchored with boulders suspended from ropes. It had had two rooms linked by a passage, with a third room no larger than a closet, behind.

'How did you all fit in?'

'It was a tight fit, right enough, but we did.' Flora Kate

had had seven children. 'It was cosy, in the winter, not like yon flimsy contraption we rattle around in now.'

The flimsy contraption was a servicable bungalow on a hillside overlooking the sea. Kat's room was built into the roof-space, with a dormer window from which she could watch the whole life of the glen going on around her, and the boats coming and going on the the loch. A vase of plastic roses stood on the chest of drawers and the orange nylon carpet had a green and blue geometric pattern that made her eyes jump. Flora Kate gave her a folding table for her portable typewriter and told her she could borrow Michael's car any time she wanted. Michael was one of her sons, absent on a fishing boat.

'But I couldn't borrow his car without his permission,' Kat protested. 'What if I damaged it?'

'Ach, away with you. Have you seen it? It's that red peril there by the old house.' Alongside an antique tractor with a bird's nest in the engine and a chimney made from beer cans, the red peril was a retired Post Office van lacking its back door. A broody hen glared out from its nest among some fleeces inside.

'Well, if you're sure . . . ?'

'It'll do it good to get some exercise,' Flora Kate assured her. 'It gets awful rusty, sitting there all the time.'

IV

Driving Michael's van proved to be a feat requiring considerable mechanical skill. As the only girl in a family of five brothers, Kat had never had to do her own engineering and now she found herself confronted by a range of controls that were kept together by string and wire, clothes pegs and old rags.

Flora Kate, who could not drive herself, initiated Kat with well practised skill.

'You pull this wire thing here, slip the peg round it to hold it, turn the key, push that pedal and at the same time flip that wee switch.' It worked. With a belch and a roar, the ancient vehicle jumped off its parking lot, slewing in the mud, and kangerooed onto the road. 'Let go the clothes peg when you reach the cattle grid at the end of the road,' shouted Flora Kate, 'and if you need petrol, don't put in more than four pounds worth at a time, for she leaks.'

When she reached the church, she found several cars already parked by the road and groups of people heading towards the sombre grey building. It wasn't Sunday; had she mistimed her visit to the priest to coincide with a funeral? No: the notice board informed her that she had merely chosen the time of the daily weekday Mass. But so many people? And not dressed up for a smart occasion but for the day's work: men in overalls, women in anoraks and headscarves, some carrying baskets. She thought of the Sunday-best congregations of her childhood: had they ever flocked to church mid-week between the milking and the shopping? Standing back, hesitating, she suddenly felt an urge to go inside with them. It was years since she had been to Mass and her motives now were born of curiosity. She had read of the strong faith of the islanders, and heard the comments of the old priest on the boat. It would be interesting to witness it at first hand. All part of her research, anyway. And why should she feel this need to justify such a natural action to the sceptical side of her mind: there was no reason why she should not attend a service in a church to which she had been baptised.

She stood at the back of the church and looked up the aisle. Above the altar, painted on to the wall and occupying the entire height between altar and ceiling, was a picture of the crucified Christ looming over the sea. The perspective of it, with the predominant head and shoulders, was presumably inspired by the Salvador Dali Christ. Though crude in comparison, with strong, almost garish colours, it had a gut-wrenching impact that hit her with such force that she gasped.

She sat right at the back of the long, narrow nave and took in her surroundings. It was a simple interior, unadorned by any of the glitzy ornaments she was accustomed to. The walls were whitewashed and stained by damp round the high clear-glass windows. The pews were narrow and uncomfortable and arranged for maximum seating capacity.

A bell announced the entrance of the old priest from the boat. The congregation stood, and the Mass began. To her delight, it was in Gaelic. The nasal cadences were music to her: she longed to be able to join in, not from any religious fervour but because to do so would make her part of the scene, not just a spectator. Listening, watching, she experienced a feeling of timelessness, as if she was participating in some primal rite that went way back beyond Christianity to the dawn of existence. It was a weird sensation.

She stayed in the church when the service was over, until everyone had gone. Then she went outside and hung about for a while, giving the priest time to disrobe. Then she went round to the door of the presbytery, joined on to the back of the church, and rang the bell.

A nun came to the door.

'Father will be with you directly,' she said. 'When he has had his breakfast.' She sounded rather disapproving, as if Kat should have known better than to call at such an inauspicious time. She ushered Kat into the parlour, a room lined with bookshelves and religious paintings, with a crucifix on a plinth on the mantlepiece, a statue of the Virgin Mary in a powder-blue robe, standing on a flower-strewn rock, holding a rosary, and shabby, comfortable looking armchairs. A peat fire burned in the grate, even in this midsummer weather.

There was a sound of distant voices, the clink of china, the smell of fried bacon. Kat sat in one of the chairs and thumbed through a holy newspaper, hoping to give the right impression when the priest saw her.

'I'm sorry to keep you waiting.' He must have gobbled his breakfast. 'Sister told me to ask if you would like coffee?'

'No, thanks.' Now she had him, she didn't want to lose his attention until her quest was fulfilled.

'It was nice to see you in the church. Did you enjoy the service?' She suspected he was pulling her leg and glanced at his face. It was hard to tell whether the shrewd eyes were serious or not: she had a feeling that he was too perceptive to be hoodwinked and decided he would prefer honesty to polite dissemblance.

'I liked listening to the Gaelic,' she said, 'and I just love that painting.' He might not approve if she told him of the queer feeling she had had, of participating in a primal ritual that had nothing to do with Christianity, let alone the Catholic Church. 'I called round to see if I could look up those ancestors of mine. You remember, I asked if it would be all right, when we met on the boat?'

'Indeed I do. All we need is some dates, and then I can fetch the relevant register. Do you know any of their birth dates?'

'There is only one, actually, Father. You see, they were twins, my ancestors who emigrated: a boy and a girl. I don't know what month they were born, but they were twenty-three years old when they took the ship in 1851.'

'So we are looking at the year 1828. All we need now is the names.'

'Francis and Catriona Macdonald.'

'Bear with me while I look out the register. I'll not be long: we haven't had such an enormous number of births on this island in the last century and a half.' He left the room, shuffling slightly on the carpet, his shoulders stooped. Kat paced the room, restless: this was a momentous milestone in her life. From the facts she was about to learn, would stem all knowledge of her roots.

'Here we are.' He held a large book, with floppy leather covers, worn at the edges. 'Let's put it here by the window, so we can see.' He laid it on a table and opened it and together they bent over the thin spidery entries, brown and faded, but easy enough to read. Father Campbell ran his crooked forefinger down the list of names. There were a number of Macdonalds, spelt in a variety of ways, but no Francis.

Kat felt disappointment extinguishing her excitement.

'Don't give up, yet,' said the priest. They could have been born at the end of 1827 or the beginning of 1829, and still have been twenty-three in 1851.' He was about to turn back the pages, when his finger shot out and stabbed at an entry half way down the page. 'Ah! What about that!' Her heart pounding, Kat leant forward and read, hesitating over the pronounciation:

'Catrìona and Prainseas Macdonald, born 3 October 1828. . .' her eyes flew to his face. 'But. . . ?'

'In Uist we use Prainseas for Francis,' he told her, smiling at her obvious pleasure, 'though they may have used the more common gaelic translation, Frangan, to address him.'

'Oh! Quick, let's see the rest.' The twins had been born to Màiri and Aonghas Macdonald, residents in the township at Rubha na h-Ordaig, Island of South Uist, on 3 October 1828 and baptised a month later. As the date sank in, Kat gave a yelp of astonishment.

'That's my birth date,' she exclaimed. 'Isn't that bizarre! I was a twin, and I was born on the same day as my namesake who was also a twin.' She started down at the page. 'I guess you get coincidences like that the whole time,' she said, slowly, glancing at him. He shrugged.

'Coincidence is a funny thing,' he said.

V

She stood, naked in front of the mirror in her room and examined herself. A suspicion, which had started as no more than a vague uneasiness, had grown in her mind until she could no longer ignore it. She was still as skinny as a boy, her stomach as flat as ever, but then, it would be, after only seven weeks. Her breasts were unusually tender, and perhaps slightly swollen, marked by blue veins she had never noticed before. She had been aware of a fluttering nausea for the past few mornings, though not enough to put her off Flora Kate's porridge. She stared at her face, so familiar and yet so unperceived. There were dark circles under her eyes, but her pale complexion always exaggerated any sign of strain or fatigue and, after all, she had endured a broken love affair, a traumatic month of frantic preparations and a long journey. It wasn't surprising, surely, if she looked rather fragile. She tried to think calmly: could she have been so careless in her last, miserable attempt to patch up her shattered relationship with Johnny?

'*Ignore it, and it'll go away!*' That had been their devil-may-care philosophy, when she and her friends had fussed over unwritten essays, or impending examinations, or unpaid bills. She made a face at herself in the mirror and pushed her fears to the back of her mind. There were far more exciting things to do than worry about something that might never happen. She pulled on her jeans and a sweat shirt and turned her attention to the day ahead.

There wasn't a cloud in the sky and Flora Kate had made up a gargantuan picnic for her almost entirely composed of starch. If she wasn't pregnant, she would certainly soon look as if she were unless she took a great deal of exercise! She spread her map on the bed and traced her proposed route out to the south-eastern tip of the island; a ten-mile round trip that would take her to the ruined township at Rubha na h-Ordaig. In her shoulder bag she took her notebook, her wild flower book, the picnic and a sweater.

'You can drink from the burns quite safely,' Flora Kate told her. 'We may be behind the times in some ways, but we don't have the pollution yet.'

At the end of the road she climbed upwards over turf and rock, through clumps of reed, bog myrtle, cotton grass and heather. The heather was not in flower yet except for, here and there, patches of bell-heather. She passed peat hags, ugly great scars surrounded by stacks of drying peat bricks. In the bottom of one, she saw a splash of vivid pink sphagnum moss. From the shoulder of the hill she looked down through the valley, along a string of lochs to a distant range of hills beyond which lay her destination. She let out a long sigh of appreciation and started off down the track, leaping the ruts, springing from rock to rock, so light-hearted that she almost believed she could fly. She stopped for breath at the bottom; she was in a bowl of moorland surrounded by receding ridges of hills. At her feet lay the first of the lochs, its dark, peaty water as still as glass, its surface dotted with water lilies. A small fish leapt a few inches into the air – she heard the plop as it landed and watched concentric circles spreading outwards.

Above the ridge of hills on her left a large bird swooped sideways on the air currents. She stared after it, her eyes narrowed against the glare of the sun. A golden eagle, she was convinced. She walked on, brushing away clouds of small flies that persisted in following her. How could anyone have left this place voluntarily, whatever the pressure applied? She would have stayed, hiding, if necessary; fighting for justice. She balanced across a slippery plank that bridged a torrent of foaming, peaty water.

It was impossible to believe that people could have been so unfairly treated, so recently. Surely some of the accounts had been exaggerated? She scoured the slopes with her eyes as she walked, looking for signs of deserted buildings. She passed a concrete base marked 'school' on her map: too recent for her needs. It must be the one Flora Kate's father had walked out to every day, barefoot, carrying his lump of peat for the school fire, and his piece of barley bread; three miles out and three miles home again in the evening, winter and summer, sun or rain, gale or snow. Flora Kate was great for the stories of the past, telling them with a relish that brought them vividly to life.

The track took her over bog; here and there her foot sank into the dark, wet peat. A wide burn crossed her path, its bridge long gone. She crossed it on stepping stones and knelt to cup the water in her hands and drink: ice cold and pure. The track skirted an arm of the sea that cut in across the moor, the beach strewn with debris enmeshed in seaweed. Ruins scattered the green pasture but these were not the ones she was seeking. She climbed again, her ankles, bare below her rolled-up jeans, scratched by sharp grey heather twigs. Panting, hot, muscles aching, she came over the final ridge and there lay her destination. A sea loch, connected to the ocean by a narrow rock passageway: a perfect haven surrounded by hills with a burn tumbling in at the head of it, and gently sloping grass round its edge.

On the emerald-green sward at the mouth of the burn, she could see piles of stones, scattered but clearly definable as ruins. She climbed down and stood among them. A skylark rose from a patch of bracken, its clear song filling the morning with exquisite joy.

She wanted to cry, to shout, to sing: above all, she wanted to share it with someone. She walked slowly among the ruins, with that ache of loss in her heart that she so often experienced.

At home, they were always teasing her for being a loner; for her love of solitude, her passion for the high and lonely places. '*You're a misfit. Always off on your own, you're so aloof, so buttoned-up. We can't get close to you.*' So had said her mother, chiding her once for not wanting to join in a family outing. And it was true, she loved more than anything else to be away on her own. But whenever she experienced this exultation of freedom and beauty, there was always this strange, secret longing to share it, as if she was mourning for someone. She had never mentioned it to anyone, not even to Johnny. Although she mocked herself for doing so, she believed it was something to do with having lost her twin brother at birth.

She found a comfortable hollow against one of the ruins and sat down. Taking out Flora Kate's picnic, she unwrapped a bannock, generously filled with crowdie. She gazed at the ruins. If only she could bring it all back to life, see it as it had been . . .

. . . a sharp cramp gripped her lower abdomen. She gasped, crouching forward, clutching the agony of it. For a moment it threatened to consume her, and then, gradually, receded. She straightened up, trembling. Almost at once, another, even sharper, pain clawed at her and as she fought to contain it, realisation struck her. She was having contractions . . . she was . . . another cramp gripped on to the one already in her, tearing her apart . . . she couldn't even cry out . . .

CHAPTER 2

'Catrìona!' She opened her eyes. She must have dozed off, sitting in the sun in the lee of the house. Waking so abruptly from sleep, she was disorientated for a few moments. She looked around, letting the scene imprint itself on her consciousness until it became familiar once more.

Of course, she was in her own township at Rubha na h-Ordaig. The house behind her was her own home, in which she had been born and brought up. Around her were the other houses with their squat, thick, dry-stone walls and thatched roofs, grouped round the burn that ran in a ceaseless, foaming cascade from the upper valley, down over rocks into the loch below her. It was a scene she knew so well that she could reproduce it in her mind with her eyes closed. The sun was hot, in a cloudless blue sky; perfect midsummer weather, with long warm days stretching into nights that were never quite dark.

'Catrìona!' Her twin brother, Prainseas, who they called Frangan, emerged from the house, stooping through the low doorway beside her. '*Am bheil thu dol a dh'éiridh?*' For a moment, his words were a meaningless babble of nasal assonance in her head; she felt a sharp stab of panic. What. . .? But then the sounds sorted themselves out and made sense to her. 'Are you going to get up?' He stood looking down at her, his face so like her own with the high cheekbones, wide-set eyes and pale complexion, framed by a shock of dark hair. He towered over her, hands on hips, bare feet brown and sinewy on the turf. His homespun breeches were patched and his collarless shirt darned and stained with age. 'I thought you were supposed to be helping with the hay.'

She scrambled to her feet, heavy with sleep; she was conscious of a slight headache. An illusive memory tugged at her mind, just beyond recall . . . something she was supposed to be doing . . . ? She tried to remember, but whatever it was slipped away and was gone. She stretched, cat-like in the sun, blinking, her head barely reaching Frangan's shoulder. On the small strips of field behind the township she could see a line of people working methodically with pitchforks, lifting the cut hay, shaking it out and turning it to dry.

'Ach, don't nag at me, Frangan. I've a headache and it's too hot for haymaking. Besides, I can't endure listening to Beathag and her constant blether, on and on about her wretched sheep. I did a fair spell yesterday, which is more than you did if I remember.' Frangan had spent much of the previous day up on the hill with their uncle, Tómas, helping him to sample the latest distillation of the *uisge-beatha* that flowed from Tómas's still whenever he could lay hands on grain. He had appeared in the evening, watery eyed and unsteady on his feet, and slept too deeply for nature, on the wooden bench in the house. Their mother, Màiri, had been so angry that she had told Tómas she would never speak to him again.

It was a bad time for Frangan, these summer months when all the younger men of the community had gone off to join the east coast drifters that had arrived in Castlebay, following the herring. Normally, Frangan would have been among the first to go and sign on for the two months they would be plying the western waters, but he had been held up by a festering wound in his arm that would have made him redundant on the boats, and by the time the poison had worked its way out of his system, the fleet had long sailed.

'You are just an idle *caileag*,' he said, dodging the light punch she aimed at his chest.

Old Peigi Campbell came toiling down the slope, a creel of peats on her stooped back, an apron over her long skirt, a woollen shawl over her head and shoulders, even in this midsummer heat. Thick stockings lapped her boots.

'Don't look, it's the *cailleach*,' Frangan said: the old woman. Catrìona and he had grown up knowing they must never look Peigi in the eye, for she was known to have the magic in her and could turn you into a slug. Indeed, if anyone passed her, on their way to take out a boat, they would return to their homes and not put to sea that day, for it was believed that she could arrange shipwrecks. She was also known to have a way with plants and could supply remedies for a variety of ailments ranging from *stopadh* – tight bowels – to *leum droma* – lumbago.

'I'm not frightened of her!' Catrìona felt her drowsiness slipping away and her usual energy returning. Anyway, Father Eóghan told me there's no such thing as witches and it's a sin to believe in magic. So!' She twirled around in front of him, doing a neat little dance on the turf with her bare feet. 'Forget the hay. Come away with me up the burn and we might get some trout.' She glanced at him, assessing his mood. Usually, she could bend his will to suit her own whims and he had never been one to go looking for routine work, always opting for adventure or intrigue. He glanced up at the haymakers, hesitating. Then he turned and faced the loch and the strip of land that separated it from the open sea.

'I'd a mind to take the boat out and try for ling,' he said. 'There's plenty about at the moment and,' he looked over his shoulder and lowered his voice, 'I've still got that barrel of salt I "found". It would be a good thing to use it up before the factor takes it into his head to come looking for it.' Frangan's life was hedged about with the need to hide the evidence of his many nefarious exploits. Indeed, it was a miracle that he had escaped serious punishment for so long.

'Well, I'm not in the mood for all those lines and hooks, so you'll just have to find someone else to go out with you.' One of Frangan's fishing lines, which he had also 'found', had a hundred hooks on it, each one a vicious barb that had to be baited and the last time she had consented to go out with him she had torn her finger badly.

'Ling is fetching a good price on the Clyde just now, Catrìona, and we are behind with the rent. Everyone else is busy at the moment. You'll have to come.'

There was always something. If it wasn't the rent arrears, it was a leak in the roof or the spoiled harvest or the cattle disease. You had to be pretty sharp to escape the endless round of boring tasks that made up each day if everyone was to survive. The last time she'd stolen a few hours holiday and gone away up into the hills to be on her own with her dreams, she had returned to find she had forgotten to milk the cow and it had trampled through the oats in its discomfort. She sighed.

'Very well, I suppose I shall have to. You collect up the gear while I tell Mother.' He disappeared round the back of the house to where he kept those things it was best to hide from prying eyes, under a peat stack. Catrìona ducked in through the door, pausing to let her eyes adjust to the dim interior before turning to the left into the room, whose only light was provided by one small window, set into a wall that was as much as six foot thick. The midden stench was powerful in the summer heat. Unlike most of the other houses in the township, they kept their beasts separate, though still within the same building, in pens partitioned off to the right of the door.

Màiri Macdonald stood over the fire in the middle of the room, stirring a pot that hung on a chain from the blackened rafters. Catrìona stood watching her for a moment, frowning. Caught in the narrow shaft of light from the window, her mother looked horrifyingly thin and frail, even with her thick woollen shawl and knitted coat and the big apron over her skirt. She was stooped over the fire, coughing as the smoke from the peat curled up towards the roof, to hang, trapped under the sods and straw until it found its way out through a hole cut in the thatch. She looked suddenly old and her hair, tied back into a bun at the nape of her neck, was already white, though she was not yet out of her forties. Her face, once so fine and strong, was now gaunt. Catrìona wanted to snatch her up and carry her out into the sunshine and sit her down on a grassy seat and listen to the once beautiful voice telling the old stories she and Frangan had grown up to. This haggard crone was a travesty of the mother who had brought them up single-handed and filled them with their spirit of adventure and their rebellious natures that had given them the courage to conquer adversity.

When you live with things, Catrìona thought, you don't notice their slow disintegration until it is too late and they fail to function altogether. It was the cough she had that was the trouble. They had all ignored it, pretending it would go away. What else could a person do, with no money, and even if there was money to spare, no access to proper medical care? The *cailleach* had recommended mare's milk as a sure cure, but it had made no difference, and had been difficult to procure, nursing mares being reluctant to be milked. Now Catrìona could see what the cough had done. She wanted to shout with frustration, but what was the point? And Màiri would reprimand her for showing lack of restraint. Forcing herself to sound natural, she stepped forward, avoiding the droppings from the hens who roosted in the rafters, the sand on the earthern floor gritty under her bare feet.

'Frangan and I are away in the boat, Mother, to try for some ling.' Màiri straightened up, easing the chronic ache in her back that was caused by rheumatism from the dampness of the house. She was still able to stand ramrod straight and never would a word of complaint pass her lips.

'If it's that salt he's trying to finish up, it'll not break my heart,' she said. 'If the factor were to find that barrel in the peat stack, it would be transportation for us all.' Màiri was not supposed to have known about the extra supply of salt, and it was a measure of how things had changed, that she did not insist they returned it to the laird's store whence it had walked.

'He did not steal it Mother.'

'Of course he did not. God forbid that my own family should ever stoop to that! But it is a thin line between keeping what you find, and stealing.'

'If the laird's fishermen are careless with the laird's possessions, and leave them lying around, it is hardly our responsibility.'

'If that particular fisherman spent less of the laird's time helping Tómas to sample the *uisge beatha* he brings down from the still he has in the hills, he might be more careful with the laird's things.' Màiri's disapproval of strong spirits led her to blame most of the ills of the township on the whisky that her brother-in-law, Tómas, spent so much of his time distilling.

'Well, if we get a good haul today, it'll need all that salt to preserve it and that will be the end of it. The Ferguson boat is leaving for the Clyde any day now and we should get enough to pay off what's owing on the rent.'

Màiri nodded. 'All right, be off with you and mind you take a shawl.' She lifted the pot and hung it on a hook higher up the chain. 'I'll have a good broth for you when you come in. God go with you.' She had had a dread of the sea ever since it had robbed her of a husband and a father for her twins, only a month after their birth, twenty-three years ago. It was, like her cough, one of the things they did not put into words. She was a practical woman and she accepted that, to survive in these hard times, she must allow her children to use the boat, but she was never easy when they were at sea.

II

There was no sign of Frangan outside. In fair weather the township boats were kept over on the beach on the seaward side of the arm of land that encircled the loch. She could hear the water from the burn, tumbling down over the rocks. She would so very much rather be up there, idling along the bank, fishing for the numerous brown trout, dreaming her impossible dreams. She hitched up her long linen skirt and tucked the hem into the waistband at the sides, leaving her legs free. She wore no petticoats in this hot weather, to hamper the freedom of her limbs, though her mother scolded her for her free and easy ways.

'I won't have you behaving like some of the other girls, they've only themselves to thank for their punishment,' she would say often enough, when news of a new scandal in the township came to her ears. The last one had been one of Ealasaid's many daughters, a vacant-eyed creature with not much sense in her head, who had led so many of the local lads astray that she was unable to name the father of the child that she carried now like a pumpkin on her skinny frame. Catrìona would laugh at her mother and dance in front of her to tease her, saying she had more sense than to land herself with a bairn and all the drudgery that went with it.

Running easily across the stones, picking her way through the bracken and reeds, she came to the top of the grassy ridge where she stopped, From here she could see down to the beach. Frangan was sorting out a tangle of lines. If she stayed up here for a few minutes before joining him, she need not get involved with the muddle of lethal hooks. Frangan had a way with him, of enticing her to take on any task that his impatient nature found too slow or tedious. She ducked out of sight and looked back whence she had come.

The township lay below her, a haphazard cluster of ramshackle hovels, crouched among stones and bedrock, on the poorest of their meagre land, chosen for its unsuitability for cultivation as much as for its proximity to the burn. Three children were playing some sort of throwing game behind one of the byres; their thin voices came up to her, laughing and calling. A haze of peat smoke hung over the roofs, seeping out through the thatch, filling the air with its acrid smell. It was her home and she knew every stone and corner of it, and she knew as well as everyone else who lived in it how impossibly insecure was their right of tenure.

Right of tenure! That was a flight of fancy: in truth, they had no rights at all for they were not even cottars, though they did pay rent, and were merely tolerated because this corner of the island was too remote to attract the incoming sheep farmers who were leasing the laird's more accessible pastures. Thus it had been, for three precarious generations, ever since her own great-grandfather had led them here. She looked down at her house, slightly larger than the others, with its few distinctive features that set it apart; small differences that reflected her ancestor's previously elevated social standing. Outside there was the other small window that made it different; none of the other houses had windows. Inside, with the partition between themselves and the beasts, and the few sticks of crude furniture that had been constructed over the years, their house was sumptuous compared with most of the others, where owners shared the same room with their animals, living at the upper end of a sloping floor so that the midden fluids ran away from them out through a hole in the wall. The other houses contained no more furniture than driftwood planks, barrels and box beds, whose wooden ceilings were essential to protect their inhabitants from leaks in the thatch and droppings from the poultry which roosted in the rafters.

She mused, as she so often did, on what their lives would have been like had her notoriously pugnacious ancestor, Aonghas, not stood by his convictions and refused to be dominated by his landlord-kinsman, Macdonald of Boisdale.

Aonghas had been Boisdale's close cousin and tenant, having previously been dispossessed as tacksman to Boisdale's half-brother, Clanranald. As tacksman, leasing his land at a nominal rent, he had been responsible for supplying soldiers for the chief's army whenever called upon to do so. After the disastrous defeat of the Jacobite rising in 1746 however, no chief would ever again have a need for soldiers and so the position of the tacksman as recruiter was obsolete. Boisdale took the land in feu farm and Aonghas became his tenant.

Aonghas then sublet his farm to a number of cottars, but unlike many, he had had no reluctance to work on the land himself and he had, so it was told, always been a just landlord. That had been a hundred years back. Then, after a ridiculous squabble with the priest over ordering his men to work on a holy day, Boisdale had turned his back on the Catholic church and taken upon himself the Protestant religion. In itself, that would not have been too much of a problem for his people: indeed Clanranald himself had become a Protestant, but was known still to be sympathetic to the old faith. Boisdale, however, filled with all the single-minded zeal of the convert, had not been content with just his own change of heart. He was determined to inflict his new beliefs on his tenants.

Catrìona had been brought up on the stories of what had happened: of Boisdale's attempts to change the lives of his people. For a while they had gone along with him with good-humoured tolerance, taking no heed of his rantings but without antagonising him. He was, after all, their landlord. But then he had gone too far. It was discovered that he was undermining the authority of the Catholic church and arranging for the children to be taught heretical practices. It was even rumoured that he had forced some of the children who shared his own children's tutor, to eat meat on a Friday.

Aonghas stormed in on his cousin and confronted him with this heinous crime. It was perhaps a story that had grown more powerful with the telling, over the years. Boisdale stood his ground. Aonghas threatened him. Boisdale shouted that if his cousin continued to thwart his actions, his lease, which had almost expired, would not be renewed. Aonghas drew himself up to his full height and faced Boisdale. He would rather live as a pauper, free, than be tenant to a heretic, he said. He flung his plaid around him and stalked out. Within hours, he led a column of his cottars away from their homes, a straggling crowd of people, herding their animals and their poultry along with them. They carried their few possessions on sledge-like carts and on what horses they owned: precious roof timbers, meal and potatoes and seed for next year's crops. It was fortunate for them that the month had been November and the harvest all gathered and stored, but winter conditions made the establishment of their new township very hard.

There had been some fifteen families in all, in that defiant procession of refugees. They had come out here to an uninhabited wasteland that had been thought too isolated to have been settled before. Officially it had been common land, so by appropriating it the little community virtually had become squatters. They had lived for a while in daily dread of Boisdale's revenge, but because of their remoteness, they had been too far away for him to bother with and the land too poor for him to want it for anything else. As time passed, also, he mellowed and became more tolerant of the faith he had abandoned – with an eye to the fate of his immortal soul, some said.

And so they had stayed and cultivated what soil there was, making narrow strips of field wherever they could and creating *feannagan* – lazy beds – for their potatoes in all the barren pockets among the rocks.

Adopting Aonghas as their leader, this little outlaw band had managed to create a self-supporting community, making no demands on anyone and causing no trouble that might bring them to the notice of their landlord. For Boisdale was still their landlord although it was common land, and Aonghas insisted that they paid him rent in the hope that they might thus establish some sort of security. This rent they had paid with grim determination, year after year, in kind – meal, animals, wool, – or in the few pounds they were able to earn at the fishing and the kelp.

Apart from the rent, they had needed little money in their self-sufficiency. Aonghas himself had taught the children to begin with and there had always been a good replacement teacher in each successive generation. And each generation had also its quota of young people who went out from the township to learn new skills or take to the boats and sail to distant lands, returning with enough tales to enlighten the long dark hours of winter. There was plenty of fish in the sea and the poor soil on their scanty fields produced rye, oats and barley, a little flax and of course their staple food – potatoes. They had hand-querns to grind their grain for the bread which were kept hidden away, for the miller at Smerclete was empowered to destroy hand-querns to ensure his multures. They did whatever building or joinery was necessary themselves. The women spun and wove the wool and flax, and made all their clothes and bedding. There was a crude kiln for the firing of their clay pots and Anndra had an anvil for the smithying. What they couldn't manufacture themselves, they did without. And little had changed over the hundred or so years that passed since Aonghas's self-imposed exile from his more prosperous lands.

A hard existence, Catrìona thought, watching the bustle of

life below her as the people went about the tasks that made up their daily struggle for survival; hard, but free. Independent. Even now, with a laird from Aberdeenshire who had bought the island in 1838 when she was a child of ten, and who had made many changes and turned hundreds of people off their crofts in order to make way for more lucrative tenants, the little township at Rubha na h-Ordaig had somehow escaped notice and managed to live as before.

As she stood there, a man came into sight on the far side of the loch, striding along the upper path that led from the track down to the township. There was something familiar about the way he moved. She narrowed her eyes, shielding them against the sun's glare. It was impossible to see his face at that distance but she did not need to; she knew only too well who it was. She stood very still, watching that familiar, loping stride; then she turned and ran down to the beach, out of sight beyond the ridge, to where Frangan was heaving the boat over the stony sand to the water.

He had loaded the lines, the mast lay ready to hoist, lug sail attached, oars adjacent. In a pail lay the putrid remains of a chopped-up conger eel, waiting for her to bait the hooks. She added her weight to his and the boat slid into the water. She climbed aboard, nimble as a monkey, wet to her knees, and crouched in the bottom ready to raise the mast. Frangan gave a final mighty shove, swung himself on board and grabbed the oars. He rowed them out from the shallow water, nodded to her and she heaved the mast upright, secured the rope and adjusted the sail. A light breeze filled the much-mended brown canvas lug and the boat pulled away, wavelets slapping the wooden hull.

'I think Ruairidh Campbell is come home,' she said, casually, her fingers busy sorting out the lines. Frangan, his hand on the tiller, looked ahead beyond her shoulder, watching for the white turbulence on the sea where the water washed over a barely submerged rock that was the fishing ground they were seeking.

'That'll set some hearts fluttering,' he said. 'I can think of several who had long faces when he went away.' There was no irony in his voice. She knew well enough that it never crossed his mind that his twin sister, his *alter ego*, could possibly cherish romantic feelings for any man. As far as he was concerned, she had him and that was quite enough. She refrained from comment.

Frangan stood up, released the sail, furled it and took up the oars.

'Right now, get the line over the starboard side,' he ordered. She dropped a line securely tied to a heavy stone weight over the side, paying it out till the weight touched the bottom. Each of the vicious looking hooks attached to the next part of the line must now be baited with a lump of the eel. With a grimace of distaste, trying not to breathe in too deeply, she threaded each stinking morsel on to its hook and paid it out over the side. When the last of the hundred hooks was baited and disposed of and the second weight with its marker buoy thrown over the side, she leaned over and washed the slimy muck from her hands.

'Eeuch! How I hate that job,' she groaned. It never occurred to her to refuse to do it, however, for the boat was heavy and she was not strong enough to keep it in control with the oars, an essential part of the operation if they were not to foul the line or get caught in the hooks.

'We might as well get some pollack for the house, while we are waiting,' Frangan said. While Catrìona would have been perfectly happy to sit and dream as the long line made its catch, Frangan was incapable of inaction. He let the boat drift away from the buoy and they fished with lines attached to traces of hooks decorated with hen's feathers. The boat rocked easily on the swell as they fished, watched by a family of puffins who bobbed close by, unperturbed by their presence. As in everything else they did together, they worked as a well-trained team, their movements synchronised to avoid any muddle or tangle of gear.

Between them they hauled up a couple of dozen good sized pollack. Then Frangan, never content to stay at one occupation for too long, hauled in his line, winding it on to its wooden frame. 'That's plenty,' he said, 'let's get the long line up now.' He heaved at the oars with all his strength, to row them back against the tide. Watching the muscles bunching on his arms and thighs and neck, Catrìona smiled. He never did things by halves, Frangan, not even the simplest, day-to-day tasks. He reminded her of one of those sudden squalls that sometimes blow up on a calm day, whose progress you could watch as a dark turmoil racing across an otherwise smooth sea. He rushed through life like that, giving all his energy in brief spurts and then losing interest and dashing off to something else. He was bored with the fishing, now, she knew, and would hurry them through till they were finished. Perhaps he had an assignation for later in the evening: he had been paying attention to one of Beathag's girls, Liùsi, recently and Catrìona had not failed to notice a decidedly come-hither gleam in her bold eyes, though she was barely sixteen. None of Beathag's daughters had a reputation for chastity in spite of the tight rein she tried to keep on their lives.

Frangan held the boat steady on the oars; Catrìona reached out, grabbed the buoy and began to haul in the line. Standing in the bottom of the boat, legs braced, she pulled it up, hand over hand, peering down into the water to see if they had caught many fish. As the hooks rose towards the surface, she saw the silvery shapes, dancing around the line, and felt them jumping and jerking.

'There's a good number,' she gasped. 'Are you ready?'

'Of course; get on with it!' It was always an exciting moment, however many times you did it, when the first fish broke the surface, and it required perfect team-work to get each one into the boat without tangling the line or getting caught by one of the flailing hooks. With a mighty heave, she brought the first long, eel-like ling in over the side, fighting furiously. While she held the strain on the rest of the line, Frangan grabbed the slithering body, yanked it off the hook and into the creel, and clipped the hook onto its cork retainer. Only then was it safe for Catrìona to bring in the next hook. Side by side they worked, keeping up the rhythm, muscles aching, until the whole line was neatly coiled round its stretcher and the wicker creel satisfyingly full of fish. As well as ling, they had caught a number of ugly dog-fish, a few cod and three haddock. The dog-fish twitched and flexed among the limp bodies; they always took a long time to die.

'That'll take care of the rent arrears at any rate,' Frangan said as they set the sail and headed in towards land. 'I'll take them across tomorrow.'

'And how will you explain away having a surplus of salt when there's been such a shortage, may I ask?' She wasn't really concerned: Frangan had a rogue's luck and a jaunty disregard for authority. Somehow, he always managed to talk himself out of trouble.

'By making sure that nobody challenges me,' he retorted. 'I shall go over on the morning tide and have that catch stowed away on Ferguson's boat before the factor or any of his precious men have tasted their porridge.'

Impatient though he was by nature, Frangan was far too well trained in subsistence not to finish off every job he undertook. When they had the boat safely beached, the fish had to be gutted before they were ready to be carried up to the house and packed in the salt. By the time they had completed this operation and thrown the guts to the voracious gulls who appeared as if summoned by some avine bell as they started the messy work, the sun was low on the western horizon.

'Let's bathe,' Catrìona said, looking down at her hands, dripping with fish-slime. 'I smell worse than the bait pail.'

'There's not much point for me to wash till the fish are into the salt,' Frangan replied, heaving the creel on to his back. 'You stay; I'll go on up.'

'If you've plans for a moonlight walk with Liùsi, you'll need to get a good scrub yourself when you've finished,' she taunted, leaping out of reach as he aimed his foot at her, 'though I daresay she's not over particular.'

The twins had not been told, until they were ten years old, that their father had drowned, not from any storm, but because he had fallen overboard while tending his nets, and, in common with practically every other islander, had been unable to swim. Catrìona could remember very clearly how shocked she had felt. *Why don't people swim?* she had mused, to Frangan. *'It can't be difficult, if animals can do it. Dogs don't sink, nor horses, nor cattle, nor sheep, so why should we?'* Frangan had grabbed the thought with his usual quick enthusiasm. *'Just think, if we could swim: we could go over to the near islands and hide there. We could play all day and no one would be able to make us do the things we didn't want to do.'* *'But how would we learn?'* *'Let's take the dog and watch what it does.'* And that was what they had done. Without Màiri's knowledge, for she certainly would not have allowed such a thing, they had gone off to a bay out of sight and watched closely as their dog rushed in and out of the water, retrieving a stick of drift wood. *'It paddles its legs,'* Frangan said. *'That's all it does.'* He had plunged into the sea, up to his chest, and without any sign of fear, lifted his feet and paddled frantically with arms and legs. And he had stayed afloat. Catrìona had been considerably more cautious to begin with, but within only a few days they had both become entirely at home in the water and able to swim out of their depth. Their worst obstacle had been the extreme cold of the water. When they demonstrated their new ability to the other children of the township, they had become celebrities. The more adventurous of their contemporaries had demanded to be shown how to achieve this new dimension and it was not very long before their community became known as 'The Swimming Folk'.

Frangan set off up the beach with the fish. Catrìona waited till he was out of sight and then, glancing round to make sure she was alone, she pulled off her shirt and skirt and stood shivering slightly in the evening air. Throwing back her head, she lifted her arms and reached out towards the setting sun. The glowing sky filled her with a primal yearning that she often felt when faced by the beauty of her island home. She was disturbingly conscious of a curious stirring in her loins.

She ran down the beach into the water, submerging completely in its icy depths, gasping at the cold, exulting in the freshness of it. She washed herself all over, hair and skin, rubbing herself with a handful of ribbon-weed whose jelly-like surface made excellent soap. Back on the beach she stood, dripping, scooping the water off her boyish body with her hands. She squeezed the water from her long, thick hair, wringing it out like washing, and scrambled into her clothes. Her shirt stuck to her small breasts, showing her nipples erect with cold.

As she stooped to pick up the box of fishing lines Frangan had left for her to carry, she noticed a movement out of the corner of her eye. She straightened up and scanned the cliff top. She saw the back view of a man, rapidly receding from view, dropping out of sight below the ridge before she could identify who had been spying on her.

Angry, she stamped her foot. It was not that she minded particularly, having no reason to be ashamed of her body, but it was irritating to know that one of the men had, as it were, taken advantage of her without her consent, and, more annoying still, without her knowing his identity. How long had he been there, watching her?

She pushed the incident out of her mind. It was far too perfect an evening to spoil with petty feelings. She crossed the beach, trailing her bare feet in the sand, and climbed towards the ridge. Half way up, she stopped and sat on a rock and let the tranquillity of the scene soak into her bones. The strange, poignant yearning persisted – half joy, half sadness – an ache that made her want to cry. *'You're too dreamy, that's your trouble,'* Màiri scolded her often enough. *'You let your mind go wandering off all over the place and you never concentrate on what you are doing. You'll dream yourself away to some distant land, one of these days, and the wind will change and you'll find you can't get back!'* Màiri never had time for daydreams, using all her energy to provide for herself and her children.

Catrìona was restless this evening. And she knew that her restlessness had been caused by the return of Ruairidh Campbell whom she had not seen since she was a hot-blooded girl of eighteen, five years ago, in the autumn of 1846.

CHAPTER 3

Memory came in flashes so vivid that she could see the quizzical lift of his eyebrow and the lean tautness of his body and the wild disorder of his crow-black hair. And she could smell the damp sourness of the room in his parents' house and hear the moan of the wind in the reed thatch and the cracked misery in his voice the day she had last seen him.

He had always been different from the other boys in the township and had come in for a fair amount of teasing, which had left him unmoved. It wasn't that he had been weak – far from it: indeed he had been as tough as a raw-hide thong, capable of scaling the most dangerous cliffs for gulls' eggs and had had a deadly aim with a catapult. But while his contemporaries were content to follow the well-trodden paths of their fathers, spending their days in drudgery on the land and their nights in horseplay and conviviality, he had fretted against the monotony and spent long hours off on his own pursuits.

She remembered a barren hillside in winter. She was thirteen, a skinny slip of a girl not yet grown to woman-hood, lagging behind the other girls of her age who were burgeoning into pubescence with sly jokes behind hands and whispered confidences out of earshot of parents. Catrìona had no interest in their prurience and spent more and more of her time on her own in the high and lonely places she loved.

This day she had climbed the hill to look for lichens for her mother's dyeing. There was a particular silvery one she was seeking, that gave a deeper tan colour than the others. The wind was coming out of the north-west, carrying with it all the bite of the ice floes it had kissed on its way. She stood facing into it, letting its freezing particles sting her skin. She thrived on extremes of weather, always seeking the most exposed viewpoint when the Atlantic gales battered the western shore, or the sunniest corner in summer.

She held her woollen shawl wrapped closely round her and laughed into the wind, letting it lift her hair and stream it out behind her. Then she spread her arms so that the shawl billowed like wings. She felt she was so much part of the elements that she could almost fly.

'Be careful, Catrìona Macdonald; remember what happened to Icarus!'

She spun round, her laughter frozen, her cheeks smarting with cold.

'Ruairidh Campbell! You shouldn't creep about like that!' She pulled the shawl round her again, embarrassed to have been caught in one of her private moments. She hardly knew Ruairidh, except as one of the young men in the community. He was nearly twenty and their paths seldom crossed. 'And who is Icarus anyway?'

'I would hardly describe it as creeping. Icarus was a foolish boy who thought he could fly. His father made him wings and stuck them on with wax. He flew too close to the sun and that was the end of Icarus.'

'Because the sun burnt him up?'

'Because the sun melted the wax.'

'Oh!' Ruairidh was full of that sort of knowledge. His father, Mìcheil Campbell, had once earned his living teaching the children of the richer folk further up the island, but he had had a strong sense of justice and a burning ambition to change the imbalance of social privilege. He had spoken out against the unfairness of the landlords in the way they treated their tenants, and he had incited the people to demand their rights. His fiercely rebellious spirit had led to his eviction from a decent croft on the west side and he had removed his family to the community at Rubha na h-Ordaig. He it was who had been responsible for the fact that most of the children in the township could now read and write after a fashion and speak English. Ruairidh himself, more at home with books than on the end of a *cas-chrom*, the 'crooked-foot' foot plough they used on the tiny fields, was hoping one day for a scholarship to a university on the mainland.

Impervious to the icy wind, in just a wool shirt and leather jerkin, over his breeches, he struck a chord of recognition in Catrìona, who sensed a restlessness of spirit in him that matched her own and that none of her contemporaries shared.

'If I made wings, I'd have more sense than to fasten them with wax,' she said. 'I'd tie them on with rope. What are you doing up here? I thought Frangan said you were all off to cut tangle for the fields?' He made a face at her, his eyebrow shooting upwards, his eyes sparkling with fun.

'If you ever have to spend a day in February up to your thighs in the sea, cutting seaweed with a blunt toothed *corran* you will understand why it is sometimes necessary to find some other task when the men go off to the islands.' Indeed, she knew only too well, having listened to Frangan often enough, for the boys went with the men from an early age. 'If you come with me, I'll show you what I'm doing,' he added, 'though there's some who might tell you it hardly qualifies as an excuse not to be helping with the tangle.'

He led her further up the hill to an abandoned peat hag, a great dark maw, with pools of water in the bottom. He leapt down, agile as a cat, and scrabbled with his hands in the *caorain dhubh* – the crumbled remains of broken peat that had been left behind, too small to bring down in the creels.

'Look!' he called, 'what do you think of that!' She stared down. He was flourishing a skull in his hands: unmistakably, a human skull, greyish, with peat embedded in the eye sockets. 'Isn't he a beauty!'

'But . . . who . . . ?' Incomprehension made her feel stupid. Should she know whose remains these were? He climbed up out of the pit and stood beside her holding out the skull for her to inspect. She touched it with her finger but did not take it from him.

'I'm going to take him down to show my father,' he said. 'I think he may be thousands of years old.'

'How can you tell?' There was something uncanny in the thought of this man having been up here all those years ago.

'I can't, but the fact that he was in the peat means he could have been here for an awfully long time. Don't you long to know what was it like here, then?'

It was just the sort of speculation that intrigued her. 'Yes, and what was he doing to die and be left up here?' It was difficult to picture any other age than her own. Ruairidh adopted a mock sepulchral voice:

'I think he was up here, hiding from his wicked brother who wanted to kill him so he could inherit their father's croft. But his brother found him and slew him with an axe, leaving him to the hoodie crows.' She shuddered.

'Poor man, like Cain and Abel. Perhaps this was the wicked brother who the good brother killed!'

'Could be, or the father, slain by both his sons.' She giggled; people of her own age would never play guessing games like this.

'Or maybe he was just an idle fellow, who wouldn't help the other men cut the tangle. He came up here pretending to be busy and fell into a peat hole and drowned.' Ruairidh tweaked her hair.

'Don't be impertinent,' he said.

Among other vivid memories she had kept in her head all these years, was one of coming upon Ruairidh one fine spring day when she was about fifteen and had been sent out to the *feannagan* – lazy-beds – where the men were preparing the soil for the potato sowing. She was carrying a pail of *deoch mhineadh* – spring water with oatmeal stirred into it – to refresh the labourers, for 'lazy' was a solecism for the back-breaking work that went into the construction of the *feannagan*. As she came up the track, swinging her pail and humming to herself in the warm spring sunshine, she could see the men bent over their spades, digging up the dark peaty soil in tiny plots, tucked into every possible hollow among the rocks. Creels of seaweed littered the ground, waiting to be spread as fertiliser before the seed potatoes were planted.

And there was Ruairidh, squatting on his haunches by the path, staring down at the ground with an intensity of concentration that stopped him hearing her approach till she stood right by him. When her shadow fell across whatever it was he was looking at, he waved her impatiently aside.

'What is it?' she asked, and then her eye was caught by two metallic black beetles who seemed to be locked together at their heads.

'Stag beetles, fighting,' he hissed. 'Very unusual to see them here. Look at their antlers!' He was completely absorbed, a million miles from the digging men behind him.

With the good natured lack of criticism that was inherent in the nature of the islanders, no one seemed to care that Ruairidh was more likely to have his nose in one of his father's books than his hands on a spade. It was not idleness but temperament. *'If it was up to that boy alone to work their land, the Campbell family would have starved long ago,'* Màitri used to comment. And then, when Catrìona was eighteen, he had won his scholarship to go and read Classics at the university in Edinburgh. He had a wide knowledge of Latin and Greek, having grown up under a father who had filled his head with learning and it was the priest who had suggested that his name be put forward as a possible candidate.

II

He had gone in the spring of 1846, for the examination in Edinburgh, at the expense of the township, all of whose families had dipped into their near-empty purses to finance his journey. She could remember so clearly the day he set off, sailing across the bay with his father to catch the boat down to the Clyde. It was the first time she had looked at him with a woman's eyes and something had stirred, disturbingly, in her heart. He had gone right round the township, clasping all the eager hands, thanking each family for their generosity. Dressed in a new suit, spun, woven and stitched by the women, his tanned face alight with excitement, his eyes dancing with vitality, he had kissed Màiri on the cheek, shaken Frangan warmly by the hand and then, with a smile, he had hugged Catrìona for a moment and said in her ear:

'Spare a prayer for me, my little fellow truant, I'm going to need it.'

Confused for a moment, she had just managed to murmur: 'God speed,' before he was gone.

It had been an unusually mild spring that year, with nature unfurling its shoots and buds too early, and then perishing in a later spell of cold. Ruairidh was away for a month or more and when he returned, his scholarship secure, it was with worrying news of a potato murrain that had already devastated Ireland and was even now sweeping the mainland.

'It won't get out this far,' Frangan had predicted. 'How could a blight cross the Minch?'

How indeed! The summer brought the worst drought in memory, withering the grass and drying the springs that fed the burns and wells. There was an unreality in the shimmering, sun-scorched days that spread anxiety over them all and filled Catrìona with a sense of foreboding.

Since his return, she had become ridiculously shy of Ruairidh, avoiding him when she could because she didn't know how to handle her new awareness of him. He seemed not to notice, treating her still as he had when she was a young girl, in the days when she had reacted with the innocent ease of a younger sister. Now, her senses stirred in a most confusing way, she couldn't meet his eyes and felt agitated most of the time.

Once, when the priest had ridden out with his assistant to say Mass in the township and they had all gathered on the hillside, Catrìona had looked across to where the men stood, heads bowed, hands clasped, and encountered a look from Ruairidh that made her heart thump. It was an intent, searching look, almost as if he was seeing her for the first time. When he caught her glance, his eyebrow went up and it was his normal, quizzical expression again. After that, though she still avoided him, it was with a sneaking wish that he would seek her out.

Then the drought was broken by violent storms. The parched ground became waterlogged, forming great pools and swamps that made any outside task impossible and rotted the feet of the sheep. The mud and rubble that was packed between the inner and outer walls of the houses, for insulation and to help hold them together, oozed and swelled with the rain that poured from the thatch. Depression hung over the township, as oppressive as the low ceiling of cloud that disgorged its moisture in an apparently ceaseless flow.

When the storms passed and the clouds rolled away, the sun shone down on a new land. What little grazing they had for their few animals at Rubha na h-Ordaig was verdant and, better still, after the rumours of blight, the potato haulms in the *feannagan* were lush and green.

But the relief they celebrated with laughter, dancing and song, with stirring tunes from Tómas's pipes and lengthy epics from the Bard, was only to last for a few days. In August, came the sickening answer to Frangan's lighthearted response to the first report of the potato murrain. How could a blight cross the Minch!

III

It came on the wind, wafted across like particles of dust in the still rain-moist air: invisible spores of fungus, floating in on the early morning mists, silent and deadly. One evening, the potatoes were healthier looking than they had ever been. The next morning, when the *cailleach*, old Peigi, went up to look for a lost ewe, she came almost running back down, her rheumy eyes wide with shock.

'The *buntàta*' she gabbled: 'the potatoes. All spoiled. It is the devil himself has come to punish us!' The people streamed out of the houses and ran up to the *feannagans* with Peigi raving behind them. And it was indeed as if the devil had vomited out some ghastly foetid spume all over the year's crop. The haulms were black and withered into glutinous ribbons of slime.

'It can't have reached the tubers yet,' cried Tómas, 'we can dig them up and save them yet.' His rich voice gave them hope as someone ran for a spade. It was Frangan, so confident that they were out of reach of the deadly spores, who snatched the spade and plunged it into the soil. There was a moment of hushed expectancy as he levered up a clod and sifted through it with his fingers. Then, with a grimace of disgust, he held up a tuber, its skin wet with a putrid excrescence that stank of evil.

'Holy Virgin! We shall starve!' Peigi threw up her arms and screeched in terror. Everywhere people started to dig: you could almost hear the frantic prayers . . . Please God, let my *feannagan* have escaped.

Catrìona, standing back, watching in fascinated horror, was suddenly aware that Ruairidh was beside her, also looking on, a grim expression on his face. She felt his hand, gripping hers for a moment, as if to give strength.

'This will be a disaster,' he muttered. 'This is the worst thing that could happen to the island. How can I go away and leave my own family to starve?' She stared at him, all her recent shyness forgotten.

'Surely it isn't as bad as that?' she said. 'There are other things to eat than potatoes.'

'Not much,' he said. 'Look at our fields. All we have room to grow are potatoes and so little else that our meal chests are seldom even half-filled after the harvest. What can we eat in the winter, when there are no fish? We can slaughter the beasts, one by one, until we have none left and then what? And without beasts, how can we pay the rents?'

'But other people will have rye and oats and barley, out on the machair where there is good soil. Everyone will share: it is the nature of our people.'

There was bitterness in his eyes as he looked down at her. 'Don't you know what has happened over the years?' he scolded. 'Ever since Clanranald discovered that kelp would pay his debts?' He was still gripping her hand. She glanced down, and he released it, leaving the imprint of his fingers on her skin.

'I know that when Clanranald was the laird, he brought in a lot too many people to work at the kelp,' she said. 'And I know that folk up the coast have been crowded into smaller and smaller holdings to make more land available.'

'Yes. But not only have the machair lands been divided and subdivided so much that there is barely room for one family to build a house, let alone grow grain, even worse, the kelp workers had to labour such long hours that they had no time to tend what little lands they had.' His voice rang out, harsh and angry. 'Their wages were so low that they could barely exist, yet they had to work the kelp because their holdings were too small to support them.'

'But surely, by the time Gordon of Cluny bought the land, six years ago, the kelp work had finished long ago.'

'Indeed. But the people were still there, with their mean plots. You can't grow oats on a strip of land no bigger than a plaid. If you were to go up the island and look at all the other townships you would hardly find a handful of any sort of grain. If this murrain has hit the whole island, as it surely must have done, then I'm afraid it will be a hard winter for everyone.'

IV

The physical effect of the blight was not felt immediately, for the potatoes would not normally have been harvested until October so there was still food to eat. But the unbalanced weather that had dominated the year and provided ideal conditions for the fungus spores to travel and flourish, caused other problems which offered a more immediate threat. The rain, falling on parched ground, had swept all the accumulated debris into many water supplies: discarded refuse and the juices from middens were washed indiscriminately into springs and water holes, with the result that many people fell ill. Typhoid epidemics erupted throughout the island, adding to the misery that prevailed.

Ruairidh's father, Mìcheil, was found on the hillside, wandering in a sick delirium. Raving mad, with the fever in him, spouting out long texts from some Latin book he had been reading. They carried him down to his house and Ruairidh and his mother nursed him and would let no one else near for fear of spreading the disease. And then his mother had taken the illness herself, within twenty-four hours only and still Ruairidh would let no one else risk infection by coming in to help nurse them. It was one week before Ruairidh was to go to Edinburgh to start his studies.

'They are both so ill that I believe they may not recover.' Ruairidh came to the door of his house to accept gruel for them, from Catrìona, sent by Màiri.

'Let me come in and help,' she said. 'I could maybe wash your mother and make her comfortable.'

'No!' He put out his hand as if to ward her off. 'Thank you. There is no need for anyone else to catch the disease.' He looked haggard: his usually cheerful expression frozen into lines of anxiety.

'There must be something I can do.' She wanted, desperately, to help. The thought of germs was unintimidating. If God wanted you to die, then die you would, however much you protected yourself. Her own aunt, her mother's sister, had refused to go outside in the rain last year for fear of catching cold and had died in her bed from a seizure.

'Even a trained physician could not help them now, I think,' he said. 'But there is one thing you could do. Could you ask Frangan to go for the priest?' His eyes avoided hers in his wish not to upset her. 'They would like that.'

'Oh Ruairidh! Do you really think . . . ?' But he shook his head and put his hand on her shoulder for a moment. She heard the sound of human distress from inside the house.

'I must go in to them,' he muttered.

'Yes. I'll go and find Frangan at once.'

But by the time Frangan had been retrieved from the shore where he had been mending fishing gear and dispatched on one of the township's skeleton ponies and by the time he had ridden as far as Bornish and found the priest and returned with him, it was all over. They had died within hours of each other, ruptured and torn apart inside by the violence of the disease. The priest said prayers over their bodies and then went out into the open and said Mass for the township who waited for him on the higher ground, a forlorn group of people whose faces reflected the anxiety each one felt for their chances of survival over the coming winter. The women, wrapped in their shawls, wept for themselves as much as for Ruairidh's parents who were now beyond the need for sympathy. The men, bare heads bowed not only in prayer but to hide their feelings, must each have been preoccupied with thoughts of how they were to find food for their families during the hardest of the winter months.

Màiri had invited the priest to take a meal in their house before setting off back. He sat on the bench, holding a bowl of broth, thickened with oatmeal, his thin, tired old face weathered by the storms he had endured over a lifetime of trying to serve people who clung to a proscribed religion and language.

'What will happen to us, Father?' Màiri asked. 'We have managed to survive out here, all these years, a burden to no one, raising our children to be useful to their country if only they were given the chance. Now we face starvation and we have no means to combat it.'

Others who had come in to be near the priest, murmured their agreement. 'What can we do to save ourselves Father?'

'Many people are talking of joining those who have emigrated over the last hundred years,' said the priest, handing his bowl to Catrìona and accepting a piece of barley bread. 'They talk of a good life over the sea; better than the life here at any rate.'

'But even if we wanted to leave our homeland, how could we pay our passages?' Tómas's deep voice boomed out. 'We haven't the price of a boll of meal among the lot of us.'

'I believe there are offers of assisted passages. I have heard tell of some folk getting loans which they repay when they have established themselves in their new lives. Indeed, in the past, when the lairds have wanted to clear their lands for the sheep farmers from the south, they have even offered to pay the fares themselves, in some cases.'

'But who wants to go!' Eilidh, timorous and tearful. 'This is our home.'

'For some, it is the lesser of two evils,' said the old man, getting up. 'I cannot advise you. It may be that you, out here, will manage to keep going. Your conditions are superior to those of many of the other townships where they live like penned animals, so cramped are their dwellings and so meagre their holdings. You don't have much land, I know, but you have space to breathe.'

Ruairidh himself laid his parents in coffins and the men of the township carried them away to the burial ground and dug the two graves and gave the responses to the prayers intoned by the priest. None of the women went out, for it was not the custom, but they prepared a wake for the return of the men, in Màiri's house which was the biggest.

Tómas handed round a flagon of *uisge-beatha* and faces glowed red in the firelight. Ruairidh was gaunt, hollowed eyed, grim-faced; but he made the effort to respond to the sympathy of his neighbours and as the fiery spirit took effect, the feeling of doom made way for the warmer suffusion of nostalgia. The Bard recited a long poem about a time when they would all meet again in heaven: Beathag keened mouth-music, taken up by the other women, filling the crowded room with an unearthly cadence that seemed to hang in the rafters with the peat smoke. Màiri, whose voice had once been the best in the township but was now cracked by hardship, sang a well-loved song which reminded Catrìona of other, happier times when they had gathered to celebrate rather than to mourn. There were tears in her eyes as she listened, unable even to hum the refrain. Ruairidh stood near by, and she glanced at his face and saw naked anguish. He was going across the loch tomorrow, to board the boat that would carry him away. What was left here to bring him back? There was desolation in her heart.

V

'Will you take these stockings across to Ruairidh Campbell,' Màiri had said, in the morning, holding out a pair she had knitted for Frangan for the winter. 'Tell him they are a gift from me and he's to mind and keep warm and dry on the boat.' Catrìona took the bundle and went out. Cloud hung low over the township; the water of the loch looked grey and sullen and she had to jump to avoid stepping on a bloated dead rat that lay in her way.

The door to Ruairidh's house stood open and she went inside. At first she thought the room was empty, but then, through the dimness, she saw him. He stood near the rack of shelves that formed a dresser, built into the rough wall. He was holding a book, his head bowed over it as if he was straining to read the page but then she realised that he was weeping. She hesitated, uncertain whether to creep away or stay. Guided by instinct, she moved forward to catch his attention. He raised his head. With an exclamation of anguish he dropped the book, flung his arms round her and buried his face in her hair. She held him for a long time, soothing him with gentle hands. The room was bare; no trace remained of his parents, nor even of himself. What few possessions he had that were not tied into the bundles he was taking with him, were packed into the meal chest for shelter from the dampness that would pervade the house once it was deserted and fireless.

Gradually she felt the tension go out of him, but still he clung to the warm security of her arms. She felt entirely maternal. Eventually, he disengaged himself and stood back, his eyes searching her face. She reached out and brushed his cheeks with the back of her hand, wiping away the tears.

'I'm sorry,' he muttered. 'Not a very manly exhibition I'm afraid.'

'Don't be foolish. Why should the expression of grief be confined to women? Here. These stockings are from my mother. She says you are to keep warm and dry on the boat.' He took them.

'She is so kind, your mother.' He held them up. 'Poor Frangan: I daresay he'll be a pair short this winter!' He was himself again.

She bent and picked up the book he had been weeping over. It was a collection of poems. He took it.

'Catullus,' he said. 'My father's favourite. He gave me this the day before he took the sickness. I told him I couldn't possibly take it and he said . . . you take it, and when you have finished your studies and are a rich, famous professor, you can give me a new copy.' His voice faltered.

'He was so proud of you. They both were.' And now she had to take her leave of him without showing her own distress, because the thought that he was going away and she might not see him for years was almost more than she could bear. She hardly knew him and yet she felt almost more in tune with him than with Frangan. She held out her hands. 'Goodbye' she said. He took them in his, stared down at her for a moment and then, very gently, kissed her on the corner of her mouth. She stood quite still, longing for him to take her into his arms and prolong the embrace, but he dropped her hands, stood back, and smiled.

'Goodbye, dear little truant,' he said. 'I shall think of you, out there on the hillside, spreading your wings and dreaming your dreams instead of helping the other women with the crofts.'

VI

For a while, after he had gone away, Catrìona was desolate. But she was young and full of vitality, and gradually the memory of him faded, though it never vanished. Now and then there would be news of him from travellers. Not long after his departure, they heard that he had abandoned the Classics and was now studying medicine instead.

He would make a fine physician, Catrìona thought: he cared so deeply about things.

And now, he was home. After five years. Why? He had not finished his training, she knew that. He had nothing here, except the shell of a house, patched up by his neighbours and used as a spare byre in his absence. He had no family here; he had been the only child of his parents and what cousins he had had emigrated long ago.

She got up from her perch on the rock and walked slowly back home. Passing Tómas's house, she heard a burst of male laughter followed by the hum of voices and then more laughter. And then she heard someone calling out Ruairidh's name. The men were obviously having a welcome home gathering in Ruairidh's honour; no doubt there would be some sore heads in the morning. She heard no women's voices and knew that her presence would not be appropriate and had no wish to join them anyway: she was shy of seeing Ruairidh again, for one thing and besides, the men got so silly when they started in on Tómas's *uisge-beatha*. Frangan would be in for another scolding from their mother.

CHAPTER 4

I

Catrìona tossed restlessly in the box-bed she shared with her mother, trying not to disturb Màiri in case she should start her coughing. She heard the sound of voices on the night air, muffled through the walls, as the men made their way home from Tómas's house. There was a scuffling in the doorway and she heard Frangan, stumbling in, cursing softly as he tripped over the milking stool. Fortunately for himself, Màiri was still in the deep sleep that comes before the lighter sleep of dawn, for he was no match for her scathing tongue when he was silly with drink. Catrìona grinned to herself in the darkness. She dared not whisper a greeting to him and lay listening as he rootled around in the darkness and flopped into his own box-bed, no doubt without even removing his breeches. Within moments, it seemed, the room resounded with the vibrations of his snoring. Still Màiri slept on.

Catrìona could neither sleep nor relax; her mind raced like a boiling cauldron, her body was tense, her skin itched. Finally, moving with controlled stealth, she climbed out of the bed and tiptoed across the room, past the fire, damped down for the night and smouldering, past Frangan, now rumbling gently and hunched on top of his heather-filled mattress; past the dog who opened one eye, stirred and lazily thumped its tail on the earthern floor. She eased the door open and stepped outside. All the township lay bathed in the green light of the moon, the humped roofs crouching like sleeping cattle. She leant against the wall of the house and took deep breaths, forcing herself to relax. Gradually the peace and the beauty of it soothed her and she felt calm. It was never quite dark at this time of year; she could see the gleam of the loch and the contour of the hills.

Here, in the old days, her grandfather used to sit on a

bench against this very stone she was leaning on. She could remember his stories so clearly – the *seanair* – who had been born not so long after the battle at Culloden, and who had grown up in the terrible times that had followed. Life had been easy enough before: her great-grandfather, Aonghas, he who had been tacksman to Macdonald of Boisdale, had raised his family on tales of the past, the good times when the clan system had still existed, patriarchal, feudal and successful. Within their clan, every member had claimed kinship with the chief and bore his name.

'*He could call on any of us, at any time, to go to battle with him,*' the old man used to say, sitting here with his pipe, upright and proud. '*Young Clanranald had not the time to call on the Uist men, when he went off to join the Prince, so it was mostly his people from the mainland that he took. But if he had called on his islanders, they would all have followed him. As it was, they stayed here, and everyone of them was loyal to the Prince when he came here to hide, though the price on his head would have kept a family for life.*'

It was a story they had heard over and over, they and all the other young people who used to gather round the old man when he was in the mood, and they never failed to beg for it again. The story of when Prince Charles Edward Stuart had come across to the islands to hide, before he'd fled back to France. She and Frangan used to act it, as children, playing out the desperate scenes with light-hearted enthusiasm. Frangan, of course, played the Prince, while she played the part of her ancestor, Flora. Frangan's portrayal of the fugitive in the cave had been a masterpiece of courage and pride, though they had always used the cave in the hill above the township, not the one in Glen Corodale where the prince and his followers had really hidden. That was too far to go for an afternoon's game.

They had never carried their acting games further than the poignant farewell between the prince and Flora, in a hotel parlour in Portree. Frangan, every inch a prince, with the price of £30 000 on his head, bowing over her hand and murmuring, 'Madam, farewell. Who knows? For all that has happened, we shall meet at St James yet.' That had always been the finale to their game; to them, that had been the end of the good times. They found no romance in the sad skulking of Young Clanranald, or of his escape to France with his new wife, disguised as Mr and Mrs Black. The old ways had gone: crushed out of existence with the lives that had been spent at Culloden. An exasperated and ruthless government had seized the opportunity to abolish forever the power of the clan chiefs, whose arrogant disregard for parliamentary law had been such a thorn in their flesh for so many centuries. Young Clanranald, once so daring and brave, had allowed himself to be seduced by the glamour of London society. Fêted by the highest of the land, dispossessed of his tartan, his sword, and his partiarchal rights, he turned more and more to the attraction of the gaming tables and the dance floors. Stories crept back to his island people, so that when he came up to his estates, he was eyed sullenly by the people who would once have greeted him willingly as their chief.

Catrìona moved away from the houses, down to the shore of the loch. Choosing a rock above the mouth of the burn, she sat, pulling her shawl round her. In only her shift, the night air was cool, but she preferred to be out here with her thoughts, not trapped in the airless bed with her mother. She wished her grandfather was still alive. She could not miss her father, named Aonghas after her great-grandfather, having never known him, but the old man had been such a central figure in their lives and she missed his quick humour and his endless fund of stories of the past and of how life had been when he was a lad and a young man.

There had been the false prosperity of the kelp boom, before the eighteenth Captain of Clanranald sold his lands, and precious little justice there had been in that for the workers. Her own father and grandfather had been involved, like most others, slaving all the daylight hours, cutting and processing the seaweed for impossibly small wages. During those years of peak profit to Clanranald, at the beginning of the century, he had imported more and more people, settling them on tiny plots of land, kept deliberately inadequate to support a family so that they were forced to supplement their incomes by working at the kelp.

'*It was not an easy life,*' her grandfather told them during the long winter evenings round the fire in the room, when everyone gathered to reminisce and hear the old stories. '*We would be out there in all weathers as long as it was light enough to see, men and boys and sometimes even the women. We would be cutting the tangle, wet through, maybe, and if the place was far from the township we would be sleeping in some damp hovel there, to be up at dawn. We would be living on* deoch mhineadh *and shell fish from the rocks. And when the weed was cut it would be burnt at the kilns to make the kelp that was keeping Clanranald from the debtors prison.*'

Catrìona stretched out her bare foot towards the water that tumbled over the rocks into the loch. That had all been before she was born, before the government lifted the import duty on foreign stuff that was cheaper than kelp, killing the market. By the time she and Frangan were of an age to learn, all that was left of the once thriving kelp industry, was a bankrupt Clanranald, chief in name only to an island crammed full of people, with no work, insufficient land and no prospect of betterment.

'*It would have been better for us,*' her grandfather used to say, '*if we had gone with that first ship in 1772, to Ile de St Jean. My father, your great-grandfather, he that was the tacksman, had the chance to go with Captain Macdonald of Glenaladale.*'

'*Why did he not go, Grandfather?*' They knew all the answers, but loved to hear them intoned in the old man's compelling voice.

'*He did not go because he would not leave his homeland. Captain Macdonald, who was at Culloden, said that there was no security left for Catholics and that is why he went. But my father would not believe that Macdonald of Boisdale, his kinsman, would let his people be persecuted for their faith. He was wrong, of course, and Boisdale became violently opposed to the Catholics, evicting them if they refused to follow his heretic ways. And that was how, as you all know my father lost his position as tacksman and why we came to live down here in poverty and hardship, no longer sharing the privileges we once enjoyed. And, more important, that is why we are free, today, and will continue to be so as long as we continue to pay the rents.'*

Now she let her mind wander back to the subject that was the main cause of her sleepless night. The return of Ruairidh Campbell. Five years is a long time especially if you are young and passionate. She had enjoyed several amorous flirtations and now and then her body had yearned to give way to the ardent demands of her suitors, but she had never allowed herself to be lured off to the remoter places where other couples strayed during the long light summer evenings. She had never been sufficiently fond of anyone to be prepared to risk losing her freedom in one of the hasty marriages that took place every autumn.

From time to time, stories had drifted back, via the travellers, of Ruairidh's success with women. A rich widow, a beautiful dancer, a pretty little tavern wench; each of the stories had brought her acute pain, which faded over the weeks as pain always does. The worst had been a rumour that he was about to have to marry the daughter of a local official. Perhaps that was why he had come home: to collect up the rest of his possessions and settle his affairs.

A clink of stone on stone brought her out of her reverie. She looked up, unalarmed, for there was no danger here in the township. A man stood watching her from across the burn, a shadowy figure in the undark night. The moon lit his features, showing the gleam of amusement in his eyes, the humorous mouth under the crow-black hair and the curiously cat-like grace of his lean, hard body, in breeches and a shirt. And she heard his voice again for the first time in five years, a deep voice, as familiar now with English, no doubt, as with Gaelic, and still with that slightly ironic inflection, half teasing, when he was not being serious.

'Miss Catrìona Macdonald! Waiting for the *each-uisge* if I'm not mistaken.'

'Ruairidh Campbell, as impudent as ever! There is no such thing as a *each-uisge* and well you know it,' she retorted, keeping her shawl close about her skimpy shift. He came across the burn on the exposed stepping stones and sat on her rock beside her. She could sense the laughter in him.

'Indeed you are wrong. I know very well he is real: the water horse who changes into a handsome young man at night and comes to make love to all the pretty girls.' His proximity unsettled her. She stared ahead, all too aware of his eyes on her profile. 'Do you know his weakness, the water horse?' He taunted her. Of course she knew, but she said nothing, worried about what Màiri would say if she were to wake and come looking for her and find her so immodestly clad in the presence of a man. 'He likes to have his head rubbed. When his chosen victim runs her fingers through his hair to please him, she feels the bits of seaweed and the grains of sand, and then she knows that at daybreak her lover will turn into a savage water horse and drag her into the loch.'

She tossed her head, and turned to look at him. 'It's the *uisge beatha* that has your tongue,' she taunted him. 'I was passing Tómas's house, earlier.' She peered at him through the half light, trying to assess whether he was as befuddled as Frangan had been. She heard his chuckle of amusement.

'It's possible to enjoy a drop or two of your uncle's medicine without losing your grip on reality,' he said.

'Reality! And you talk to me of water horses!' she mocked him. 'So, if you are not drunk, city ways haven't taught you sense, even after all this time,' she said. 'I'd have thought five years learning to be a physician would have knocked the nonsense out of you.'

'Five years! Have you been counting, little Catrìona?' His voice was full of amusement.

'Why should I count?' she retorted, 'though I could name you many who did. I happen to remember that it was near Frangan's and my eighteenth birthday, in October 1846, when you went away, that's all.' She wondered, uncomfortably, how much of his departure he himself remembered, and whether any of that final day had meant as much to him as to her. Of course he would by now have let himself forget that moment when he had wept in her arms and she had held him like a child. Nor was he likely to remember that kiss, so light and yet, to her, so intimate that it had stayed with her all this time.

She was conscious of his shoulder, close to hers. This Ruairidh, gently mocking her in the moonlight, was quite a different man from the one she had carried in her heart all these years, his lithe body honed by poverty and hard work. She had no doubt that he would have seen and experienced things way beyond her imagination and that he would regard his native land and people as lamentably ignorant and unsophisticated. Passionately, she wanted him not to despise them for having remained the same.

'You have grown up,' he said. 'But not so much so that you have given up being a mermaid, I'm happy to see.' She remembered the man whose back view she had seen from the beach.

'So it was you, Ruairidh Campbell, who was spying on me this afternoon!' she cried. He laughed and she was glad of the dim light that hid her easy blush.

'I swear I did not mean to spy on you,' he said. 'In fact I had gone up on the cliff to enjoy the view that I've missed so much over the years. Truly I had no other intention. I came over the brow and there you were.' He didn't sound too apologetic.

'How long were you there?' she demanded, 'watching me.'

'Just long enough to know that it would be honourable to turn my back,' he retorted. She felt his hand on hers for a moment. His voice was low, no longer laughing. 'Don't be embarrassed, Catrìona. I'm sorry.'

She muttered some sort of acknowledgement. 'How long are you home for?' she asked.

'Until October. I have to study for my final examinations next year.'

'Why did you not come back before?' she asked, regretting the words as she spoke them, knowing she sounded plaintive.

'Ah! Did you miss me then?' He was laughing at her again.

'Certainly not! What makes you think anyone would miss you when there's plenty of other men on the island.'

'Indeed there are, but not one of them has managed to lead Miss Catrìona Macdonald to the altar, I'm told.' So! He had asked about her. No doubt there had been plenty of ribaldry, earlier in the evening when they had all been swallowing back the *uisge beatha* in Tómas's house.

'I have no intention of spending the rest of my life slaving for any man,' she retorted, flouncing. 'And I suppose, that with all those fancy city women we've been hearing about, you never had time to feel lonely or homesick.' He chuckled, obviously delighted to have won such a reputation.

'What terrible tales have you been hearing? Did the priest never tell you not to listen to gossip?'

'We heard you might be getting married,' she muttered, dreading the moment when she must face the knowledge that he was irretrievably committed to some other woman.

'Married!' His shout of amusement rang out and she felt a stab of relief. 'I don't know where that came from. I have no intention of marrying anyone for many a year to come. Apart from the fact that I've not met any woman in the city who has tempted me to give up my freedom, I have barely enough money to feed myself with, let alone support a family.'

'Oh.' She flashed a quick look at his face, a pale blur in the moonlight. 'And what about all those women they say you've been seen around with.' Even to her own ears her voice sounded childish and petty.

For a moment, he was serious. 'O Catrìona, you can have no conception of how homesick one can be in a city, how lonely among those crowds.' All at once she saw again the young man, weeping in her arms and she wanted to comfort him in the same way.

'I think I can guess a little,' she said gruffly. She tried to dismiss, once and for all, the parade of flashy women who had peopled her imagination for so long. 'So, why didn't you come home before, if you were so homesick?'

'Money.' He said it lightly, but she read bitterness in his

voice. 'My scholarship doesn't give me enough to live on and buy all the books and equipment I need. I have to do manual work in the summer holiday to earn enough to last me for the year. I usually go down to one of the farms in the Borders.'

'How will you manage next year, if you aren't earning now?'

'I was lucky. I wrote various things for periodicals and newspapers, and I've been commissioned to do a series of stuff that will pay me better than any farm work. I thought I could come back here and study and do my articles at the same time.'

'Why did you give up the idea of reading Classics?' she asked. 'You seemed so set on it.'

'I think it was when my parents died that I changed direction. I felt so angry that there was no proper medical care for them. I daresay all the physicians in the world could not have saved their lives, but it seemed to me such a waste of two good people, dying so young because none of us knew what to do for them.'

'Do you like living in Edinburgh?' she flipped at the burn water with her foot.

'No; it is worse than hell. I live in the oldest part of the city where hundreds of people crowd together in tenements that should have been demolished years ago. They live like maggots crawling in a piece of cheese. The poverty is dreadful, and the disease. Everywhere there is corruption and despair. The people are unfriendly and cold, and there is a biting wind round every corner that cuts you in two. We talk about the bad living conditions here, but truly we live in paradise compared with the poor quarters in the city.'

'How can your bear it? I should go mad if I had to live like that without any of this.' She spread her arms to embrace the peace and beauty of the sleeping township, quickly folding them again when she remembered the scantiness of her apparel.

'I put up with it because the work I do and the work I shall do when I am qualified is more important to me than anything else in the world.' He spoke with such emphatic conviction that she knew, with a stab of dismay, that indeed his vocation would lead him through life and would surely keep him away from his native land. Intuition told her that any woman who loved him would have to forsake everything to follow him. She stood up.

'I must go back before my mother wakes and comes looking for me.'

'She would most certainly not approve, if she is still the Màiri I remember,' he commented, the laughter back in his voice. Standing, he reached out and touched her cheek. 'You look like one of those sea-nymphs in the stories.' She felt his fingers smoothing her hair back behind her ears. 'Have you come out of the loch to seduce me, little mermaid?' For a moment she thought he was going to kiss her and she knew if he did that she would not stop him. Then, seeing his grin, she twitched herself out of reach, breaking the spell.

'Certainly not,' she snapped. 'Don't flatter yourself.' She turned and left him, very aware of his eyes on her back, on her bare legs below her shift. She sped away back up to the house, hearing his laughter long after she was out of earshot.

CHAPTER 5

I

The township was stirring into life when Catrìona came down from the pasture carrying her milking stool and pail. It has been an effort to wake up, after her disturbed night, but once outside, the fresh air and the walk up to find the cows had restored her vitality. Having milked the two cows, she had lingered, basking in the warmth of the sun, lulled by an elusive contentment she could not quite explain. The early mornings were almost the best time of day when the light had a particular clarity and the air an intoxicating zest that gave her a feeling of omnipotence.

In her childhood, when there had been more beasts and more land, the women and children used to move up to the *airigh* – shielings – for the summer weeks while most of the men were away on the herring boats. This practice had given the young crops, growing in their unfenced rigs close to the township, a chance to mature without the threat of trampling feet and snatching teeth. Now, they drove the beasts out by day to wherever they could find fresh pasture, sometimes trespassing on land that had once been their own common grazing and had now been leased to a sheep farmer from the Lowlands. They took turns to watch over them, driving them back to the houses at night. If word came that the shepherds from the south were on the prowl, they fettered them with a rope *buarach* and let them feed nearer the growing crops.

She could well remember those long summer days in the upper pastures, when the women had had little to do but watch the animals and make butter and cheese with which to pay the rent. The first task on arrival each summer had always been to repair the tiny huts that were their temporary shelter, built of stones and turf. The children would be despatched to collect fresh heather, bracken and rushes for the roofing and bedding and Màiri used to offer a reward to whoever brought in the biggest load, usually a newly cooked pancake from the girdle, lavishly spread with honey from the three hives communally owned by the township. When it rained, which it frequently did, they would cram into the huts and sit close, telling stories and singing the old songs. The earthy humour of people who had endured every sort of hardship and still managed to see the funny side of life was infectious and the children learned, at an early age, the fine line between malice and wit. It was in those days that Màiri had been the most popular personality among the women, leading the songs, telling the best stories and the most amusing jokes. Respected for her integrity, she had also been admired for her warmth and kindness, her sense of fun and her sharp intelligence. That had been before her cough had claimed her vitality. Catrìona sighed: she remembered those times as holidays, vibrant with laughter, when no one had seemed to have any worries and when, as children, they had been unaware of any feeling of insecurity. It was then that she had first started to go off on her own, wandering away into the hills, lying for hours in the heather, dreaming and letting her mind explore new ideas: ideas often germinating from conversations with Ruairidh.

Ruairidh! She was all too aware, this early morning, of his presence, somewhere down there in the township, still asleep maybe, or perhaps already away on one of his solitary rambles.

Peat smoke hung over the houses as people blew up the embers of their fires. Here and there she could see figures busy about the day's tasks. Beathag stood in her doorway, her massive bulk swathed in a huge apron, her sleeves rolled up over arms like tree-trunks, her head tied in a kerchief. Even her voice, as she called out a greeting, was gargantuan. Beathag's enormous girth was nothing to do with greed: who could be greedy when there was barely enough food to go round and plenty of physical exercise needed to produce it? She had some disease for which there was no known cure.

The shepherd Beaton, whose family were known to have healing powers through the use of herbs and who had been employed throughout the islands for generations had tried several of his potions on her in the past, but with no effect. Beathag had a personality to match her bulk, and kept her flock of children, each as thin and waifish as she was colossal, in firm control.

' 'Tis a wonder you managed to be up so early, with the late hours you keep Catrìona Macdonald,' she boomed, her eyes twinkling with shrewd provocation.

'It's never difficult to get up on a morning as fine as this,' Catrìona retorted, refusing to be stung into a sharp reply that would set Beathag rumbling. To be sure, you couldn't sneeze in this place without the whole township knowing about it.

Frangan was waiting for her, near the peat stack.

'Did you get that barrel of fish across to Ferguson's boat in time?' she called. He shook his head, grinning wickedly at her.

'I did not. Such a disturbed sleep as I had, what with you creeping around like a ghost all night, that I missed the early tide. I shall go over tonight.' She made a face at him. Was anything ever private in this community?

'You were fairly noisy yourself, last night,' she retorted. 'How could anyone be expected to sleep with the din of your snoring? I daresay you'll be suffering from a sore head this morning?'

'Not at all. Do you want to come across in the boat with me this evening, to take the fish and visit the inn?' As she hesitated, knowing that Màiri did not approve of her going into the inn, he added: 'You need not, unless you want to. Ruairidh said he would like to come so I shall have company anyway.' Unlike his sister, he hated to be on his own. With most of his contemporaries away with the herring boats just now, he would be claiming Ruairidh frequently as his companion, for as long as he was home, no doubt!

'I might,' she said, trying to sound off-hand, knowing she would be there whatever Màiri might say.

The day stretched out interminably as she went about her normal tasks, half of her alert, watching out for Ruairidh.

Màiri set her to carding the wool she was spinning from the last shearing. They worked together outside the house, discussing the various uses the finished yarn would be put to as they worked. Catrìona teased out the raw wool between wooden carding combs that were like large butter pats covered with thin steel hooks. It was a job she enjoyed for the satisfaction of the finished product though it was hard work on the arm and shoulder muscles, raking the matted wool this way and that, over and over again, with the heavy cards, pulling out all the fragments of briar and bracken and heather that each tuft contained. Màiri took each *rolag* – the fine web of carded wool, soft and light as gossamer, joined it to the thread already spun, and twisted it deftly onto the whirring *fearsaid* – spindle – driven by the wheel she turned with the treadle.

'Frangan should have new breeches,' Màiri said, hardly looking at her busy fingers that released each strand at just the right thickness.

'You need a warmer blanket for yourself,' Catrìona insisted. 'That is to be the first priority.' Màiri pursed her lips and shook her head.

'I have all I need,' she said firmly.

They worked in companionable silence for a while. A pair of terns darted over the loch, diving and piping angrily at a herring gull that had lumbered into their territory. Watching them, Catrìona forgot what she was doing and let her hands lie idle in her lap. How wonderful it would be, if one could just spread one's wings and fly off anywhere one wanted. She remembered the story Ruairidh had told her, about Icarus. . . .

'Catrìona! You are dreaming again: I am nearly ready for another *rolag* and you've hardly started on that one!' Màiri's voice made her jump. She snatched up the carding combs and resumed her work. 'You are your father's daughter, God rest his soul. There were times when you could have a whole conversation with him and know that his mind was ten million miles away.'

'What was he like, our father?' It was a game she and Frangan often played, trying to lure Màiri away from whatever was occupying her attention, by asking her to talk of their father. Sometimes, they could divert her for hours, but at others she would refuse to be drawn and quickly bring them back to the matter in hand.

'He was as good a man as you could ever wish to meet,' was the reply, 'but he had the dreaming in him, just as you do yourself. I often told him he spent more time with his head in the clouds than with his feet on the ground.'

'I wish we had known him.'

'Wishing will get you nowhere and I'm needing another *rolag* if you please.' It was not one of her days to be drawn.

'Was he anything like my uncle?'

'Like Tómas? Indeed he was not! He was never one for the *uisge-beatha* whatever Tómas may tell you to the contrary!' Catrìona ducked her head to hide her smile. If her uncle, Tómas, were to be believed, her father had been happy enough with his dram and a good companion over the drinking of it, but kept well and truly to heel during the all too short period of his marriage.

'It wasn't the drinking I meant,' she persisted. 'Tómas is a good, kind man, whatever you may feel about his weaknesses and I love him dearly. And he loves you.' Màiri's stern features softened reluctantly into a smile.

'Yes indeed; and I love him. And of course he has your father in him in many ways, in the laughter and the fun in him. But I won't have you thinking your father was ever in the condition Tómas gets himself into sometimes, and Frangan too, I'm disgusted to see.'

Catrìona raked and counter raked at the raw wool, her mind drifting off again towards the subject that seemed to occupy it obsessively. As if she could thought-read, her mother suddenly said:

'Have you seen Ruairidh Campbell yet?' Catrìona glanced at her, reading nothing from her impassive face.

'I had a quick word with him,' she said. 'Yesterday.'

'He will have changed a lot, I daresay. Grown away from us. Learnt city ways.'

'Maybe.' She tried to sound indifferent. 'He is certainly very taken with his work.' Her arms ached from the carding.

She rested them, while Màiri gave way to a coughing fit. On an impulse, she said: 'Mother, would you ask him about that cough of yours. It seems to get worse every day.'

'Nonsense. It is just a tickle in my throat. It will go and there is nothing anyone can do that will hurry it on its way.' As she spoke, Ruairidh himself came into sight, walking along the bank of the burn holding a dead otter in his hand. Seeing the two women he came across.

'Good day Màiri,' he called. 'It's fine to see you again.' He bent to touch her forehead with his lips: she had been like an aunt to him, when his parents were alive. If he noticed how much she had aged, he did not show it. Straightening, he grinned mischievously at Catrìona who refused to meet his eyes. 'Catrìona!'

'Good day to you, Ruairidh,' she murmured, her eyes bent over her work.

'Welcome back,' said Màiri, swallowing hard to supress the cough in her throat. 'It's been a long time and we have missed your company sadly in your absence.' She had always had a soft spot for him.

'Too long,' he replied, dropping onto the ground beside her spinning wheel, 'and I've missed you all and it is a tonic to be home.' Impertinently, he stretched out and removed the carding combs from Catrìona's hands. 'Let me see if I can still do that,' he said.

'Where did you find the otter?' Màiri asked.

'Up along the burn. He hasn't been dead long. I thought I might trap a few more and cure the skins: I could do with a good warm rug in my room in Edinburgh.'

'There are too many about just now and they are taking all the fish,' Màiri said. Catrìona watched as he fumbled with the cards and laughed at his clumsiness.

'Here, give them back to me,' she said. 'Or we shall be here all day.' His fingers touched hers as he handed them back and lingered for a moment. She was conscious of her too-easy blush and let her hair fall forward to hide her face.

'Are you coming across with Frangan and me this evening?'

he asked, 'to deliver the fish he wants to send down to the Clyde.' He knew better than to mention the inn.

'I might,' she said, grudgingly, not looking at him.

'That isn't very polite,' said her mother. 'You go, and enjoy the change of scene. You spend too much time on your own.' She touched Ruairidh on the shoulder. 'It will be good for Frangan to have you back,' she told him. 'He was not able to go on the herring drifters this year because he had an infected wound and he needs the company of a young man to keep him steady.' She lowered her voice. 'He can be wild in his ways and he is over fond of the *uisge-beatha*. Will you do me the favour of trying to steady him.'

'I'll give him my company when he asks for it Màiri, but you cannot ask me to preach to him. He won't look on me as a friend if I act as an uncle, and I'm only six or seven years his senior.' Ruairidh stood up and gave her a reassuring smile. 'But don't worry your head about him. He doesn't strike me as a dissolute man: he's just young and maybe restless and bored. I'm not a heavy drinker myself – I've had to witness the consequences too often in my work – so I'll not be leading him astray at any rate.' She nodded, knowing the truth in what he said.

II

They sailed on the last of the tide, carried round the point and along the south coast of Loch Boisdale by the strong current and a fair wind in the lug. The two men talked easily all the way over and Catrìona was content just to listen, and watch the shoreline and the evening sky. A warm glow of happiness filled her: she didn't need to join in the conversation – just to be there on this perfect evening was enough. Ruairidh spoke of conditions on the mainland, of the price of things, and of politics. Frangan fired interminable questions at him, mainly about the quality of life and the availability of labour.

'Why, don't tell me you are thinking of leaving here?' Ruairidh said, glancing at Catrìona as he spoke. Frangan shrugged.

'Sometimes I wonder if it wouldn't be more exciting,' he said. 'There is so little, here, for a man to do.' It was the first time Catrìona had heard him express his dissatisfaction with his lot, though she knew him well enough to have known for some time that he felt caged and restless. 'It was all very well for our ancestors, when they had more land and when they were forever going off to fight with the chief: life was exciting, then!' Frangan still had, hidden in the thatch, a broadsword that had belonged to their great, great-grandfather and that had, so Màiri said, been used in many a bloody battle before the final one in 1746. When they were children, he had often taken it out and used it as a prop in their many games of make-believe. Catrìona laughed.

'I believe you would be perfectly content if you could spend your life fighting,' she said.

'It would certainly be more fun than digging peat and spreading seaweed all day,' he muttered.

'Did you ever think of going over the sea to one of the new countries?' Ruairidh asked, his voice serious. Frangan nodded, watching the sail.

'Often,' he said. 'Maybe, one day I might. But I couldn't go and leave my family here. Would you come with me Catrìona?' He was half joking, but she knew he was also testing her out.

'If you were to go on one of the emigration boats I'd not try to stop you,' she said, 'but I wouldn't come with you. This is my home.'

The subject was dropped as they ran in towards the stone jetty below the inn at South Lochboisdale. Ruairidh climbed over the side, and made their line fast to an iron ring set into the jetty. He held out his hand to Catrìona and she took it and let him help her ashore, though she was as nimble as a cat and would normally have scrambled ashore with the line herself. The strong grip of his fingers on hers made her reluctant to meet his laughing eyes.

Ferguson's boat lay moored alongside, a sturdy craft already well laden for its next trip south. The man Ferguson ran a lucrative two-way business. He shipped out cloth, butter, cheese, fish, black cattle, kelp, paying the vendor considerably less than he would receive on resale down on the busy wharves of the Clyde. He would return with an assorted cargo that would include such coveted luxuries as tea, tobacco, sugar, salt, *uisge-beatha* and ale, as well as meal to supplement the meagre supply of locally grown grain. He was a shrewd businessman and he drove a hard bargain, but he was known to help people out if they were in dire need, lending rent against such securities as livestock or wool. He was also known to be on the side of the cottars, in opposition to such men as the minister and the doctor, who held big farms *in lieu* of salary and were all too willing to terminate leases in order to gain more land.

'The sooner we get rid of this, the better,' Frangan said, tapping the barrel they had heaved up out of the boat. 'Let's go and find Ferguson. He'll be in the inn.' Padding across the stone slabs in their bare feet, the three of them crossed the jetty and came to the slate-roofed inn. A babble of noise came from the open door; Catrìona hung back, thinking of Màiri and her opinion of girls who frequented the inns and took strong drink. Ruairidh, seeing her hesitation, said:

'We won't tell your mother, and I shan't let Frangan get drunk. Come in and listen to the talk.'

The room inside was dim after the evening light outside. A press of heavy-faced men stood drinking ale and discussing island business. Ferguson, a large man in a suit with a waistcoat and a watch chain across his protruding belly, was among them. Tufts of white hair sprouted over his ears and fringed a bald dome, accentuating a florid complexion. They were arguing without rancour about the price Ferguson was offering for a bolt of cloth that would have taken weeks of work to create from the raw wool through to the final waulking. When the deal was concluded, in Ferguson's favour, he turned with a genial smile that embraced the three who had just entered.

'And if I'm not much mistaken, Frangan Macdonald will be in a hurry to deliver merchandise he has "found" lying around the island somewhere?' There was a roar of laughter and Frangan grinned. They were safe enough among these men; the factor's people knew better than to be seen in these parts where they were treated with sullen hostility.

'It is a barrel of ling that I have Mr Ferguson,' he replied. 'Every one caught and cleaned by my sister and myself yesterday.'

'Ling, is it! And are they salt or dried?' He knew fine that they could not have been dried since yesterday. His eyes were alight with mischief.

'They are salted, Mr Ferguson.' Frangan held his gaze, head up and shoulders back: proud and independent, Catrìona thought, watching him.

'Salted? Well, well, what a lucky fellow you are to have salt available. I was just hearing from the factor himself this morning how they have gone short of salt themselves, due to the carelessness of one of his men. He was asking me to keep my ears open for news of that salt.'

'Indeed?' Frangan knew as well as the rest of them that Ferguson was just teasing him, and that he had no intention of betraying him. But he hated being made fun of. 'Will you be buying the ling Mr Ferguson, or shall I take it across to the mainland myself?' Ferguson laughed and clapped him on the shoulder.

'That's the spirit,' he said. 'I like to see a man stand up for himself. And I daresay you would take it across yourself in that little boat of yours.'

'Of course!'

'And he would, too,' Ruairidh murmured in Catrìona's ear. 'And you'd go with him no doubt?' She glanced at him and saw what she read as admiration on his face. She shrugged.

'I'd go if he asked me to,' she said. Ferguson was following Frangan out to inspect the fish. Catrìona and Ruairidh stood outside the inn watching the two men haggle over the barrel. Ruairidh chuckled.

'I suspect that Ferguson has met his match in your brother,' he observed. She smiled.

'Frangan has a way with him, and I think Mr Ferguson secretly rather admires him. Certainly he pays him a fairer price than he pays to some.' Eventually they seemed to come to a conclusion that was mutually satisfactory, for both were in a good humour when they walked together back up to the inn.

'Let us seal our bargain with ale,' said Ferguson and you will be my guests.' Catrìona declined, though she sipped from Frangan's tankard and made a wry face. They sat on a settle and listened to the flow of talk around them.

'They say Colonel Gordon is determined to clear off the last of the small tenants.'

'That man! He'd sell his own grandmother!'

'They say there is talk of his building a pier at Lochboisdale, and a hotel; maybe even roads. Think of that!'

'It would provide work for some, right enough.'

'Some. But not all. And where will we all live if he takes our holdings from us?'

'You'd think he might have had enough by now, with the hundreds of people he has shifted from their homes since he bought the land.'

For Catrìona, the talk was just a background of noise, making little impression on her. She was more aware of the proximity of Ruairidh on the settle beside her and though he listened to the talk, throwing in the occasional remark himself, she had a feeling he was as conscious of her as she was of him.

When they came out from the inn it was nearly dark, as dark as it would get. They let their eyes adjust before unfurling the lug and pushing out from the jetty. It was possible to navigate from the shape of the coast: Frangan knew every crag and inlet and he knew where all the submerged rocks lay. The tide had turned in their favour and they made fair progress back towards their own beach. Without the sun, the night air was sharp: Catrìona pulled her shawl over her head and round her shoulders. Beside her, Ruairidh began to hum an air she knew so well that she found herself adding the words before she had time to reflect on their meaning: '*Siomadh oidhche bhá sinn . . .* Many a night we sat together in the byre, and when I sought to leave you your arm would hold

73

me . . . ' And the final verse, *An cuimhneach leat an cómhradh*
. . . Do you remember our conversation in the little bed in
the back room? . . .'

III

Màiri was sitting in her chair near the fire, her thin face
illuminated by the flickering flame from the *cruisgean* on the
wall. She had her spinning wheel beside her but her hands
lay idle in her lap. It was unusual to find her inactive. She
looked pinched and anxious.

'Mother, you look worried. What is the matter?' Catrìona
went to her, peering at her through the gloom while Frangan
stirred up the fire and lowered the pot of broth on the chain
that hung over it.

'Tómas was over to Daliburgh on the horse,' she said, her
voice hoarse. 'He met the priest. Father Eóghan says there is a
stranger arrived on a boat recently, come to survey the crofts
for Colonel Gordon. He says there is talk of . . . evictions.'
The word caught in her throat and brought on a coughing fit.

'Evictions! Again!' The conversation in the inn, earlier,
came back to her. There had been so many evictions in the
past, so very many, as well as a large number of emigrations
by folk who had had enough of being pushed around. Those
who were left would joke about how there soon wouldn't
be any people left. But those things had all been happening
further north and the little community at Rubha na h-Ordaig
had come to believe it could never happen to them. That they
were safe, down here in the south east corner of the island,
forgotten, almost, by the new laird who was so determined
to redistribute his land to make it profitable.

The twins had been ten when the debts of Ranald George
Macdonald of Clanranald, eighteenth Captain of their clan
had forced him to sell South Uist to John Gordon of Cluny
in 1838. Catrìona could remember only too well the anxiety
of the islanders, for Gordon had a reputation for ruthlessness,
a reputation he quickly lived up to. Within a few years he had
evicted hundreds of the subtenants, or cottars, from his land,

joining their many small plots into larger, single farms which were invariably managed by incomers from the mainland.

'But surely he can't evict anyone else! Not us, down here at any rate. Where could we go?' Catrìona came closer to the fire to peer into the pot. Somehow this new threat couldn't touch her present mood which was all of sunshine and dreams. It was words, only. They would be all right.

'He can do whatever he likes, and we are all in his power.' Màiri's bitter voice expressed the feelings of all the tenants on the island: people who had once been proud and free and independent. People who now were caught up in a tangle of misfortune that had started more than a hundred years ago, on a bleak moor above Inverness in a sleety gale on the morning of 16 April 1746.

IV

'They are saying he wants to turn all this part of the island into one big sheep farm,' said Anndra, a slow, heavily built man who always managed to hear things before anyone else. 'Not one person to be left, only his own shepherds who will come over with the sheep, not even local men.'

The people from the fifteen houses in the township gathered round the door of Beathag's house, discussing among themselves the threat that hung over their lives. Catrìona stood back, only half listening, trying not to show her awareness of Ruairidh, who had come out of his own house, and stood leaning in the doorway, observing the scene. He no longer belonged, she thought: he was an outsider, come back to spectate. She wondered how he saw the scene before him: the half-naked children, laughing and calling to each other as they played, dodging in and out between the houses; the hens scratching in the rushes that grew near the water. What was in his mind as he looked at the people around him; the women in their long skirts and shawls and knitted jerkins, the men in their breeches and waistcoats, all with faces weathered by the harsh climate, strong, raw-boned features moulded by hardship. She longed to know what thoughts he had, to produce that enigmatic smile that was half sad, half affectionate. While the talk ebbed and flowed around her, she thought back to the night before and to the conversation they had had beside the burn, the night before that. She thought of his lightning changes of mood, one moment amused and teasing, the next serious, or bitter, or gentle. She tried to concentrate on the present moment.

'But there is nowhere left for us to go! How will we live without any land at all.' Eilidh, always timid and worried, was now almost in hysterics, her eyes swimming with unshed tears. Ever since her mother had died, Eilidh had been a little soft in the head. She lived in dread of being taken advantage of by every man who crossed her path, despite her sixty odd years and her shrivelled, warty body.

'Don't bother your head, Eilidh, I'll take care of you;' the rich, robust voice of Tómas, rang out over their heads. He stood near the door, his face florid from a lifetime of alcohol, his stance kept steady with the help of the wall. 'You and me can go and set up home together in one of the old deserted shielings.' Good natured laughter erupted for a moment and died. Anxiety damped the spontaneous humour that usually lightened even the most solemn occasions.

'Can we not persuade the man that our land here is too poor for sheep?' one of the men called out.

'If he has eyes in his head he'll see that for himself right enough,' shouted Beathag, waving her plump arms. 'Look at the condition of our cattle; look at my poor sheep.' Beathag kept her scraggy sheep down near the house, treating them like pets and hand feeding them scraps from her cooking pot. They were grazing now beyond the cluster of houses, guarded by her dog whose job it was to keep them away from the crops.

Catrìona's eyes wandered over the crowd: these were the people she had grown up with, every one of them as familiar to her as her own family. It was impossible to believe, on this hot day in midsummer, that this was not just a dream, that tomorrow life would go on the same, the life they were all accustomed to, hard but endurable, with many compensations for the bad times.

A raucous caterwauling heralded the eruption of two tom cats from Beathag's byre, spitting and snarling. One leapt up the wall, on to the roof and challenged the other, arched into a hoop of erect fur. Another ripple of amusement lightened the solemn faces for a moment; flickered and died.

'Who is this stranger? Has anyone seen him; talked to him?' It was Beathag's voice, demanding, belligerent.

'The priest says he is Gordon's agent: a Lowlander,' Tómas supplied.

'A Lowlander! So he won't even have the Gaelic I suppose.' Beathag again, full of contempt.

Catrìona put her shoulders back and lifted her chin high. 'We shall have to speak English to him I daresay!' Her voice, carefully pronouncing the unaccustomed language, learnt from Ruairidh's father so many years ago and never used except in mockery, carried on the clear air, making them all laugh. Fighting the urge to look across at Ruairidh, she bobbed and held out her hand to Tómas: 'Good day to you, sir,' she said, still in English, 'pray help yourself to our land.'

'Catrìona, if you see the man, be polite I beg you,' Màiri rounded on her daughter sternly. 'There is no sense in tangling with him: he will have authority to do whatever he chooses.'

Catrìona tossed her head and her eyes narrowed. One or two of the younger ones murmured their approval at her show of spirit. Frangan come over to stand beside her, facing the crowd.

'Surely we should show some sort of protest,' he called out. 'Remember the stories about how the people fought at Sollas, two years ago!'

'And where did that get them?' shouted Uistein, Beathag's brother who now and then brought a sheep's carcass he had 'found' into the township for speedy disposal into many eager cooking pots. 'A lot of spilt blood and broken bones and then what? Some were in jail, they all lost their land and it is said they are mostly off to Australia any time now.'

'That may be, but even so, no Gordon of Cluny is going to turn us off our land if I have anything to do with it, and that's for sure.' Frangan stood firm, he who had so recently admitted that he had often contemplated trying his luck over the sea.

'Except that it isn't our land, it's his, and we owe him rent.' Màiri's voice wavered as one of her coughing fits shook her.

'Rent! It is himself should be paying us rent, if he wants to take over the land we have worked since the beginning of time.'

'Don't speak like that, Frangan Macdonald. In this mood you and your sister'll get us all turned out. You were always a wild pair, with only your poor dear mother to control you.' Eilidh's petulant voice made Catrìona scowl. Màiri coughed and turned away to spit blood onto the ground. Catrìona went across and put her arm round her shoulder.

'Don't worry *eudail*,' she whispered, 'whatever they may say, you have Frangan and me to protect you.' They never spoke of the terrible disease that was burning up Màiri's lungs: there was no point for there was nothing anyone could do. As she straightened up, she caught Ruairidh's eye. He was frowning. Had he seen Màiri's sickness already!

Suddenly his voice rang out carrying a note of authority that made everyone turn towards him and listen.

'I know I must seem like a stranger among you now,' he said, 'but it is not how I feel. All the years I've been away, my heart has been here, and it always will be.' Catrìona's eyes never left his face. 'I believe the twins are right and that you – we – should make some sort of effort to hold on to what we have. If we let Gordon clear us from this place we shall have little alternative but to leave the island and though there are many who feel that is a desirable solution there are many who would never be happy in a foreign land.'

'But what are you suggesting we do? Fight them with stones, like they did at Sollas?' Anndra's voice brought murmurs of agreement.

'No, that doesn't work. But I'll tell you what does have

some effect. To bring the matter to the attention of the newspapers.'

'Newspapers? How do we do that, from here? Who is there on this island who can present our case when everyone is against us? The Bard Séumas Macdonald, spoke up from the edge of the crowd. 'The priest would not do it in case they expel him and leave us without the sacraments. The minister, the doctor, the teachers, all are too keen on keeping in with the laird to risk losing their privileges by speaking up for us. There is no one who would take our side.'

'I could do it,' said Ruairidh quietly. 'I write for various publications and at least two of them would, I think, publish a report on what is happening. Indeed, there are several people who have already taken up cases on the mainland and had them exposed in the newspapers. If enough fuss is made, they start making enquiries in Parliament.'

'But is there time?' cried The Bard, himself no mean wielder of a pen, but unable to express himself in English.

'Who knows?' Ruairidh shrugged. 'But it is worth a try. I can send something on the next boat that leaves.'

'Ferguson isn't leaving for another couple of days, he told me last night,' said Frangan.'Carrying that barrel of ling for me, nicely preserved in the laird's salt, if I have my way.'

'He'll have us all transported,' muttered Màiri.

Ruairidh glanced at the anxious faces around him. 'I can't promise any results,' he said. 'But it is worth a try. Meanwhile, if the man comes out here, we must be civil, and present our case in a balanced way, explaining that we have nowhere else to go and that the land is not good enough to support all those big Linton sheep they bring over.'

V

The loch was joined to the sea by a long, narrow channel between rocky cliffs. Entrance by boat was only possible at slack water; otherwise the ocean rushed in and out in an unnavigable frenzy of rapids and swirling currents. Once inside, the loch formed a perfect sheltered harbour. In calm weather, most of the township boats were kept outside, like Frangan's, beached on the shore beyond the ridge. In the winter and when storms threatened, they brought them all into the loch on the high tide and beached them below the houses, as safe as if they were up on the summer pasture.

High above the township Catrìona sat leaning against a slab of lichen-covered stone, her skirt hitched above her bare knees, her sleeves rolled up. She turned her face to the sun, narrowing her eyes against its glare. Beside her, the dog lay, half asleep, gauging her mood.

Apart from the bell heather, the heather was not yet in flower; the bracken was still young, uncurling tender shoots among the bog myrtle and milkwort. She could smell crushed thyme and moist, peaty soil. Away in the distance the golden eagles swooped over their eyrie: she remembered how she and Frangan had tried to get up to the nest, years ago, and been attacked savagely, lucky to get away with their eyes, so Màiri had told them. She reached down and plucked a tiny, yellow tormentil and held it in her fingers. Skylarks rose and fell filling the air with their song and a chord of yearning stabbed her heart. She thumped the ground with her fist.

Never would she consent to leave her home! This was her land, her birthright, her heritage. She would fight to the death, if necessary but she would not go! She glared at a gull eyeing her from its perch on a stob. Gordon of Cluny indeed! Most likely he couldn't speak the Gaelic either. And what did he know of the islands: he may have purchased the land but he could never, never own the people. Nor begin to understand them.

She had been reared on folklore and legend, inextricably interwoven with a devout faith that had influenced her ancestors almost unchanged since it had come to the islands with missionaries from Ireland in the early sixth century. What did Gordon of Cluny know about the centuries of Norsemen who had never managed entirely to conquer them and who had finally been driven away! What did he know about the Lords of the Isles; those arrogant, proud chiefs who scorned the mainland government and refused to follow their laws! How could he ever understand how every member of the clan family had been independent and equal in status, looking to their chief for guidance and justice but never for oppression? How could he understand, because that way of life was over forever, trampled and destroyed in the mire and blood of Culloden Moor. How could he know of the fierce loyalty of her ancestors who had sheltered and fed the fugitive prince, with a price on his head and their downfall on his conscience – the cause of all their future troubles, shielding him from soldiers and spies thirsty for blood only a handful of miles north of where she was sitting!

No, Gordon of Cluny had no idea what he was taking on. But they would show him. Had they not, within the last few years, already managed to evade the ruthless evictions he had set in motion when he bought the land? Since her great-grandfather had led his band of rebels out here, they had survived so many previous waves of eviction and emigration. They could do it again. Even during the potato famine, they had fared better than the other townships because of their fierce independence and ingenuity, though their isolation had made it difficult for them to collect their ration of meal from the boats that had come over from the mainland.

'*They are an improvident, idle, shiftless people,*' said the politicians and the officials in charge of the Relief Board, arguing against giving aid that might stop the starving people from helping themselves. '*If we keep sending them relief, they will grow to expect it.*' But it was not idleness that had caused the famine. It was greed, partly. Greed for wealth and not their greed. They had only reluctantly adopted the potato as a staple in the first place, long before she was born, when Clanranald had introduced it just before Culloden. '*Worthless things,*' her great-grandfather was reputed to have told him. '*You can force us to plant them but the holy Virgin, will you force us to eat them!*' Soon enough the potato had caught on, growing so well on the seaweed lazy-beds.

It had been another of the injustices that had contributed towards their present crises. Even now, four years later, the land was still sour from the blight and they lived on the edge of starvation.

But she, for one, would rather live here in hardship than anywhere else in the world.

The sun was hot. She undid the upper buttons of her shirt and let the light breeze cool her skin. It was a skin which never tanned nor burned, but the touch of the sun warmed her heart. She should be helping turn the hay, or with any of the other many jobs that made up the crofter's day, but her lack of sleep last night had made her drowsy and her thoughts were too strange and disturbed to concentrate on weaving, or spinning, or threading out fish to dry, or carrying seaweed, or peat . . .

Suddenly, the dog growled low in its throat, crouching beside her, hackles raised. A shadow fell across her. Startled, she looked up and her hands flew to the buttons she had just undone.

'Don't do them up: you look very good just as you are.' An affected voice it was with English words in a pinched, mincing accent. The man behind it was fleshy, with a jowled face, sparse ginger hair and protrubant eyes. His clothes and boots were city-made, new-looking and unnatural. 'Well, well! What a delightful bonus indeed! A rustic shepherdess, looking for her lost sheep.' He reached down and pulled her hand upwards towards him, away from the buttons she was trying to fasten.. She came slowly to her feet, the hem of her crumpled skirt falling to cover her bare legs, and tried to free herself from his grasp.

'*De t'ainm a th' ort? Cia as a bheil thu?*'

He scowled at her. 'I don't speak your heathen tongue,' he said rudely. 'Talk English,' Anger threatened to choke her.

'What is your name and where do you come from,' she supplied contemptuously. 'And please let me go.' She strained away from him, but his grip was too strong for her.

'I am Donald Henderson, agent to Colonel Gordon of Cluny. I am here to survey this part of the island. The colonel has a mind to run sheep here and needs to know where the best grazings are.' He sneered down at her as she struggled to get away from him. 'I was in the township down yonder, they told me the land was too poor for sheep and showed me half a dozen mean looking brutes that they said were all they could raise. I thought I should explore, in case they were mistaken.' He gestured towards the land spread out below them. 'I see I was right. You have some good pasture here.'

'It may look good, but your flocks would eat it up soon enough and it is all we have. It would hardly be sufficient to support hundreds of sheep all year long.'

'That, my pretty, is for me to decide.' He clipped her arm round behind her back, bringing her up against his plump body. 'But my decision could possibly be influenced by a little kindness from a certain young lady.' He bent his head and tried to kiss her. She smelt liquor on his breath as his moist lips sought hers. With a frantic wrench, she managed to shove him away, thrusting at his face with her free hand. She broke his grip and stepped back, panting; furious.

'How dare you! You filthy pig! What makes you think you can come here with your barbaric ways. Have you no honour at all, to molest a woman who has no man to protect her.'

He fingered his cheek where she had struck at him. His pale eyes held no kindness and there was no humour in his laugh. 'There are many who would not consider an advance from me to be an insult,' he said. 'In fact quite the contrary.' He watched her carefully for a moment before taking a pad from the pocket of his coat and jotting on it with a gold pencil. 'I think the colonel will agree with me that this southern end of the island holds many acres of good grazing but he will, without doubt, also agree that there are at present too many people starving the land of its potential.'

'So! It's true then. You have come to evict us.'

'Evict? That is a strong word.' His voice sneered at her as he returned the pad to his pocket. 'You are all here by the generosity of Colonel Gordon.'

'What a fine gentleman you are, Mr Henderson,' she mocked him, imitating his mincing accent. 'What a gallant, honourable task you perform. No doubt you enjoy your bullying tyranny, thinking it makes you more of a man.' She held her head very high and let him see the utter contempt in her face. 'Will you go back to your southern friends and boast of the justice and integrity with which you discharge your duty?'

Her words lashed him on the raw. With an oath, he lunged towards her, catching her off balance so that they both fell to the ground. She struggled as he wrenched at her shirt, pinning her down, fumbling with the clothes that separated their bodies.

'I'll teach you to speak to me like that,' he panted. 'There's only one thing a bitch like you is good for . . . ' She felt his hand on her bare flesh and screamed, her nails raking his jowls. Suddenly, he was hauled off her and she was free. She leapt to her feet and stood at bay, grasping her torn bodice, her heart pounding in her chest.

Donald Henderson lay on the ground, face down, anchored by Ruairidh Campbell who sat astride him, forcing one of his arms up behind his back. Catrìona stared, her recent terror forgotten.

'I thought it was only in the cities that vermin emerged from the sewers,' Ruairidh was saying. 'But it seems I was wrong.'

'Let me up, damn you.' Henderson flayed the turf with his legs, powerless. It was a ridiculous sight and Catrìona wanted to laugh aloud. 'You'll be sorry for this.'

'Not half as sorry as you will be if you don't get out of my sight as fast as your fat legs will carry you.' Ruairidh released him and sprang lightly to his feet. His victim clambered ponderously upright and stood rubbing his arm, ridiculous in his humiliation. He eyed Ruairidh uncertainly and made an unwise decision.

'She had it coming to her,' he snarled. 'She led me on, hot little bitch that she is . . . '

Ruairidh's fist shot out; there was a sickening crack, and Henderson lay sprawled on the ground. For a moment, silence and immobility froze them all into a melodramatic tableau of violence. Then Henderson dragged himself on to all fours, his head swaying from side to side like a wounded animal. Ruairidh eyed him, rubbing his knuckles. He stood up, blood oozing from a graze on his jaw, one side of his face already discoloured by a spreading bruise. His voice was thick and distorted.

'You'll regret that for the rest of your life,' he said. 'I'll destroy you both if it's the last thing I do.' Catrìona shivered and took a step towards Ruairidh. The venom in Henderson's voice was almost palpable. He turned away from them and stumbled down the path.

They watched him go, not speaking until he was out of sight. Catrìona was shaking from head to foot.

'He meant it,' she said.

'Yes, I'm afraid he did.' They faced each other. Ruairidh's jaw was clenched in anger, his eyes hard. Then, seeing her own distress, his face relaxed a little and he raised an eyebrow. 'Don't look so worried,' he said. 'There isn't much harm he can do to us, whatever he may say.'

'He can evict us,' she retorted. He shrugged.

'Maybe Gordon will decide Rubha na h-Ordaig is too remote for his bloody sheep.' He held out a length of twine. 'Here, use this to tie up your bodice,' he said. She had forgotten, in all that had happened since, the event that had caused their present situation. She felt herself blushing with humiliation as she remembered what he had witnessed.

'It's all right,' he said, 'you needn't be embarrassed. I'm only thankful I got here in time to stop him.' His voice was neutral and matter of fact. Taking the twine, she tried to fasten the gaping cloth but her hands shook so much that she couldn't manage. Gently, he took it from her, drew her hands down to her sides and with quick, deft fingers, gathered the two lapels together and tied them in a firm knot. She kept her eyes averted.

'There you are,' he said cheerfully. 'One of the things medical students have to learn is how to mend cuts!' Again, his impersonal tone brought the situation down to earth. She moved away from him.

'Thank you,' she said, fingering the repair. 'And thank

you for . . . well . . . saving me.' He brushed her faltering gratitude aside.

'Forget it,' he said. 'I have.' She ran her hands through her tumbled hair, combing out the flakes of moss that had got into it during her tussle with Henderson.

'He said . . . oh God!' she covered her face with her hands as it all came back to her. 'He said that if I . . . if I was . . . kind to him . . . he might not have to evict us.' She stared at him. 'Should I have . . . ?'

He shook his head. 'Certainly not! Whatever you had or hadn't done, you can be sure his survey would have been the same. You can never look for mercy in a lecherous bully.'

'Perhaps I should have been polite, at any rate. I was so angry that I was . . . well, not very polite to him I'm afraid.'

'I should hope so. Polite indeed.' He laughed, his eyes flashing. 'I remember Catrìona Macdonald being the terror of us all, in the old days! A right *diabhol* you were when you were a little girl.'

'A devil was I!' She put her hands on her hips, the memory of her recent experience fading as no doubt he intended. 'Who was it then, who put a mouse in Seònaid Macneil's meal chest? And who tied a dead rat behind the *cailleach*'s dresser?'

'That was just fun.'

'You were always the one who played the jokes if I remember rightly,' she retorted. 'You were so much older than us and you got away with murder.' Their eyes met, and held for a moment. His eyebrow lifted almost imperceptibly and she wondered what he was thinking. She felt flustered. 'Did you see . . . was Frangan back from fishing yet?' she said quickly, turning away.

'I saw his sail but I didn't wait for him. Your mother was worried about you when that man was seen coming up here.'

As he spoke they heard a shout. Frangan, sweat streaming down his face, came running up the path.

'Catrìona! Are you safe? They told me . . . Ruairidh! ' He flung himself down on the ground, panting, taking in great gasps of air. 'I almost kill myself racing up here to save my sister from some strange man they told me had come up here, and what do I find? No stranger at all but Ruairidh Campbell!' He held his heaving ribs, his shirt drenched with sweat.

'I wasn't the stranger. I followed him up here. The stranger was Gordon's agent, Donald Henderson, and if I hadn't arrived on the scene, he would have raped your sister.'

'What!' Frangan shot to his feet and grasped her shoulders, taking in the repair to her clothing and her dishevelled appearance. She nodded.

'It's true. He . . . well . . . let's just say Ruairidh got here in time.' He put his arm round her and held her against him.

'I'll get him,' he said. 'I'll castrate him, just as we do the rams, and he'll wish he had never been born.'

CHAPTER 6

It was always in Màiri's house that the people gathered for discussion or decision-making. It had always been so, not just because it was the biggest, but also because Aonghas Macdonald the tacksman, who had brought their ancestors here, had been their leader and they had always come to him, in this house, with their problems. The practice had been handed on, even though his grandson, Aonghas, Catrìona's father had never reached an age to inherit any role of leadership. When her grandfather, the *seanair* had died, there had been no obvious successor. Tómas was a popular man, but no one took his opinions seriously; the Bard was too occupied with meditations, Ruairidh's father was dead and none of the other men had quite the stature. It was almost as if Màiri existed as a regent, not to be consulted, for she was only a woman, but to represent leadership until Frangan was old and wise enough to inherit the responsibility.

Even at midnight, at this time of year, you could see the veins on your hands without the light from the fish liver oil, burning in the rush wick of the *crùisgean*. But Màiri had lit the lamp even so, because people had started to gather, in ones and twos and it was inhospitable to receive them in twilight. And although it was not cold and the cooking was finished, she had made up the fire for the same reason, instead of smothering it in ashes as she would normally have done to keep the life in it till morning.

The room was packed with people, their faces glowing in the flickering light. As a rule, with the long, light nights of midsummer, everyone was too busy working outside to have time for *céilidhs*, and only gathered like this in the winter when even in the middle of the day it was barely light enough to work indoors without the *crùisgean* and for some weeks the sun never showed over the ridge. But such momentous events as those that had happened this day had to be shared, discussed, and judged by all the community.

Séumas Macdonald, the Bard of the township, had hastily composed a suitable poem to mark the ousting of the stranger. He declaimed it, at length, and some of the younger members of his audience exchanged hidden grimaces of boredom. Although neither Ruairidh nor Catrìona had gone into any detail in their accounts of what had happened up on the hillside, enough had had to be disclosed for the Bard to refer repetitively to the cherishing of the precious flowers of the community, and the virtue of chastity. His cracked old voice went on and on. Catrìona, standing back from the press of people round the fire was suddenly aware of a gentle pressure against her shoulder. She turned her head; Ruairidh had eased his way round to stand beside her.

The mobile eyebrow quizzed her. 'I thought he would have retired from his recitations by now,' he whispered in her ear. 'It's the only reason I came home.' Both could remember those yawns, mimed behind young hands at many a *ceilidh* in the past. Laughter welled up inside her; he put his finger to his lips and turned back to face the Bard, adopting an expression of exaggerated appreciation that made her want to laugh even more. She studied his profile; he did not remove his shoulder from hers until someone called to him from the fireside, but the contact could have been inadvertent she told herself.

'Ruairidh, give us a song. Show us that Edinburgh hasn't made a Lowlander of you!' He moved away from her then, thought for a moment and nodded.

'*ó ho nighean, é ho nighean, ó ho nighean a' chinn duibh àlainn;* his clear voice rang out, carrying the haunting air; other voices took up the chorus. 'O my maiden, é my maiden, o my maiden of the beautiful dark hair . . . .' Catrìona knew the love song as well as the rest of them but she did not join in. His voice alone sang the verses and she sensed his teasing eyes on her averted face.

'*Ach mas e 's gun d'rinn thu m'fhàgail . . .* ' 'But if you have left me and prefer a new lover, my thousand blessings with you for ever; you have left me like a lamb without a mother.'

When the song was over Catrìona glanced across the kitchen and saw Tómas, leaning heavily against the dresser, laughing at her. She stuck her tongue out at him, looking hastily around to make sure her mother was not watching. Màiri, she knew, would have a fit if she discovered the easy relationship between her daughter and her brother-in-law.

But now the time for pleasantry was over and the real reason for the gathering must be brought out for an airing.

'What will we be doing about the stranger?' It was Eilidh's voice, querulous with anxiety. 'He has come to burn us out of our homes.'

'That won't happen, Eilidh. You've been listening to gossip. Those days are past.'

'I heard they was driving folk from their homes and burning the thatch even now, on the mainland,' put in the Bard, whose outlook on life reflected many years of reading Job. 'Someone told me they are herding the men in pens, like cattle.'

'Surely not, these days. That was how they were going on in the early days, over on the mainland in Sutherland and such places. All that is finished, now.' Tómas, his optimistic nature fuelled by the contents of the flagon he passed, with magnanimous generosity, around the assembled company, stood near the door, exuding heady fumes that made Màiri frown with distaste. 'What do you say, Ruairidh? You've experience of the happenings over there.'

Everyone in the room turned to look at him; he hesitated. 'I don't get about much,' he said. 'We are kept pretty busy in the hospital where I am training.'

'But you must hear things, man. Edinburgh is, after all, a city.' Beathag's deep, strident voice demanded an answer.

'Yes, well, of course I hear things. And it is true that there have been burnings and even deaths, they say. Death from indirect effects of eviction, I must add, not murder.' His face was serious now; gone was the quizzical humour that Catrìona was beginning to find irresistible. 'Many of the stories go back to the early days, however.' He stopped but their expectant silence forced him to continue. 'I believe it has been worst in Sutherland, as Tómas says. Hundreds of people driven from their crofts and forced to move to makeshift hovels on the coast. Made to take up fishing when they had never seen the sea before. Even when they'd been good tenants and their rents were up to date. Oh yes, there are some pretty bad stories right enough. But you have to look at the other side to make a fair judgement. Often the land was giving poor yield, there was overcrowding, disease, starvation. When the potatoes failed for the first time, five years back, there was terrible hardship . . . '

'. . . and so there was for us, too. Was it not worse for us, so far from the Relief Board?' said the Bard. 'But we still chose to stay in our homes – not to be shifted off somewhere else.'

'But at least you had roofs over your heads and stone walls to protect you.' His quiet, sure voice was magnetic, Catrìona thought, and everyone else in the room felt it too, she could tell. 'Some of these people were living in huts rigged up from blankets. Some were even living in the open.' His voice was harsh, his profile stern. Looking at him, Catrìona thought again how much he had changed – or not so much changed, maybe, as developed. No one, living here in isolation, had the experience to expand their horizons to the extent he had. He had always had strong convictions; now he had acquired a deep, angry social awareness that fuelled his driving ambition to change the lot of the poor and needy. His medical vocation had been born out of bitterness, after the death of his parents who might, he had believed, have been saved with proper medical attention. It had then turned outwards, to embrace a whole multitude of ills. He would never be content, now, to return and practise his skills among his own people, when there were others, worse off, on the mainland.

The conversation continued, well into the small hours. It was mainly speculation, flung back and forth across the fire, interspersed by songs and stories of the past.

Tómas's flagon was dry and voices were ululant with

emotion as the final song was sung. They had talked themselves out, with no conclusion. Conviviality and fatigue had softened the sharp edges of the crisis. Towards dawn a terrible coughing fit siezed Màiri. Quietly, without rude haste but with the instinctive courtesy that knew how best to help, the people left the house and went to their homes.

Ruairidh lingered until Màiri was calm and settled among the woollen blankets in her box bed.

'That cough,' he said in a low voice, as Catrìona and Frangan stood in the door to bid him good night; 'it is bad I'm afraid.'

'But what can we do?' Catrìona felt drained after the long, eventful day. 'It seems to be getting worse every day.'

'There is nothing you can do, here.' He sounded bitter. 'There are no potions that will cure the consumption in her.'

II

News filtered through of the progress of Donald Henderson as he made his way up the length and breadth of the island, and as he got further away, the menace of him seemed to grow more remote. Perhaps, after all, nothing would happen; perhaps he had forgotten his humiliation; perhaps he had forgotten his promise of revenge. But the threat of him hung over them even so, like a haze across the sun, so much filling the minds of the older people that nothing else was important, such as enforcing the strict rules that generally governed courtship.

The hot spell showed no sign of breaking and the ceaseless round of work continued on the tiny strips of land that they called their crofts. There was the hay to finish, the meagre oat crop to cut and stack, the beasts to tend and keep off the fields. There were the fish to catch and dry, the wool to spin, the yarn to be woven. There were the peats to be carried and the water to be fetched from the spring.

It somehow happened that whatever task occupied Catrìona each day, Ruairidh contrived to pass by and stop to lend her a hand, or talk. She tried to ignore what was happening to her because she knew that he would soon be returning to his studies and it might be many years before he came back, if ever. She hid behind quick laughter and light-hearted teasing, like an elusive will-o'-the wisp, but she enjoyed his company and the strong compatibility of their natures and now and then grew serious and listened gravely to his tales of life in the city.

No one seemed to notice that Catrìona volunteered more often than anyone else to keep watch over the township's beasts, wherever they were to be pastured during the day. It was a long haul up into the hills and tiring in the heat. Because he had been away so long, Ruairidh's absence from the communal activities in the township was unlikely to be noticed and besides, didn't a medical student work hard enough and deserve a rest! He had long ago given up his parents allotment of land, keeping only the house, and even that was used by his neighbours cattle when he was away.

'What will you do, when you are qualified?' Catrìona sat perched on a rock, her bare feet dangling, her fingers busy knitting up wool into winter stockings. Ruairidh lay on his back in the heather below her, his eyes closed, his Edinburgh pallor already tanned dark as leather.

'Oh, I don't know.' He opened one eye for a moment to look at her face and then closed it again. 'When my parents died, I thought my vocation lay in coming back here to try to help people like them, and like your mother. After a couple of years in Edinburgh, however, I realised how badly the poor people there need medical help.' He sat up abruptly, all indolence gone. 'O Catrìona, you have no idea of the conditions some of those people live in. There is poverty and hardship all over the highlands and in the islands, I know that and I know that sometimes people live in conditions no better than their animals endure. But they have space and air and . . . freedom.' He threw his arms wide. 'Look at what they have. I've already described to you how the poor people in the cities live in dark, rotting tenements, hundreds of them to a building, with no clean outdoors to run to. They cannot support themselves off the land: they must

have money to buy food and clothes, or starve and die.'
She watched the passion in his eyes, the clenched muscles
in his lean cheeks, the restless fidget of his spatulate fingers.
'How would someone like the *cailleach* survive in conditions
like that? And your mother: right enough she is sick – very
sick,' he glanced at her, for she had not yet dared to ask him
what hope there was for Màiri's recovery; 'but at least, here,
she has a whole community to look after her needs, if not
her health. Milk, meal, eggs, fish – all are provided for her,
and wool,' he added, pointing to her knitting. 'There are
peats for her fire and oil for her *crùisgean* and there is even,
occasionally, meat to go in her broth. All free.' He spread
his hands. 'The only thing she needs money for is her rent,
and she has her beasts to earn that for her every year, and
Frangan to drive them to the sales. It is a frugal life, I grant
you, but my God, Catrìona, it is paradise compared to how
she would have to live in the city.'

Catrìona laid down her knitting. 'Calm yourself,' she said.
'You get so worked up. I'm not disputing any of it. I just
asked you what you wanted to do when you qualified. Now
I know the answer.' She spoke lightly, to hide the desolation
in her heart.

With another of his lightning shifts of mood, he was on
his feet, standing close, looking into her face. Up went his
eyebrow, all the indignation gone. 'So, what is the answer?'
There was an ironic note in his voice.

She shrugged. 'Why, that you will settle in Edinburgh, or
Glasgow maybe, one of the big cities anyway, and help the
poor people there.' She flicked a pellet of moss off her skirt,
trying to sound casual, unable to meet his eyes.

He reached out and took her hands and pulled her off
the rock, holding her imprisoned against it. She smelt his
healthy, male sweat and felt the hardness of his spare body
and heard the laughter in his voice as he murmured: 'Wrong'.
His breath stirred the fine tendrils of her hair around her ear
as she averted her face, suddenly shy. 'That is the answer I
would have given you when I came off the boat. Now –
well, I seem to have changed my mind. Since I came home,

I have a very strong urge to follow my original plan, and come back here when I'm qualified. I want to live among my own people.'

His lips, light as a whisper, brushed over her ear, followed the line of her cheek, touched the corner of her mouth. Disturbing instincts in her loins chased caution from her mind; she moved against him; all inhibition fell away.

III

In this uneasy time of waiting to see what was going to happen, many of the usual practices were suspended in uncertainty. People hurried about their daily tasks, always watching the track, listening for rumour, conjecturing: there seemed little time, and less inclination, for following old customs.

Catrìona and Ruairidh were well aware that in less troubled times their courtship would have been beset with all the customary rules and regulations that had governed young people since time began. In the old days, had Ruairidh wished to marry her, though marriage was not a word either of them had yet mentioned, he would have come on a visit to her house, bringing with him an older friend, Séumas the Bard, maybe, as one of the most respected members of the community. After greetings and conversation had been exchanged, in a leisurely fashion, Séumas would launch into a description of Ruairidh's virtues, heaping good qualities on his head. If Catrìona had been interested, she would have stayed in the room to listen and would have made her pleasure obvious; if not, she would have left the room and gone outside. No one had the heart for such ritual now: who could think of marriage or indeed anything beyond the question of what was going to happen to the land and what they would do if they were turned out of their houses.

Everything seemed to conspire to make the hours they spent together perfect. It was as if God himself had blessed them, though Catrìona knew better than to put this theory to Father Eóghan. The days were cloudless, the air warm even at night. Lighthearted as children they wandered through the hills, down in the straths, far from the townships that scattered the island. They found secret places, caves, inlets, tumbling burns, small lochans. They picked wild flowers, caught brown trout, built stone cairns to mark each new place where they had been happy together.

She took him to all her favourite spots, scenes of her youthful escapades with Frangan, and described their games to him: their Jacobite re-enactments with Frangan always in the leading role.

'You were so old, then' she teased him. 'Much too old to join in our fun.'

'You never invited me. I would have made a far more impressive prince than that scatterbrained brother of yours.'

'Frangan can be very royal, when he chooses: very haughty.' They were sitting on lichen-covered rock half way up the southern slope of Roneval, looking across at the little island of Eriskay.

Ruairidh pointed across the sound. 'Did you know that that house there, on the beach, is where the prince took shelter for a night, on his way to summon the clans, before it all started?'

'No. Who told you that?' He smiled lazily and turned, to lie with his head in her lap.

'While you and Frangan were play-acting, other people were busy at their books, studying the truth.'

'You studied horrible Latin and Greek, not romantic stories about the Jacobites.' She twisted a strand of his hair round her finger, leaning forward so that her own hair fell over them both. 'And I happen to know that the prince landed on the mainland, at Loch nan Uamh, when he came over from France.'

'Wrong! That was later. His ship, the *Du Teillay*, put in to Eriskay before it got to Loch nan Uamh, when they saw what they thought was a hostile ship, apparently chasing them. The prince went ashore and was offered the hospitality of that very house there.' It was the crudest of black houses, a squat hump of stone and rushes, by the shore. 'The story is told of how the prince was so overpowered by the smoke inside that he had to go out and sit on a peat stack to get some fresh air. The woman of the house came outside and scolded him for being too fastidious!'

Catrìona gazed down across the water to where *Bliadna Thearlaich* – The Year of Charlie – had begun. 'Poor prince Charlie. Can you not picture him, even now, sitting down there, so full of hope?'

'It was there that Macdonald of Boisdale came to him and told him that he should go home; that his mission was futile.'

'What did he say?' Ruairidh sprang to his feet, drew himself upright and threw her a haughty look.

'He said: 'I am come home.''

Catrìona beamed with delight. 'Oh my love, why did you not play with us as children! You are right, you would have made a wonderful prince. Just as good as Frangan.'

To discover perfect harmony with another person was, to Catrìona, an unending wonder; every hour they shared was a new, exquisite joy.

'You are lovely, do you know that? All of you, so beautiful: like one of the paintings the rich people hang on the walls of their fine houses. I could spend my life looking at you, and caressing you like this.' They were up on the high plateau, where mossy turf enmeshed with wild flowers grew in tiny pockets among great rocks and boulders.

'I'm not stopping you,' she murmured. He made her feel lissom, langorous, voluptuous, as if there was nothing in the whole world except their own, private places, filled with love and pleasure and laughter. 'And do these rich people display unclothed women on their walls?'

'Indeed they do. They call it art.'

'Art! I call it shameless!'

'And are you shameless then, my little temptress?'

'Only for you. Not for all the world to see.' She laced her hands behind his head and stared up into his luminous eyes. 'Tell me about those fine houses. Do you go to many of them?'

'Now and then, as an assistant to one of the doctors.'

'And is that where you meet all those fancy women?' He laughed down at her, teasing her with his eyebrow.

'Of course. Can you not picture the scene. Queues of society ladies, lined up for my delight, wherever I go, in my threadbare student's suit.' She pinched the skin on his neck, hard enough to make him flinch. 'Hey, vixen!'

'Tell me the truth about the women. I want to know.' She was only half joking. He pulled away from her, leaning on his elbow, smoothing her hair away from her face.

'I'll tell you about them, and then we won't talk about them again, because they are not important. There have been a few, Catrìona, I can't deny it. But they were just passing experiences, no more. A man gets lonely; he goes off to the tavern maybe, has a drink or two, and a wench catches his eye.'

'I heard there was a dancer, who lived with you.' It was best to spill it all out, than to let it fester in her heart when he had gone. His fingers touched her cheek, her throat, her neck.

'Yes.' He was laughing at her. 'Her name was Dolly. She was a bad dancer, had a filthy temper, and her breath smelt like a midden.' He ticked them off on his fingers: 'then there was Liza, who was so mean she used to steal my money if she could get her hands on it; and Annie, who had never heard of washing; and Bess, who drank gin like water and made Beathag seem slim.'

'Oh.' She giggled. 'All right, let's forget your fancy women.'

Early one evening, when they had been over to Glendale to collect cockles, raking them up out of the sand and carrying them home in rush creels slung on their backs, they came up over the peak Cruachan and stopped to rest their loads in a dip the far side. Just below them, beyond a sharp shoulder of rock, they saw a thin spiral of smoke, almost invisible on the clear air. Ruairidh grinned, put his finger to his lips and went forward to investigate. Creeping up, he inched round the rock, ducked back and beckoned to her. She went to his side and peeped round. A crude turf shelter that would not have fooled the excise man, half concealed an ingenious contraption of makeshift tubes, funnels and tubs. Tómas was bent over, inspecting the contents in the main reservoir. He sensed their presence and swung round, his expression of alarm changing to one of open delight.

'Catrìona! Ruairidh! Do you have to come creeping up to scare a man like that. I thought the excise man had got me at last!' He shook his head at them.

'Shame on you Tómas Macdonald! You know quite well you have the excise man on your side.' Ruairidh said, coming forward to finger the still admiringly. 'It wouldn't be difficult for him to catch you at it if he wanted to.'

'Maybe, but you gave me a fright even so.' He moved away to sit on a rock close by, motioning to them to join him. Catrìona dropped down onto the turf beside him and Ruairidh perched on a tussock of dried silvery moss. 'You two seem mighty pleased with each other's company,' he observed, his moist eyes full of humour. They exchanged a look that would have betrayed them to the most impartial of witnesses, causing Tómas to chuckle. 'But I won't be telling tales on you,' he said. 'How did you know I was up here?'

'You were as conspicuous as the sun at noon,' Ruairidh said. 'How long have you been using this place?'

'Not long. It's difficult to find running water in these hills, in a place where one isn't too public and where those prying shepherds from the south don't keep appearing on the skyline.' He jerked his head back towards the burn that ran down past them, disappearing under the turf some distance beyond the still with the hollow reverberation of a subterranean torrent. 'And I'm finding it harder and harder to get grain.'

'You'll manage, as long as you have a ready market,' said Ruairidh cheerfully. Tómas nodded.

'Oh yes, and there will always be a ready market for the *uisge-beatha*. But to tell you the truth, I'm thinking of moving across the water.'

'Across the water! To the mainland?' Catrìona felt a tug of dismay: Tómas was almost a father to her. To lose him was unthinkable.

'Away with you lass. What would the likes of me be doing on the mainland! No, no! I've been hearing stories about the Stack Islands.' He pointed towards the south, across the Eriskay Sound. 'I've never been down there myself, but someone was telling me that yon castle would be a fine place for my still. No one goes there and there are no sheep so no shepherds.'

'The castle? I've heard about that place. It has ghosts, they say.' Catrìona tried to remember what stories she had been told, but could not.

'The castle is big enough for me and a whole family of ghosts; they won't bother me. It is a ruin, now, but I don't mind that.'

'Will there be water?' Ruairidh said.

'That is the question. The man who built the castle in the old days lived there with thirteen children, so I'm thinking they must have had water.

'Why did he live there?' Ruairidh asked. 'It must have been mighty precarious, perched up on top of the Stack.'

'He was a wrecker. The Reaver, they called him. He used to light fires on the rocks and lure the ships off course. He had to live in a remote place. Up there, he had a fine view all round and he could drop stones on anyone climbing up to catch him.'

'His poor wife! Think of how hard her life must have been with all those children to watch. The castle has a sheer drop all round; they would have fallen over the edge whenever they went outside.' Catrìona had seen it from the sea, fishing with Frangan.

'He lived alone to begin with. Then he was lonely, so he came on a raid to this island and stole away a young girl for his wife.'

'So she was a prisoner?' Catrìona exclaimed.

'The story goes that she was a willing prisoner.' He shook his head. 'Women are fanciful creatures, right enough.'

'Wouldn't it make life very difficult for you, if you have to go all that way every time you have to tend the still?' Catrìona asked, gazing across to the distant crags of the Stack Islands.

'That is the point. There is a new excise man and I'm told he is very persistent in his duty. If the Reaver managed to evade the law for all those years, he must have had a mighty good stronghold.'

They sat in silence for a while, each with their own thoughts.

'Tómas, do you think we shall be evicted, this time?' Catrìona asked, smoothing her skirt over her drawn-up knees. He pulled an empty pipe from his pocket and sucked on it, making a wet gurgling noise.

'I am thinking that we have been very lucky not to have been disturbed before now. Maybe we shall be left alone again, but I have a feeling in my bones that it is our turn next.'

'What will you do, if we are turned out?'

'Me? I shall offer Colonel Gordon of Cluny a generous dram of thrice distilled *uisge-beatha*, wish him *"slàinte agadsa"* and ask him if he would be so kind as to go away and leave me in peace.' They left him, humming to himself, muttering all the brave things he would do when faced with eviction.

One day, when the sun was particularly hot and the sea was at its deepest blue and calm as glass, Catrìona stood on a rock looking down into the water, a mischievous smile on her face.

'Shall we swim?' she said.

'I haven't swum since you and Frangan were bairns and had the rest of us goaded into trying to keep up with you,' he confessed, standing behind her, wrapping his arms round her. 'Perhaps I've forgotten how.'

'I'll race you to the rabbit island,' she said, pointing to the small, grassy islet about two furlongs from the shore. They stripped off their clothes, laughing in their haste and flung themselves into the water. It was icy cold, despite the hot sun. Gasping, they both struck out for the island, flailing the water, neck and neck to begin with but then, better practised, Catrìona pulled into the lead and reached the islet well ahead. Exhilarated, they ran across the springy turf to the far side, to a sheltered dip overlooking the ocean. Their lovemaking was passionate, and as natural and free of guilt or shame as the mating of wild animals.

Later, they swam slowly back, side by side. They dressed and wandered homewards, hand in hand, saying the things that all lovers say, believing, like all lovers, that they were unique.

'How sad for the world, not to know such perfect joy.'

'Can such happiness last forever?'

Catrìona stood on the edge of the cliff, arms outflung, head back, hair flowing in the wind. Low on the western horizon a line of cloud was building up, only just discernible through the haze. With an uneasy stirring of premonition, she said:

'Perhaps not, but whatever price we may pay for it, we have had this, which is more than many others ever have. If we were both to die now, it wouldn't matter.'

CHAPTER 7

I

The weather broke. A gale blew in from the west battering
the island with mighty waves which had built up unchecked
across the whole of the Atlantic ocean and now pounded the
western beaches, tearing at the white sand, pouring through
gaps in the dunes to flood on to those parts of the machair
that lay below sea level, drowning the tiny strips of crops.
It was impossible to walk upright against the force of the
wind.

At Rubha na h-Ordaig, the men brought the boats round
from the open bay, through the narrow channel at high tide,
and beached them at the head of the loch. Frangan was away
up the valley, looking for a stray horse, so Ruairidh brought
his boat round for him, just before the storm broke. They
were lucky to have had time to do so. Even sheltered as they
were, tucked in under the eastern hills, their precious vessels
would not have survived such seas.

The wind ripped at roofs, worrying away at any loose
edges until great swathes of thatch tore off and scattered,
leaving skeleton rafters that soon collapsed unless they were
well secured. The noise was a continual roar, punctuated by
high screeching and the thumps and bangs of flying debris.

Catrìona, stimulated by the excitement of such violence,
forced Ruairidh to struggle along the burn, through the valley
and up the lee slope of Maraval. As they neared the summit
the full force of the gale howled round them and they had to
lie on their stomachs and crawl to a point where they could
see to the west. The mighty waves looked like mountains
marching in across the boiling sea. Now and then a tall plume
of water rose, higher and higher in slow motion, to hover,
towering over some rock or islet before descending in white
victory. Such was the strength of the wind that they could feel

salt spray on their faces, even at that distance. Catrìona tried to talk but the words were snatched away before she could form them. Ruairidh shook his head and dragged her back down into the shelter of the eastern slope. Pressed in under an overhanging rock, they strained together, each fired by some primal urge that had been roused by the elements.

By evening, the shore was littered with distressing evidence of boats that had perished in the storm: planks, timbers, spars; a barrel of lard, a broken oar, a cabin trunk, flung up onto the beaches to prove that taking passage to a new land was not always the solution to problems. In spite of the law that had been passed, making all driftwood government property that must be paid for if collected, people crept out from their townships like ants, to carry away any flotsam and jetsam that could be used, struggling home to hide their finds or build them into the fabric of their homes so that they quickly became integral and absorbed by peat smoke.

II

By the morning, the storm was beginning to blow itself out. Catrìona, waking early, discovered that Frangan had not slept in his bed. He had not come in by the time she and Màiri retired to sleep the night before, but as he was frequently out till late there had been no reason to worry. She stood, eyeing his empty bed. Perhaps, by the time he had found the stray horse he had been searching for yesterday, it had been too dark to return; perhaps he had sheltered in some bothy up the valley. He would return presently. She did not disturb Màiri who was still sleeping; there was no point. Frangan was often up and out before Màiri woke. She dressed and crept outside to inspect the aftermath of the gale.

The wind was still strong, but it no longer took her breath away. The air was clear and fresh; the smells that usually clung to the township had all been swept away. Debris lay caught up against walls and in crevices: mostly roof debris – dried reeds, bracken, heather. Standing in the doorway, smiling into the early sunlight that filtered through high, scudding fingers of cloud, Catrìona saw Ruairidh standing over by the boats beached near the mouth of the burn, where he had found her that first night after he returned home. He saw her and waved. She ran to join him; even in full sight of the houses she could not but throw herself into his arms and lift her face to be kissed. But his response was less prolonged than usual and she stepped back and looked up at his face.

'What is it? Have I done something wrong?'

'No, of course not,' he reassured her quickly. 'How could you? I love you.'

'Good. So what is the matter?'

'Tómas's boat isn't here.'

'But . . . ' She looked around at the row of beached boats. Tómas's was unmistakable because he had secured part of the figurehead of a wrecked ship to his prow, giving the boat a jauntiness that the others lacked. He had found the figurehead washed up one day and said it would do instead of a wife for him: just as beautiful, he said, but less trouble. No figurehead adorned any of the boats lined up now.

The tide was coming in. The last time it would have been possible for Tómas to have taken his boat out of the loch was about six hours ago, when it had been dark and when the wind had still been raging. Neither he, nor anyone else would have attempted such a thing: to have done so would have been certain disaster, and why should he have wanted to anyway? She stared at Ruairidh, her eyes wide with apprehension. Then a thought struck her.

'I know what will have happened,' she said. 'He will have been away at his still, before the storm, and when you all brought the boats round no one noticed that his was left behind. It will be there now to be sure, on the outside beach,'

'If that is so,' he said, 'it will have taken a rare pounding. Shall we go and see?'

Together, not particularly alarmed, they climbed the ridge and stood looking down on the seaward shore. The sand was strewn with flotsam and jetsam, including a dead cow and a whole tree that must have travelled many miles to reach this treeless island, but there was no trace of Tómas's boat, either pulled up above the tide mark, or smashed to pieces on the rocks that lined the bay.

'It will have been swept out to sea,' Catrìona said uncertainly. 'The wind was from the west; if a wave had come high enough to float it, it would have blown it out into the Minch.'

They looked at each other, and she saw that Ruairidh was as worried as she was herself. It did not feel right: Tómas loved his boat. Even if he had been at the still, he was weather-wise enough to know when a storm was coming. If he had not managed to get back in time to move his boat on the last incoming tide before the storm, he would certainly have taken every precaution to make sure it was safe from the sea. He would have summoned a team of helpers and manhandled it half way up the ridge to be sure of escaping any big wave that might wash it out to sea.

'He will be in his house,' Ruairidh said firmly. 'Let's go and see.' Even from where they stood, they could see that no smoke hung over Tómas's roof. But nor did it hang over several other of the houses: some folk were still sleeping and had not yet blown up their fires. Tómas was seldom up early. They walked down towards the township.

Tómas was not in his house and the ashes of his fire were cold: so cold that they felt damp. There had been no embers there for many hours.

They stood looking down at the dead fire, surrounded by the disorder of Tómas's domesticity.

'He'll be up Cruachan,' Ruairidh said.

'He would never have stayed up there in the storm.'

'Perhaps he was tasting his *uisge-beatha* too liberally and didn't notice the storm.' Catrìona smiled briefly but shook her head.

'You know fine that he doesn't get drunk like that. He is pickled in the stuff; it hardly touches him. If it had been Frangan . . . oh! Frangan!' Her hand flew to her mouth as she stared at him in dismay.

'What about Frangan?'

'He didn't come home last night. I've just remembered.

He was away after a horse, as you know, yesterday. When he didn't come home I thought he must have sheltered in one of the bothies up the valley.'

'The horse he went to look for, it was Beathag's wasn't it?'

'Yes. She was in such a dither about it. You know what she's like about her beasts.' Ruairidh took her hand.

'Come,' he said quietly, and led her outside. He pointed across to Beathag's house. Her horse, hobbled by a rope *spearrach* cropped at a tuft of marram grass close to the door.

At first, she couldn't take in what it meant and then the full implication struck her like a physical blow.

'Frangan must have come back last night after all, if he found the horse. So where is he? Him and Tómas?'

'And Tómas's boat!'

'O Ruairidh!' He put his arm round her shoulders and his touch gave her strength. 'What shall we do?'

'First we must make sure they are not up Cruachan at the still. Will you come with me?'

'Of course. But what about mother? She was still asleep when I got up. Should I . . . ?'

'No. Why worry her? Let her think he came in late last night and left early this morning. She will think you have gone up to do the milking.'

'Yes. And I must do that, too.'

'There isn't time; we must go up to the still at once. Ask someone else to do the milking for you. Look: there's Liùsi, going off to do hers. Tell her it is for Frangan she will be doing it!'

Liùsi was inclined to flounce and toss her fair hair, but she would have milked a thousand cows for Frangan and waited while Catrìona fetched her pail.

Catrìona and Ruairidh strode away together towards the distant hump of Cruachan. They did not speak, saving their breath for the climb. Catrìona tried not to think of what they would do if the two men were not up at the still. So many possibilities flooded her mind and each one more terrible than the last, because of the missing boat.

Not only was there no sign of Tómas nor of Frangan, but the still itself had disappeared. They came round the shoulder of rock to where they had sat talking with Tómas so recently, and found nothing. The burn ran gurgling past towards its subterranean passage. The turf shelter had been dismantled and scattered and the ramshackle bits and pieces that made up the still were not there.

'Are you sure this was the place?' Catrìona knew it was, as she spoke, and to confirm it, there on the ground was the blackened patch where the fire had been.

Suddenly, simultaneously, they remembered their conversation with Tómas.

'Holy Virgin! They've taken it across to the Stack Islands!' Ruairidh's voice was hoarse with incredulity. 'But they can't have done such a crazy thing, not during a storm.'

'Could they have gone before the storm broke, and got stranded there?'

'Not if Frangan was out looking for the horse. Even if he brought it back early in the day, no one could have put to sea yesterday, not even on such an urgent mission as saving Tómas's still.' He looked at her. 'Who told you he had gone after the horse?'

Catrìona reflected, her mind dazed with worry. 'I can't remember: oh, yes!' A new and horrifying thought occurred to her. Slowly, massaging the pain of tension in her temples, trying to stay calm, she went on. 'He was not in his bed when I woke early on the morning of the storm before it broke. I was looking for him, to bring our boat in on that tide. I asked Beathag if she had seen him, and she said . . . '

'. . . he'd gone to look for her horse?'

'Yes.' She frowned, desperately trying to remember. 'No! Oh dear God! She didn't. She said some of the men had gone to look for her horse and he had probably gone with them. That's what she said. And I, fool that I was, assumed that that was what he was doing. That was when I asked you to bring the boat round for him.'

'So he could have disappeared the day before the storm?

Can you remember if you saw him come in, that night?' She shook her head miserably.

'No. I know he wasn't in when I went to bed that night either, because I remember thinking . . . ' she glanced up at him, '. . . thinking how unfair it was that he could be out as late as he liked without Mother saying anything, while I must always go to bed at the same time as her.' She gave him a wry smile.

Ruairidh turned and stared out across the sound towards the Stack Islands, trailing off the southern end of Eriskay, hidden from view by Ben Stack. Although the wind had dropped considerably, even since they had set out, the sea was still rough and menacing, with white peaks to the waves. It would be a while yet before it would be safe to take the boat out.

'They could have gone the day before yesterday,' he said. 'If they misjudged the wind that day and took longer than they'd anticipated, they would have stayed the night, intending to come back yesterday.'

'And then been trapped by the storm?' Catrìona narrowed her eyes, searching the eastern entrance to the sound as if, even now, she might see the boat making its way back. 'It is still so rough; they must be there yet.' Hope flickered in her heart. Of course that was what had happened.

III

The township hummed with Tómas and Frangan's misadventure. It would certainly serve them right; teach them a fine lesson. Two nights on the Stack Islands with no food or bedding and in a storm, too. Perhaps Tómas might decide that his distilling days were over. Perhaps Frangan might have been put off strong drink for ever. A certain amount of satisfaction could be detected in some of the voices that speculated on when the truants would return.

Catrìona could not give her mind to anything else and she knew from his face that Ruairidh was as worried as she was. They had managed to pacify Màiri, who was grim-faced in anticipation of her son's return, and they had convinced the rest of the community that it was only a matter of hours before the boat with its distinctive figurehead would be seen sailing into the loch. But, though the sea had grown calm and the wind had died away to a whisper, there was no sign of them.

'I wish they would come.' She stood on the highest point above Rubha na h-Ordaig, scanning the sea with restless, anxious eyes.

'They must come soon,' he reassured her, but his voice lacked conviction. And then they saw Liùsi running towards them, and heard her frantic voice. They went down to meet her; she was sobbing, panting, hysterical.

'They've found the figurehead . . . Tómas's boat . . . wrecked . . . round in Glendale . . . ' She clawed at Catrìona, her face, usually so bold and cheeky, contorted with grief. They ran with her, down to the township. It was true. Someone had come over from Glendale, bringing the splintered figurehead. Not much of it remained, just half the woman's painted face and neck – but enough to recognise it. Catrìona turned it over and over in her hands, unable to speak.

IV

They had to wait three hours for the ebb tide so that they could get the boats out of the loch. It was impossible to sail out against the incoming tide, which boiled in through the narrow passage with all the force of a waterfall. Every one of the nine boats owned by the township put to sea, each to search a different area. There were so many creeks and bays and rocks and islets, where the timbers of a wrecked boat could have landed . . . where a body could have been thrown up.

Catrìona and Ruairidh headed south for the Stack Islands. What wind that was left after the storm had backed right round to the east, so it was an easy haul and they had the current with them. It was a long way: six miles or so and it took them more than three hours before the biggest of the Stack Islands lay abeam, with its jagged-toothed ruin on top. They had hardly spoken: what could they say that wasn't painful speculation.

Catrìona stood and furled the sail and Ruairidh took up the oars. Their eyes raked the barren rocks, and the grassy cliffs of Eilean Leathan – The Stack. It was almost impossible to believe in the storm that had raged with such ferocity such a short time ago. The water under the lee of the Stack was glassy-calm and so clear that Catrìona could see the waving fingers of sea-anemonies, deep down, clinging to the rocks as they inched in through the narrow creek below the ruined castle. She scrambled up from the boat onto a sea-weedy rock and tied the line round a jutting crag. Ruairidh joined her and they stood, hand in hand, gazing up the steep cliff to the Weaver's Castle.

It was a desolate spot. The ruin, little more than a tumble of stones, stood high on a pinnacle of rock, approached by a path with dizzying drops on either side. Had the two men reached their destination, unloaded the still and been on the way home when the boat had foundered, or had they been on the outward journey? The only way to find out was to climb up there and see if the still had been installed. Sheer cliffs enclosed the creek, white and stinking with guano from the huge colony of gulls who nested on the ledges, their harsh cries echoing and re-echoing around them. It was eerie and unnerving. They started to climb; a perilous ascent; one wrong step would have brought a person plummeting down a precipice, bouncing off jagged rocks into the sea. Catrìona tucked her skirt up and set her eyes ahead, not liking to look to either side of the path. Near the top she suddenly stopped,

'Listen!' she cried, cupping her ear with her hand. 'I can hear something . . . voices!'

'Surely not! It is the gulls.' Ruairidh cocked his head. Raising his voice, he shouted: 'Tómas! Frangan!' and the sudden noise echoed round the towering cliffs sending a screaming flock of gulls into the air.

From the tumbled ruins of the castle, two heads emerged, and two pairs of arms, waving like windmills.

'Praise be to God!' Catrìona hugged Ruairidh, laughing and crying at once. 'Oh my love! Oh thank the Lord!'

Tómas and Frangan, stubble-faced, bleary eyed, stinking of stale spirits but cold sober, greeted them with vociferous enthusiasm. They were both hollow cheeked, pinched, and starving.

'What happened?' Catrìona was incoherent with relief.

Between the two of them, Frangan and Tómas told their story. Frangan had gone up to the still on Cruachan, the day before the storm, to warn Tómas that he had seen the new excise man poking around not far from Rubha na h-Ordaig. Tómas, who had had the last one well and truly on his side, with frequent offerings of *uisge-beatha* had panicked.

'I had this feeling in my bones,' he said. 'I had heard the new man was awful ruthless and not a drinking man himself.'

The two men had dismantled the still, carried it down to Tómas's boat, together with a certain amount of the surplus spirit, going round the coast rather than through the township so as to avoid detection. The rest had been more or less as Ruairidh and Catrìona had guessed.

'By the time we had it all safely hidden away up here,' Frangan said, pointing to the ruin behind them, 'it was getting dark and the tide was against us.'

'And the weather looked uncertain, too,' Tómas added. 'So we spent the night, meaning to go back on the morning tide.'

'And by morning, the storm was brewing,' Ruairidh said. He looked around. 'By God, it must have been quite breezy, up here,' he said.

'It was terrible, I can tell you,' Frangan said. 'It was so strong, the wind, that it would have been mad to try and climb down the path to the boat, to make it secure. We lay there, in the lee of the wall and I expected to be picked up by the wind and carried across the Minch at any moment. I couldn't believe the stones weren't going to tumble down on us. And the noise of it! And then, when it dropped sufficiently for us to get down, the boat was gone.'

'No doubt you took courage from the *uisge-beatha*' said Ruairidh, dryly. Frangan laughed.

'Of course! But a man can't live on *uisge-beatha* alone. There comes a time when he must eat.'

'And it dries you up, that stuff!' said Tómas. 'You need water.'

'You mean there's no water here?' Catrìona chuckled. 'So how would you have worked your still, Tómas, without water?' He shook his head, ruefully.

'That's the whole thing about it! All that planning and trouble, and all the terrible things we have endured and at the end of it, no water! I was wrongly informed.'

'The Reaver must have relied on rainwater,' Ruairidh said. 'Poor Tómas, no one will let you forget this, ever!'

V

But the community at Rubha na h-Ordaig had forgotten all about it long before the sun set the following day.

Creeping away from the dancing and singing, the eating and drinking and story telling, that celebrated Tómas and Frangan's return, Catrìona and Ruairidh stood for a while watching the moon on the sea, their arms entwined. She rested her head on his shoulder.

'If Frangan had been drowned,' she said, 'I would have lost part of myself.'

'You love him very much, don't you,' he said. She nodded.

'Yes. It is hard to describe the way I feel about him. It is nothing like the love I have for you. It is . . . possession: as if we were two halves of a whole.' His arm tightened round her.

'There will come a time,' he said softly, 'when each of you will want to join your half with someone else. What then?'

She turned within the circle of his arms and pulled his head down to hers.

'I have no doubt that we shall solve that problem when it arises,' she murmured. At the back of her mind there lurked the ever present shadow of his departure, back to Edinburgh, at the end of the summer.

VI

Hard on the heels of the first gale, a second one raged in over the Atlantic, as if to finish off the destruction wreaked by its predecessor, screeching over the already battered houses with savage ferocity. Later, looking back it seemed to Catrìona as if these two gales had been sent as harbingers of all that was to follow.

CHAPTER 8

I

Màiri sent Catrìona across to the house of her cousin Ealasaid with the sack of yarn they had been spinning over the past weeks. Bent into the wind, she struggled through the township, taking shelter where she could from the houses she passed. Doors slammed, wisps of straw whipped past, rags and debris scattered, animals and hens huddled in the lee of walls. Frangan and Ruairidh had gone round to the beach, to see if there was any new treasure washed up during the night so she didn't tap her usual greeting on Ruairidh's door as she passed.

Ealasaid was the best weaver in the township, her loom almost filling the house. As Catrìona approached, she heard the sound of women's voices over the wind, singing the *coileach* – the quick-time, clapping song that marked the finishing of a *luadhidh*, or waulking: the shrinking of a length of cloth with hot sheep's urine.

Catrìona pushed open the door and entered. Two of the women, in rough aprons, their sleeves rolled high, kerchiefs over their heads, faced each other across the roll of cloth, clapping it as they sang

Fàil ill éileadh ho a ó éileadh,
Step out and get me a sweetheart,
Fàil ill éileadh ó ho ro i . . .

The room was heady with the sweet stench of the urine that had soaked the cloth to give it softness and to set the colours. The other women were laughing and clapping, as the song got more ribald, extemporised to include references to the love lives of those present. When the song was finished and the cloth ready to be washed in the burn, Ealasaid nodded towards Catrìona, saying with a wink: 'I think it is the *caileag* we should have been singing about.' There was more laughter, as Catrìona blushed and set down the sack of yarn.

'My mother asked if you could weave this for her please. She needs a length of cloth from the crotal skein as soon as you can manage.'

'I hope it is not intended for a suit for your sweetheart to wear when he takes the boat back to the mainland,' said Ealasaid, 'for you know what they say about the crotal lichen: what came from the rocks will return to the rocks.'

'And will you be going away with him, we are asking ourselves?' said Beathag, her button eyes sharp above her large, flaccid cheeks.

Catrìona shrugged away their good natured teasing. Nothing could touch her: she was wrapped in a cocoon of love so intense that to be parted from Ruairidh for a few hours no longer mattered because of the anticipation of reunion.

As she opened the sack to show Ealasaid the quantity and quality of the yarn, the door burst open and the Bard stumbled into the room, his white hair windswept, his eyes ablaze.

'The stranger has been back,' he announced dramatically. 'He has been serving eviction notices all over the island and now he has served one on us.'

There was a shocked silence, broken only by the wind moaning in the rafters. The women stared at him and Catrìona felt the cold shock of fear in her heart. Then there was a confusion of voices: indignant, angry, defiant, frightened.

She slipped out through the door and stood against the wall, staring across the loch towards the beach. Sheltered as it was, the water ran in angry looking peaks, and she felt spindrift on her cheeks. Frangan and Ruairidh came over the ridge, struggling crabwise against the wind, too far away to distinguish their faces. She made her way back to her own house, trying to take in the full implication and yet still so cushioned by her emotions that she could only think: it can't happen to us.

Màiri sat, slumped across the bench, her face a grey blur in the dingy light. In her hand she clutched a blood-stained rag. She lifted her head to say something but the coughing wracked her, tearing her apart. Catrìona ran to her, trying to hold her as the awful spasms consumed her.

'Don't try to speak,' she commanded, everything else forgotten except the imperative need to stop the searing force of the cough. She fetched water from the pitcher but her mother couldn't drink. She damped a cloth and sponged her forehead, smoothing back the white hair that was lank with sweat, and the sticky, claw-like hands and wrists. She heard voices, felt a quick stab of relief and turned her head.

'Come quickly,' she called. Frangan and Ruairidh were laughing at some joke as they entered. Hearing the urgency in her voice they hurried in and came to her side. She stood back and watched as Ruairidh bent over Màiri, feeling her head, lifting her wrist to test her pulse. His voice was low, soothing, very calm; his face serious and, Catrìona knew, worried.

'Can you bring blankets, rugs, anything warm,' he said over his shoulder. She collected the homespun bedding from the box-bed and helped to tuck them around the frail body. He lifted her up and put her into her chair. 'It is better for her to stay upright, than to lie down,' he said. 'Will you heat some milk?' He stooped over Màiri, listening to her breathing. 'I want you to try to drink some warm milk Màiri,' he said gently. 'It will make you feel stronger and may soothe your throat.' He turned back to Catrìona. 'Have you honey?' he said. She nodded: the township shared out the honey they gathered from their three hives and each family hoarded their crock for special days. 'Stir some into the milk,' he ordered.

The fire was low. Frangan tended it carefully, blowing into the embers until flames licked round the lumps of peat and they blazed up. Catrìona spooned honey into the warm milk, taking care not to waste any and handed it to Ruairidh, who held the cup to Màiri's lips. She took a few sips, swallowing painfully, but not coughing again. She closed her eyes and seemed to sleep. Ruairidh beckoned to the twins and they crept outside to stand against the wall, trying to keep from the wind.

He faced them, his eyes travelling from one to the other. 'I'm sorry,' he said quietly. 'I'm afraid you must prepare yourselves for the fact that she cannot last much longer.' Catrìona turned away; he made a movement towards her but checked himself as Frangan put his arms round her.

'She has tuberculosis, as you will surely have guessed. Pulmonary; that is to say, in her lungs. They call it consumption, all too aptly,' he added bitterly. 'All we can do is to try to keep her warm and calm, and get her to take a little nourishment whenever she can.'

'Donald Henderson has been back. While you were to the beach.' Catrìona lifted her head from Frangan's shoulder and wiped her eyes fiercely with the back of her hands. 'We are to be evicted.'

'What!' Both men spoke together. Frangan dropped his arms and stepped back. 'How do you know? Who said? When?' She shook her head.

'I don't know,' she said, her voice dulled with despair. 'The Bard came to tell Ealasaid when I was there. I think maybe he had been here to tell mother first. She looked so shocked when I found her.' She twisted her fingers together. 'What shall we do?'

'They can't possibly enforce such an order on your mother,' Ruairidh said. 'It would be murder.'

'Can't they! Have you forgotten Donald Henderson?' Catrìona's voice was bitter. 'He swore he would take his revenge, remember?' She stared at her lover. 'That man is capable of anything.'

'We can apply to Colonel Gordon himself.' Frangan sounded doubtful even as he spoke. 'He is supposed to be a gentleman, he must surely have some common decency.'

'Being a gentleman doesn't, I have discovered, automatically endow a person with the virtue of humanity,' said Ruairidh. 'In fact, it is often very much the reverse.'

'I think we should find out exactly what the eviction order says.' Catrìona found herself taking command. 'The Bard was never one to see the lighter side of events: perhaps he has got it wrong.' None of them were reassured by her optimism, least of all herself. 'Frangan, will you go and see what you can discover. Ruairidh,' she was conscious of a softening in her tone as she spoke to him, 'would it be an imposition to ask you if you would stay with mother? I must go for more milk: that was yesterday's and it will have turned by the evening.'

'Of course. Have you eggs? We should beat one into her next cup to give her strength.' While Frangan hurried away into the aftermath of the gale, they returned to the room, where Màiri was still peaceful. For a few moments, Catrìona stood within her lover's arms, quietly, drawing strength from his strength, courage from his love. Then she drew away and gave him a faint smile.

'We'll manage,' she whispered. 'Somehow.' He nodded. She went to the door, turned and blew him a kiss.

Struggling against the wind, she set off to find the cow, reflecting affectionately on the many facets in Ruairidh's character, and wondering if he still had any hidden ones she had not yet discovered. Now she was seeing him in perhaps his main guise, no longer the laughing, teasing companion, nor the passionate lover, nor the serious talker: now he was the compassionate healer and all his attention had been directed to his patient and she knew that nothing would divert him. The knowledge gave her great comfort.

II

There was no time to petition the laird for he was away on the mainland, too cowardly no doubt to stay and face his tenants. He left his employees to do his dirty work and gave them a free hand to do it as they pleased.

First, there came a gesture of generosity. In the name of Colonel John Gordon of Cluny, Henderson was offering to remit the arrears of their rents, to buy their crops and their beasts off them, to pay them for any work they had done in the spring and to lend whatever was needed to give them passage to Canada on boats that were even now approaching the island. Each family was to give their answer when Henderson returned. If they would not accept the colonel's munificence, they must leave the township anyway. and make their own arrangements.

With a handful of men to protect him, Henderson rode into the township at Rubha na h-Ordaig to present the terms. A drizzle of rain fell from a ceiling of low cloud; the midges were out in force, almost invisible hoards of them, raising tempers and fraying nerves and keeping everyone within the shelter of their houses. Henderson tied his horse to a stob and walked up to the first house, Beathag's, with its peat stack newly built to the side, and its stinking midden whose juices ran across the wet ground to mingle with the litter of domestic debris scattered around the walls: a pail, a tangle of seaweed, a few planks of driftwood, a pile of fleeces. He walked with exaggerated disdain, high-stepping the dirt, wrinkling his nose. He raised his whip and rapped on the door. Hostile eyes watched from every house, as Beathag lumbered out to stand towering over him, She listened to his prepared speech. He held out a paper towards her. She uttered one brief sentence, brushed the paper aside, and shut the door in his face.

Tómas came to his door, swaying slightly. He listened to the prepared speech with look of good-humoured indulgence on his face, as if he was pandering a troublesome child. Then he reached out, plucked the paper from Henderson's fingers, ripped it into pieces and let them flutter to the ground between them.

'Go back to the gutter you crawled out of, Mr Henderson,' he bellowed, for everyone to hear. 'We can manage fine without you.' Driven to a frenzy by the pervasive midges, Henderson's face was apoplectic. He raised his whip as if to strike Tómas, but checked himself and turned away, rubbing his exposed skin frantically.

Catrìona, Frangan and Ruairidh watched as he made his way from house to house, with always the same negative reception, working his way towards them. He slapped angrily at his face and neck and tried to drive off the midges by flapping his hands. Theirs was the last house, and it was almost as if he had been saving it up for the end. When the knock came, Frangan opened the door.

'Are you the head of the family?' Henderson demanded harshly.

'I am.' From the room, Catrìona watched her brother standing as tall as possible, his chin in the air, head flung back. It was a stance she recognised as one she adopted herself when on her mettle.

'On this paper are written the generous terms offered by Colonel Gordon, if you will agree to leave this house and take the ship to Canada. Shall I read it out to you?' It was rudely meant.

'No thank you.' Frangan could sound lordly arrogant when he wished. He took the paper. There was a silence as he read the terms.

'Well?' said Henderson when he had finished. 'Will you go?' Frangan looked at him. Then he screwed the paper into a ball and tossed it contemptuously over his shoulder.

'No,' he said quietly, 'we shall not go. This is our home.' He closed the door and came back into the room. 'That man is evil,' he said. 'We must think of a way of preventing this.'

All the time, Màiri sat hunched on the chair, saying nothing, nor indicating by any means whether she was aware of what was going on or not. Catrìona suspected that she was so wracked with the pain and the effort of trying not to cough that she had little attention left to spare for what was going on around her.

Each family came out to stand at their doorways, silently watching as Henderson strode back to his horse. A dog, one of Beathag's, rushed out suddenly, running low to the ground, its wall eyes glowing red, and flung itself at him with snarling ferocity. In the flurry that followed it was hard to see exactly what happened, but Henderson, fighting off the dog with yelps of anger and fear, scrambled clumsily on to his horse and kicked it into motion with savage jabs of his boots. A long strip of cloth was seen to be hanging down from the

121

seat of his breeches. A roar of derisive laughter followed him up the track.

III

A list of the 'generous terms' that had been offered by Colonel Gordon was posted in every township, alongside the eviction orders in their stark, legal language.

Every one of the families in the township at Rubha na h-Ordaig was to be off the land by the end of the week, which was in three days time, after which their roofs would be fired. At the time of eviction, each would be given a final chance to accept the terms for emigration, terms that so far everyone had refused instinctively. If this final offer was rejected, then they must fend for themselves.

'But who wants to go to Canada?' stormed Beathag, standing four square in her doorway, arms akimbo, legs straddled. 'I've heard stories about that place. They have terrible winters there, with the frost so hard it turns your breath to icicles in some parts. And besides, the conditions on the boats are terrible they say, in spite of all their grand Acts of Parliament, laying down all sorts of fancy rules and regulations.'

'Everyone knows that the Passenger Act was passed when they wanted the people to stay at home and work the kelp,' said Séumas. 'They improved the conditions on the boats so they could put up the prices and none of the poor people could afford to pay them. It'll be a different kettle of fish now, right enough, when they want us gone. You can be sure they won't be so particular about how many people are accommodated in their stinking boats.'

'I heard there was plague on one of the last boats,' said Eilidh, 'and many people died. And then when they got to the place the other side, they were put into sheds and they were still dying every day.'

'Cholera, that was,' someone supplied.

'But where else can we go?' It was a cry from every heart.

Ruairidh raged impotently, thinking of the despatch he had sent to the mainland, knowing that it could be many weeks before it took effect, if ever. Frangan incited them all to protect themselves with weapons. He fetched his broadsword from its hiding place in the thatch and swung it over his head, until Catrìona shouted sense into him, and the Bard reminded him that spilt blood would only make things worse.

By the evening, as the second gale abated, the entire island knew of the disaster that hung over them. The lucky ones were those who were spared, because their holdings were too poor to support sheep or because they had no holdings at all. The tradespeople were to stay, of course: the merchants, millers, joiners, tailors, blacksmiths, tinsmiths, cobblers and tanners, as well as the officials: the excise officer, policemen, minister, priests, doctor. But at Rubha na h-Ordaig, every family counted as a cottar, with no rights, occupying land that could be more profitably used in other hands.

Everywhere, people gathered in each other's houses to try to find some solution to their difficulties.

'You should have told him about mother, when he came to the door,' Catrìona scolded her twin. 'You should have had him come inside and see her for himself.'

'It would have served no purpose,' he said. 'I tell you, he is evil. Nothing will change his mind.'

'That is stupid! We don't know till we try. There may be a law against turning someone out if they are sick. I shall go and tell him, and I shall also tell him about Ruairidh's article that will soon be published in the newspapers for the whole country to read. That should make him think.' They were sitting round the fire in the room, having propped Màiri up in her bed for the night.

'I didn't say anything in it about evicting people who were sick,' Ruairidh said. 'I only wrote the facts as they were then.'

'He is not to know that.'

'And it will be a while before the article finds its way to Edinburgh, I'm afraid.'

'You men! Always looking on the gloomy side. You are

worse than the Bard, both of you. Where is your fighting spirit!' How could they be so abject. 'I shall go and find Henderson tomorrow and put our case to him. If he refuses to listen, we shall have to go to Gordon himself.' She felt Ruairidh's eyes on her face and saw the approval in them. 'If anyone goes, it should be Frangan,' he said. 'You are not to go anywhere near the brute.'

'I must,' she retorted. 'It was I who set him against us, after all. Perhaps it will be possible to . . . persuade him to change his mind.'

'No! Catrìona! You cannot . . . ' Ruairidh reached across and gripped her wrist. She loosened his hand, lifted it to her mouth, kissed the palm and wrapped his fingers round the kiss, her eyes dancing with mischief.

Frangan's eyes widened with astonishment. She smiled at him. 'Didn't you guess?' she said. He shook his head. 'And you my twin! I thought we had intuition between us, you and I.' Again he shook his head and she laughed softly. 'I'd have known, if it had been you,' she said. Turning back to Ruairidh, holding on to his hand and tracing the lines in its palm with her forefinger, she murmured: 'don't you trust me to be faithful, dear love?'

'Of course I trust you. It is not a question of fidelity. But I can think of only one way he might be persuaded to change his mind.' His fingers laced hers. 'And that is not even thinkable.'

'I wasn't contemplating sacrificing my virtue!' she said, making a prim face at him.

Ruairidh's eyebrow shot up. 'Virtue?' he said, softly, 'what virtue.' She grinned.

'Catrìona!' Frangan gaped at her.

'Don't look so shocked Frangan,' she flashed at him. 'Are you so chaste that you can cast the first stone?' He started to protest but she cut in. 'I hear little Liùsi and you have been spending a lot of time in the caves recently.' He was silent for a moment, torn between anger and amusement. Amusement won and the three of them broke into laughter.

'You must both see,' she went on, 'that as I was the original object of his displeasure, I must somehow try to undo the harm.'

'It would be a waste of time, and dangerous.' Ruairidh said. 'I think we should go to Father Eóghan: surely the priest has some authority.'

'Of course! What fools we are! We'll take our case to Father Eóghan. Why did no one think of that before.' Catrìona felt a great surge of relief. The priest was invincible; if he put in a word for them, no one would dare to go against his wishes.

'The priest is in a difficult position,' Ruairidh warned. 'We Catholics are only tolerated on sufferance don't forget. Any priest who seems to be inciting the people to go against the landowners might find himself expelled, and then the people would not even have the comfort of the sacraments.'

'Surely, in a case like this, he would be allowed to put in a word for us. It could hardly be called incitement; just common humanity,' Ruairidh shrugged. 'It is worth a try, at any rate. Frangan, you must go at first light tomorrow: we have so little time.'

They had no difficulty in persuading Ruairidh to spend the night in their house, in case Màiri should need more expert attention than the twins could give her. Catrìona lay on a pile of fleeces on the floor beside her mother and the two men shared Frangan's box bed.

IV

During the night, the wind dropped and steady rain succeeded the gale. By morning the ground was a quagmire, the tracks like running rivers. The hay rotted where it lay; no one noticed or cared. Of what use was hay without beasts, and who would have beasts by the end of the week? Water poured down off the hills, crept in through the roofs and the stone walls. Dampness pervaded everything: damp peats smouldered on the fire; it was impossible to dry the blankets they wrapped round Màiri.

Frangan left early in the morning, riding up to Bornish

church on Tómas's horse because their own was lame. The rain fell in a relentless deluge all day, dripping down the thatch between the double walls of the house, soaking the earth and rubble that filled the space, seeping out into the room. The dryest place for Màiri was in her bed, propped up like a tiny doll among the damp shawls and blankets, watched over by Ruairidh and Catrìona. She seemed to be fading away before their eyes, her moments of rest separated by the heart-rending spasms of coughing.

During the moments when she was peaceful, they sat close together on the bench, sometimes holding hands, talking in whispers, telling secrets and making confessions: tender exchanges, repeated by all new lovers in every language in every century in every corner of the world, and yet singular to each.

'When did you first love me?'

'I loved you, before you went away,' she told him. 'Did you not know that?'

'I wasn't sure, but I hoped you did.'

'You didn't do any such thing. You thought of me as just a child.'

'Not that last summer I didn't, nor on that final day before I left, when you comforted me. Do you remember that?' He caressed her cheek. 'I carried that memory in my heart when I went away.'

'Until the first pretty face crossed your path, I've no doubt.' He chuckled.

'I thought we had agreed not to mention all those fancy women you insist on burdening me with. Once and for all, not one of them was serious, Catrìona, I swear, and when I decided to come home, it was you I was thinking of most, on the boat coming across.'

'Really?' He nodded. She was absurdly pleased.

'I thought of you so often while you were away, and always I thought you would come back with some smart town woman, all done up in fine clothes and fancy language.'

'Shame on you! And what about you? All this talk about my little indiscretions: don't tell me you didn't lose your heart a few times over the years because I won't believe you.'

She grinned. 'Never my heart, but sometimes my head, I'll grant you. And never,' she shot him a mischievous look, 'my virtue, as you know full well, until you came back to claim it.'

They talked of what might happen to the township, and the people but they steered away from any talk of their own future. They speculated on the success or failure of Frangan's mission and tried to be optimistic. They heated milk, beat eggs into it, strengthened it with honey and gave Màiri frequent sips of it. At one point, Tómas came in, to see how she was, and stood by the bed looking down at her, an expression of sadness on his florid face.

'She is dying, isn't she?' he said to Ruairidh, quietly; 'I've seen that look before.'

'Yes,' Ruairidh told him, 'and it won't be very much longer.'

'What about the evictions? We can't let them turn her out.'

'No. It would certainly hasten the end. Frangan has gone up to Bornish to see if the priest can put in a word for her.'

But when Frangan returned, late in the afternoon, it was with a grim face and no hope.

'There was a great crowd at the church,' he said. 'All with petitions to the priest to intervene for them. Mother isn't the only one too sick to be turned out. There are many others, some as close if not closer to death than she.'

'But why couldn't he do anything?' demanded Catrìona. 'However many there are. Can't he help them all?'

'He says not. He came out and spoke to everyone. He says that Colonel Gordon owns the island and can do what he likes with it. And Gordon is a Protestant, so the Catholic church has no authority over him. The ministers of his own church have even been reading out the eviction orders in the kirks in some places on the mainland, so they say. He says . . .' Frangan hesitated, '. . . he says we must pray.'

'Pray!' Catrìona spat the word. 'He can do the praying for us. I am going to do something more positive.'

Màiri was no worse the next day, but her condition was very bad. When she wasn't coughing, she slept. There was no saying how long it would last: it could go on for weeks yet, Ruairidh said, or she could die at any moment. Each bout of coughing weakened her further and it was also a terrible strain on her heart.

Catrìona watched over her mother, prepared food for them all including Ruairidh and tended the house and the fire. The few moments when she was able to be alone with Ruairidh gave her strength and his medical knowledge was a great comfort, though he was unable to provide a cure.

Then the rain stopped and the sun came out and it was as if there was hope. The ground dried out; a light breeze blew the dampness from the houses Màiri seemed to cough a little less.

V

Catrìona, carrying water from the burn, saw a horse and rider in the distance, coming down the track towards her. There was something familiar about the man. She set down her pail and stood watching. It was Donald Henderson. He came up to her and halted, looking down at her with an unpleasant smile on his fleshy face and a gleam of triumph in his pale protruberant eyes.

'Good day to you,' he said, 'Miss Catrìona Macdonald.' He had discovered her name: this meant that he had been making enquiries about her in particular, and no doubt her family, and Ruairidh . . . She felt anger rising to conquer prudence, but she knew this might be her chance: her only chance. She stared up at him, forcing herself to smile. Could she possibly persuade him to be merciful?

'Good day to you, Mr Donald Henderson,' she said, trying to sound friendly. 'What a blessing the rain has stopped.'

'Indeed,' he agreed, in his mincing voice. 'It will make it so much easier for everyone as they move out of their houses.' He was mocking her, relishing her sycophancy. She wanted to scratch his eyes out.

128

' Mr Henderson, I was planning to come and see you.' She pronounced the English syllables carefully.

'I am flattered.' She hated him.

'My mother is dying. She has tuberculosis. She could die at any moment. She must be kept quiet and warm.'

'How fortunate for her, and you, that you have been able to draw on the knowledge of a half-trained medical student.' She bit back the hot words that threatened to escape. The man had been digging deep for his information.

'Yes, we are fortunate; and he says that if we try to move her we shall hasten her death.'

'Ah! Perhaps that would solve your problems. You'd not want to see her so sick in a ship going all the way to Canada. It can be a long voyage.'

'Please. I am asking you to let us stay in our house until . . . for as long as she lives.' She gripped her hands together, putting all the entreaty she could into her voice. 'Our presence could hardly make any great difference to anyone, if we promise to leave when . . . when it is over.'

'No!' It was a whiplash. 'What makes you think your family merits special treatment? There are plenty of sick people on this island, all thinking their plight makes them special.' His horse threw up its head and sidled, nearly throwing him. With a curse, he clung on and brought it into control. 'I want every house cleared by the end of the week and that is final.'

'And if it were your mother, Mr Henderson, dying in her house, and someone ordered you to get her out and you had nowhere to go? What would you do?'

'The cases are hardly comparable,' he sneered. 'My mother owns her house.'

'But if things were different. If she . . . '

'You are wasting your time.' Impulsively, she put her hand on the horse's neck.

'Mr Henderson, is there anything I can do that will change your mind?' As she spoke, she wondered just how far she would be prepared to go, to persuade him. But she need not have worried. His harsh bark of laughter made her flinch.

'Too late, bitch,' he said. 'You had your chance and you chose to ignore it. Did I not tell you then that you and your precious doctor would regret it for the rest of your lives.' His voice was a triumphant sneer.

'I shall appeal to Colonel Gordon. I shall tell him that you are acting from personal spite and that you have tried to molest his tenants. He must be a just man.'

'Colonel Gordon is not on the island, nor is he coming in the immediate future. By the time your appeal reached him, if it ever did, you will be half way to Canada in the first boat to sail from here. He puts all his trust in his agent. I have his full authority to act as I think best for his interests. I consider that this island is overcrowded, disease-ridden and its land poorly cultivated. Furthermore, I find the people ignorant and lazy, with minds and habits no better than their pathetic animals.'

Catrìona stepped back, her head held high, her eyes blazing.

'That, Mr Henderson, will prove to be your downfall.' With all the strength of her will, she compelled him to look her in the eyes. For a moment, it was as if she held him completely in her power: he looked almost nervous. She chose the unfamiliar English words with care.'Poor we may be, by your standards, and our living conditions may seem primitive, but ignorant and bestial we are not! You make a mistake in treating us as animals. You should have studied our history, Mr Henderson. We lost our old way of life more than a hundred years ago when our clans were broken up and our chiefs deserted us, but we never lost our pride.' Her voice rang out, full of passion; it was as if she was being directed by some outside force. Henderson seemed to be mesmerised, listening against his will, and for a moment she thought she saw uneasiness in his porcine features.

'We are Celts, Mr Henderson; our ancestors were Lords of the Isles. When each clan was a united family under one chief everyone owed loyalty to that chief but no one was his servant. When the chief called on his clan for men to fight, every able man rallied of his own free will and in return he looked to his chief for justice and guidance.' Still she held his attention, forcing her will on him.

'You find us ignorant, Mr Henderson. Simple and uneducated would be better words. Our people have an intellect far above that of your oafish Anglo-Saxon peasants: our musicians, our bards, our story-tellers can stand shoulder to shoulder with any you care to name.' She spat words at him, pouring out all the frustration and anger that his ruthless arrogance had generated. 'You can turn us out of our houses, you can force us to go over the ocean, but you will never, never break our spirit. If you send us away from our homeland you will damage the land but you will not destroy its people.'

Donald Henderson slapped his boot with his whip, as if to break the spell her words were creating. She stopped, feeling drained and impotent.

'Very interesting, Miss Macdonald. They should invite you to be dominie when you arrive in Canada. Your eloquence should certainly indoctrinate a new generation of rebels.' He was playing with her again; had regained control, in his sneering voice.

'I am not going to Canada, Mr Henderson. This is my home.' She spoke flatly, knowing she was beaten. She turned, picked up the pail of water and walked away from him across the moor. His voice, following her, was as peevish as that of a spoilt child:

'Tomorrow we shall start clearing the houses. You are sailing on that boat if I have to tie you down with my own hands.' She didn't look round. 'It will be in the harbour any time now, and we have the army and the police to help with any trouble.'

VI

'Could that be true?' Catrìona demanded of Ruairidh, who had walked out from the house to take the pail of water from her. 'Can he force us to take the boat? Would the army really come?'

'I don't know. Certainly by the time we could get any sort of word to Gordon it will be too late. What was he doing here anyway?'

'I suspect he had come to gloat. Or to test the mood of the people maybe. But Ruairidh,' she gripped his hand; 'he is determined to get us on to the first boat to Canada. How can he make us?'

'He is acting for the man who owns the island, he can make you leave it.'

'Yes, he can force us to leave the island but he can't force anyone to go to Canada against their will, can he?'

'Catrìona, I . . . '

'Ruairidh, come . . . quick . . . it's mother. . . .' Frangan called urgently from the door of the house. They hurried in. Màiri was lying on the floor by the chair, her clothes stained with blood. She seemed to be unconscious but she was still breathing. They lifted her up and tended her: her eyes flickered as Catrìona wiped the blood from her lips.

'Pain,' she gasped. 'Such pain.' She pressed her hands to her chest. Ruairidh soothed her; it was as if he had the power of healing in his gentle hands for she relaxed and closed her eyes. With his help, Catrìona set about changing her clothes and washing her.

A voice called from outside: Frangan went out to investigate. Voices, muffled by the thick walls, rose and fell. When he returned he put a finger to his lips and beckoned them to the far end of the room.

'Tómas was up the hill looking for a new place for his still: he says there is a transport boat sailing into the harbour at this moment. It'll be anchored within the hour.'

VII

Henderson returned in the morning with half a dozen ground officers, none of them local men, riding out along the track and down into the township on sturdy horses. Once again he approached Beathag's house first and knocked on the door. This time, when he had put his one brief question to her and received her answer, he turned and shouted an order to the men. They pushed past her into her house. She followed them in, shouting. The whole community stood outside their houses, listening and watching. There was the sound of voices raised and they heard Beathag's, loudest of all, yelling at them to stop what they were doing, to get out. One of the men reappeared, dragging her meal chest behind him, with her trying to stop him, screaming abuse at him, tugging ineffectually at one of the handles. She turned towards the other houses, her hair unpinned and wild, her face stricken. She held out her arms, imploring for assistance.

But no one moved to help her; it was as if they were all frozen by the horror and cruelty of it. Her bedding was tossed out and lay in a heap in the mud that was still sticky from the recent rain. She tried to collect it together, heaping rugs and blankets on to the meal chest from which they flopped back into the dirt. Her sticks of furniture came next: the planks of wood and barrels that had made up her table and bench and chairs, her stools, her spinning wheel. As each of her possessions appeared, thrown roughly out as if it were rubbish, she greeted it with a moan, rummaging in the growing pile of broken bits, pulling things out with cries of distress:

'My stool; oh my crocks; Holy Mother, my crucifix!' Her daughters stood by, sobbing, too shocked to do anything to help.

'Is there nothing we can do?' Catrìona muttered, gripping Ruairidh's arm. 'How can we just stand here, watching.'

'There are too many of them,' Ruairidh said, 'and besides, what could we do except fight and possibly kill, and that wouldn't help.'

Then the men began on her roof. They tore down the reed thatch with hooks, scattering it on the ground and stamping on it. They pulled out the turf divots and her house became a gaping, empty shell topped by a skeleton of rafters made from a crude assortment of driftwood, old oars and spars. Beathag stood amid the wreckage of her home, finally struck dumb with grief, her big, flabby face streaming with tears. All the fight had gone out of her.

The men came next to the tiny hovel where the *cailleach* had lived all her life, nearly a hundred years, some said. It was the smallest of the dwellings in the township, almost round in shape with turf piled against stone, looking more like a potato clamp than a house. The *cailleach* guarded her privacy fiercely and no one ever ventured inside. Legends, half-believed, told of the various trappings of sorcery that would be found in the dark room: broomsticks and a press brimming with magic potions and spells.

As the first man approached, Peigi herself came to the door and stood there, one hand lifted as if to ward them off, her eyes like two balls of fire, her white hair tumbled over her shoulders giving her a biblical appearance. In a high, keening yowl, she intoned a long spiel in her own language. She was the only member of the community who had refused to learn even a smattering of English from Ruairidh's father. It was an awe-inspiring sight, the little old woman with no flesh on her bones, more like a stick of driftwood than a human being, standing there venting the fury and contempt they all felt. The leading man fell back as if her words were indeed casting some magic hold over him. But Henderson, watching, called out an order and they moved forward again. Peigi, seeing that they were determined, threw herself to the ground and lay prone in her doorway, feet inside, head out. Again the men stopped.

Tómas's voice rang out: 'Watch out for the dog, Mr Henderson: it was hoping to get another bite at your arse.' There was a ripple of derision. Henderson, flushed with humiliation, took a step forward, pointing his whip at Peigi.

'Move her!' he yelled, but the men stood in an uncertain group around the prostrate figure. He strode forward, his face suffused with anger, his fleshy body bulging in his fine city clothes. He pushed through the men and prodded Peigi with his foot. There was a low growl of protest from the people watching from their doorways. He bent over her and shouted: 'get up, you old witch. If you don't, we shall have to lift you.' Still she lay there, staring up at him, rigid. He grabbed her shoulders and began to drag her clear of the doorway, her body trailing in the dirt. When he had moved her a short distance he let her go. Her head thumped onto the ground and she lay, motionless, her eyes now shut, her mouth gaping in a silent shout of outrage There was something frightening in her imobility.

'He's killed her!' screamed Eilidh.

Henderson looked around at the grim faces, visibly apprehensive. His men shifted, uneasily; the air vibrated with raw hostility – ugly, threatening. The mood had suddenly switched from dumb impotence to savage rage. The people began to move, very slowly, closing in on the tableau outside the *cailleach*'s house. Henderson glanced at the horses, tethered some distance away, and at the circle of ground officers who stood back, obviously reluctant to get involved. His visible alarm provided the spark needed to light the flame of revenge.

Frangan stooped, picked up a sharp stone and flung it with all his might, straight at Henderson. It hit his fat belly, causing him to double up with a squeak of pain. There was a high, blood-curdling shriek and stones began to fly from all directions. The ground officers dithered, torn between retreat or attack. While they vacillated, Henderson crouched down, holding his arms over his head, sobbing for mercy. The people came closer, silent, menacing, their faces distorted with hatred. They were running out of missiles but still they came on, until they formed a tight circle round the cringing man, gibbering on the ground beside Peigi's prone body.

For a moment, Catrìona thought they were going to tear him apart, like a pack of dogs at a rabbit, but no one made the first move. They just stood, watching him. He came to his feet, poised to duck again, darting furtive looks, a figure of ridicule. He glanced down at Peigi.

'She's not dead,' he panted. 'She's breathing. Look!' He jabbed his finger. 'I didn't kill her. She was just stunned, that's all.' Peigi's eyes flew open, fixing on him with a red, malignant glare. Henderson backed away, still at bay but recovering his authority. The circle of people parted, their thirst for vengeance defused. As he stumbled through their double ranks they reached out their hands and their feet to taunt him as he passed, so that he had to dodge and duck. The ground officers followed him.

He flung himself at his horse. Mounted, feeling more secure, no doubt, he wheeled, screeching curses at the men who were trying to form up behind him.

'I shall be back the day after tomorrow,' he shouted. 'I shall bring more men, and this time we shall burn the roofs.' The cavalcade moved away up the track with the loud jeers of the people of Rubha na h-Ordaig in their ears.

'We can't look for mercy now,' said Ruairidh. 'But I salute you, Frangan. Whatever may come, Henderson has had to pay a crushing price for his eventual victory.'

A group of people bent over Peigi, helping her to her feet. She stood stiffly erect for a moment, supported on either side, testing her balance. Then, with silent dignity, she shook off the hands that held her and marched into her house, shutting the door behind her.

VIII

Catrìona stared out through the open door towards the loch. 'I know what we must do.' The two men looked at her expectantly. 'We must take mother and hide in the caves.'

'But we can't possibly move her!' Frangan protested. 'She would die and besides, she is too ill to live in a cave.'

'She will die anyway, we know that; very soon. But wouldn't she rather die with dignity.' Her voice was quiet and very sure. 'If Henderson comes tomorrow, and he certainly will, and she has to be subjected to that, she will die tormented. And if she does not die from the shock of the eviction, and we have to put her in a cart and trundle her all that way, or take her across in the boat, the journey would be torture. And at the end of it what? Herded into the transport ship to die in conditions no better than a cattle pen? Or, if she were to survive that, arriving in a foreign land, with nothing but the clothes on her back, to die among strangers. Don't you see, Frangan?' She put her hand on his arm, beseeching him. 'We can put her on a litter and carry her ourselves. If we wrap her well and take it very slowly and she will hardly know what is happening. We can make it comfortable enough, and keep watch. One of the caves goes a long way back: if we are careful to leave nothing lying around, we can retreat into that if we see anyone coming. The rest of the time she'd be in the fresh air, or near the entrance to the cave, and she would be free.'

'They think fresh air is good for tuburculosis,' Ruairidh put in. 'There is even talk of setting up places for patients where they can live out of doors. I think it is a good idea.'

'But think what it will be like if we get another gale?' Frangan spread his hands. 'We'd be blown away, up there.'

'Not in the long cave, we'd be a lot more sheltered than down here. And dryer, too, when it rains. Please Frangan. We have no time left. It is not as if this would be for very long, is it Ruairidh?'

He shook his head sadly. 'No. She can't go on much longer.' He put his hand on Frangan's shoulder. 'It is a good idea, Frangan. She could possibly linger on for a few days. Would you have her witness what we have just seen. Would you give Henderson the satisfaction of ordering her to be carried out and dumped among her things in the dirt, or dragged out, like the *cailleach?* She would die in an agony of mind as well as of body. If we take her away, we won't save her life but we may save her dignity.'

CHAPTER 9

I

With wholehearted enthusiasm, the people in the township rallied to assist in what they saw as the thwarting of Donald Henderson. Perhaps, Catrìona thought, it was a way of forgetting their own problems, or perhaps this act of defiance served as each person's individual protest.

Frangan unfastened the wooden planks that partitioned off the animal pens from the living room in the house. Willing neighbours provided poles, brought out from precious, secret hoards of driftwood and they made a litter. On an island where there were no trees, and where driftwood was supposed to belong to the government, wood was hard to come by and carefully preserved. At a time when the future of each of them was threatened, it never occurred to anyone to use their energy or their possessions trying to save themselves. Màiri was sick and needed help: it was their duty and their instinct to do what they could and they did it generously.

Catrìona, watching the preparations, receiving the many offerings brought to her door – an extra blanket from Eilidh, a packet of dried saithe from Beathag, a bottle of medicinal *uisge-beatha* from Tómas, felt humbled by their charity and deeply regretted the many snide jokes she and Frangan had shared at some of their idiosyncrasies in the past. Even the *cailleach* came to the door bearing a crock containing some herbal potion she thought might ease Màiri's discomfort. Catrìona forced herself to meet the wild, staring eyes as she thanked her, and asked her how she was after her own experience with Donald Henderson.

The old crone leant towards her; she tried not to flinch from the unpleasant odour of her unclean body.

'I have put a curse on him,' she screeched. 'He won't be troubling folk for much longer,' and she rattled off a harsh cackle of laughter. 'No one abuses Peigi Campbell,' she gabbled, 'and lives to boast of it.' Catrìona took the crock from her claw-like hands and thanked her again. She felt a shiver of awe as Peigi stumped off.

When the sun had reached its zenith, a lone figure was seen riding down the path to the township, too large for the small pony that carried it. It was Father Eóghan, his black soutane bunched up over his knees, come to see for himself if there was anything he could do to help Màiri, spiritually if not temporally. The people stood watching his slow approach. His life had been as hard as anyone else's on the island, trying to administer to a people whose faith had long been proscribed, making his every act difficult. He was known and respected throughout the island, and the fact that he had made this long ride down to visit Màiri was a typical mark of his devotion to his flock.

He dismounted and someone came forward to take the pony. He was an old, stooped man with white hair and a great beak of a nose, over which he stared at them with piercing blue eyes. He singled out Frangan and beckoned to him.

'How is she?' he enquired. 'Your mother.'

'We are preparing to take her away, Father, to hide her, up in the caves.' Frangan pointed to the ruin of Beathag's home. 'The man Henderson was here yesterday. He is coming back tomorrow, to finish his foul work. Will you come to her, Father? She is in the house yet.' He led the priest through the township and the people bowed their heads in respect as they passed. Inside, in the gloom, Màiri was sitting upright in her chair, hunched and barely conscious, her pain-racked eyes half closed and unseeing. Catrìona and Ruairidh, who had followed them inside, came forward and Ruairidh bent over her, listening. He straightened and looked across at Father Eóghan.

'She is holding on, Father, but only just,' he murmured.

'It may not be possible for me to get back again,' said the old man. 'Is it too soon for the last rites?'

'No, not at all. She could go at any time now.'

They left the priest alone with Màiri, in case she should be strong enough to make her confession and then he called them back and they knelt while he prayed and annointed her forehead. Although this Extreme Unction was the prelude to death, Catrìona was aware of a deep peace in the room, and knew for certain that what they were doing was the best thing for Màiri.

II

It was mid-afternoon when the procession set off up the valley and into the hills towards the caves. Quite a party of neighbours accompanied them, at least one representative from each family in the township, carrying food, blankets, oil for the lamp; taking turns with the litter. At the last moment, Tómas emerged from his house carrying his bagpipes. He placed himself at the head of the column and led them out of the township, through the valley and into the hills, the haunting notes of the pipes beckoning them upwards. Several dogs accompanied them, running ahead, quartering the ground, putting up birds and rabbits. The sun showed fitfully from gaps in the clouds chasing shadows across the heather. Lapwings flew out from under their feet as they passed and a blackcock, scolding, rattled off out of range. Catrìona walked beside the litter, putting out her hand now and then to reassure her mother.

Màiri lay cocooned in shawls and rugs, half conscious, too ill to question what was happening. With the careful carrying of the litter, it took more than three hours to get up to the craggy peaks. Catrìona had a moment of doubt; was this really the place for her mother to die in? It was desolate up here, with great slabs of grey rock thrown up by primeval eruptions out of pits of peat where water lay, dark brown and still. The caves ran back into the southern face, overlooking the sound that divided them from the southern islands. Some were just shallow indentations, offering scant shelter, some deeper and one, approached through a long fissure opened out into a large chamber with a gently sloping earth floor.

This was the one they chose as Màiri's last resting place. It was dry, not too cold, with enough light coming in to see by without using up valuable fish oil burning the *crùisgean* by day.

Perhaps the most uncomfortable part of the whole journey was getting the sick woman into the cave, through the narrow entrance. In the end Ruairidh carried her in his arms and even with his lean frame and her stick-like body it was a struggle to get her through the constricted passage and the discomfort brought on a terrible coughing fit.

They settled her, making a soft bed of pulled bracken and heather, and rested her against the far wall of the cave. The people grouped round the entrance in the twilight. One by one they went inside to take their final leave of the dying woman. There was the occasional glisten of tears as each one stooped, touched her wasted hand, or put lips to her clammy forehead. Perhaps she knew she was dying. Catrìona watched her anxiously. Tómas was the last to go in: Tómas who had loved her in his way, his brother's wife, but been unable to win her approval by parting from his still. When he emerged, his cheeks were wet. Beathag took his hand as if he were a child. They began to walk back to the township, a silent, proud procession. While they were yet visible to the three who stayed behind with Màiri, the sound of Tómas's pipes floated up through the dusk, playing a lament that hung in the evening air long after the people were out of sight.

Màiri lingered on, her faithful attendants taking it in turns to sit with her, keep watch outside, or rest. They made the cave as comfortable as they could, but dared not light a fire for fear of the smoke that would alert anyone looking for them. They were trespassing at the heart of the sheep-run for which Henderson was evicting their township. If he found them up here while Màiri was still alive, he could even now wreak his revenge by bringing violence to her last hours.

It was a strange time, suspended between fear for the future and defiance, cut off from the world.

For a while, in the morning, Catrìona went out to keep Ruairidh company as he watched for signs of searchers.

They lay on their stomachs, side by side on the summit, invisible from below if they kept still, able to see the entire spread of the south-eastern foot of the island. Their own township lay out of sight beyond a shoulder of cliff, but they could see the whole floor of the valley to the north, and all the possible approaches. To the south they could see the hills of the other islands and the peaks of rock that rose like blackened teeth from the turquoise water of the sound. The tide was out and the white sands of Glendale glistened in the sunlight. There were people on the sands, tiny as insects, gathering shellfish from the rocks, and raking up cockles. The water was a mirror of the sky. Smoke rose from townships around the coast and they could see a few boats out by Hartamul rock, fishing for saithe and pollack.

Catrìona sighed, her heart torn by the beauty around them and the closeness of her lover. It was almost as if Donald Henderson did not exist. She lay very close to him and twined her fingers through his and teased his ear with her tongue. For a few moments, a surge of mutual desire threatened to overwhelm them both. But then he pulled away, smiled, kissed her and pushed her gently from him.

'Minx,' he said. 'Don't torment me.'

'Everything is unreal,' she said. 'Ever since the day you came back, I've been living in a dream.'

'A nightmare?' His eyebrow shot up.

'Oh yes, a terrible nightmare!' She reached out and traced his profile with her finger. 'No, I don't have to tell you: a lovely, happy dream.' He caught her finger in his lips.

'We haven't talked about the future, have we?' His voice was indistinct: she retrieved her finger.

'No.'

'You know that, until I qualify, if I do . . . '

'Of course you will,' she put in vehemently. 'Anyone can see that you were born to be a physician.'

'I hope my superiors will be as generous as you. Anyway, until then, I have to tell you that I am not in a position to support a wife. I live in one small room and can barely afford to eat, let alone clothe myself; and any spare money has to go on books.'

'Yes?'

'So if you . . . if we . . . if you wanted to come back to Edinburgh with me, you would have to find employment for the first year.' He glanced at her. 'It is a terrible thing to have to say to the girl you want to marry, isn't it!' She shook her head.

'Not terrible at all, just honest.' She touched his hand. 'Let us leave the future until it becomes the present,' she said. Her heart was heavy with the knowledge of the secret she was keeping from him. She pushed it to the back of her mind and tried to show him a calm spirit. They lay there for a while, murmuring, their hands entwined, until suddenly he looked down across the valley, gripped her hand and pointed. A column of figures came into sight from the north-west, winding along the track through the valley towards Rubha na h-Ordaig. One was mounted, the rest straggled behind on foot.

'Henderson! It must be.' There were upwards of a dozen of them, the special constables they had heard about, no doubt, shipped over from Oban to enforce law and order during this latest scourge of evictions. They filed along the track and vanished from sight.

'Now begins the heartache.' Catrìona closed her eyes. 'Thank God we got mother away in time.'

They had heard enough of Henderson's methods and seen for themselves how ruthlessly he applied them, not to be able to picture what soon would be the happening, down there in their township.

They were silent, watching, ears straining, both tense, waiting for some sign that Henderson had started his vile work.

Then Frangan called up to them, urgently, and they hurried to the cave.

The change in Màiri's condition was very marked. She lay, her head pressed back against the rock wall, her mouth gaping. There were long pauses between every breath, as if each one was her last. Now and then she gave little cries of pain. Her fingers curled and uncurled, restlessly crawling over her chest. A flicker of a pulse beat in her neck.

They gathered round her. Catrìona took her hand, whispering soothing words. It was an uncomfortable vigil, crouched down on the floor, with only the feeble flame from the *crùisgean* to light them, and it seemed to last forever. Watching the spasms of pain on her mother's face, Catrìona found herself praying: entreating: Please God, let her die now. Please God let this be her last breath. Let her free, now.

But still it went on, hour after hour, as if she were not yet ready to let go. Catrìona knew that the other two must be sharing her thoughts and prayers and the knowledge that, had they not brought her up here, her last moments would have been shattered by all the horror and violence of Henderson's vengeance. It seemed impossible for her to keep up this agonised breathing: the gaps grew longer: Please God, take her, now!

There was one, final, terrible issue of blood: it seemed to give her relief. She opened her eyes for a moment and her face was suddenly at peace. She smiled, and died.

Ruairidh felt her pulse, nodded, and gently closed her eyes with his thumb. They knelt, the three of them, round the makeshift bed, and Catrìona, her voice husky but unfaltering, led them in the prayers so familiar to them all. It was over. Outside, the dog set up an eerie howl that echoed and re-echoed round the hills, an uncanny lament.

They went out into the daylight. It was strange to find that the sun was still shining, the world still existing as it always had done, the little figures still busy far below on the sands.

They had already planned what to do and had brought up the *coibe* to dig a grave with. Having made it possible for her to die in peace, away from the ravages of Henderson and his team, they wanted her to lie forever up here, with all the island spread out below her. Later, with God's help, they might be able to get the priest to come up and say the burial: meanwhile, they knew the words, and surely God would understand.

The two men took the *coibe* and went away round the peak, looking for a suitable place to dig. Catrìona went back inside the cave to make her mother ready.

She stood, gazing down. Màiri looked so peaceful, now, it was already hard to remember her struggle. This was the woman who had given birth to her and Frangan, twenty-three years ago, and learned of the death of her husband within the same month. She had been too young to be widowed and it could not have been easy for her, running the croft and raising twins. Of course she would have had help from the community, but even so. Catrìona and Frangan had been high-spirited, right enough, and had often defied their mother's strict rule. She stooped and traced a cross on the cold brow and lightly kissed it. Then, briskly, to keep her mind from grief, she set about laying out the body for burial. She had assisted at the laying out of several of the old people in the past and knew what to do.

As she worked, she was conscious of the dog, outside, barking. Màiri's death had disturbed it; it never normally barked for no reason. She heard the scrape of feet; one of the men was coming back into the cave.

'Have you finished the digging already,' she said, without turning her head. 'I am not quite ready for you yet.' Receiving no answer, she glanced over her shoulder. Donald Henderson stood just inside the entrance, and even in the dim light she could tell he had been drinking. Slowly, trying not to show her alarm, she straightened up and faced him.

'So, I've found you, bitch.' His voice was slurred, his features distorted. 'I heard there were caves in these hills and when I found you had left the township, I knew you'd be up here somewhere. You can thank the dog for leading me to the right spot with its howling.' He swayed, and lurched towards her. She put out a hand.

'Please,' she said quietly. 'Respect the dead.'

'Dead? Oh, so she's dead already is she?' He took another step, steadying himself against the wall of the cave. 'All the better, bitch. The dead tell no secrets.' She backed away from him; he pursued her, panting and giggling to himself.

The man was half demented. He closed with her, pressing her back against the wall, thrusting himself against her, his hands scrabbling at her clothing, his face nuzzling into hers, exhuding the stench of stale brandy.

'No, please . . . no.' Vainly she struggled to push him away, but he held her too firmly trapped with his flabby body.

'I'm going to teach you, bitch,' he mumbled, tearing at her skirt with clumsy fingers. 'I'm a going to show you . . .' She couldn't move, her hands beat at him in vain . . . and then, over his shoulder, she saw a figure enter the cave. Frangan! For a second he stood there, taking in the scene and then he was across the uneven ground in one great bound. He grabbed Henderson from behind, yanked him away from Catrìona, and in a blind frenzy of rage, he pummelled him, punching at him over and over again. He took the lapels of his coat and shook him backwards and forwards like a sack of meal. Henderson staggered, lost his balance and fell heavily sideways, his head striking a jutting rock at the base of the wall with an alarming thud. He lay still.

The twins stood holding onto each other, looking down at him.

Ruairidh, coming in a moment later, found them like that, staring down at the motionless body, sprawled within only a few feet of Màiri's corpse.

Quickly he came forward, knelt, turned Henderson over and examined him.

'He's dead,' he said.

'Oh God!' Catrìona's mind was numb: none of it quite registered. 'The *cailleach* told me she had put a curse on him!'

'He deserved to die.' Frangan's voice was shaky. 'But I didn't kill him on purpose.'

'I suppose I don't have to ask what happened?' Ruairidh said, and had his confirmation in their two faces.

'He was drunk,' Catrìona said, as if it explained everything. 'He knew about the caves – someone had told him – and then he heard the dog howling. He found the cave and came in, and . . . well, Frangan got here in time.'

He nodded. 'I would have done the same Frangan,' he said. 'It was not murder.' He thought for a moment. 'We don't have much time; they could be looking for him even now. We must put him in the grave we have just dug.'

'But . . . ' Catrìona glanced again at her mother's body, neatly wrapped in its shroud of woollen blankets..

'Then we shall dig another,' he said, 'and she will have her decent burial, I promise.'

The business of getting Henderson outside was too sickening for Catrìona to watch. She left them and went up on to the summit, facing away from the cave entrance, towards Rubha na h-Ordaig. She saw smoke rising on the clear air: black smoke, more dense than that from the peat fires on the hearths. Soon, later this day, they would have to talk about the future. There would be no home for them, down there, any more. They could not live indefinitely in the caves, nor would there be any point without land to support them.

She forced herself to turn back and watch the two men now they had Henderson through the passage. They carried him, his bulk sagging between their two lean bodies, bumping on the turf. She saw the grave they had dug, some distance from the cave. They reached it and dumped their burden into the gaping hole. For a few moments they stood, heads bowed at the edge of the grave. She wondered what they were doing, until they both lifted their hands to their foreheads and made the sign of the cross and she realised they were committing Henderson to his creator. The man had, after all, been a human being with a soul. She felt ashamed, knowing that she might not have thought to do the same.

Quickly they filled in the grave, stamped down the new soil and scattered it with moss. They then selected a slab of rock that lay nearby and heaved it, end over end, to lie on top of the grave. From where Catrìona stood, there was now no evidence of a burial. Taking turns, they dug again, throwing up the peaty soil not far from the first grave. Watching them for a moment, Catrìona suddenly remembered the skull Ruairidh had found in the peat hag, all those years ago and their light-hearted guesses at how it had got there. Would another young man make a similar discovery, many centuries from now and show it to another girl and would they be equally intrigued?

She made her way back to the cave and waited for them to come, kneeling and trying to pray for the soul of Màiri, and, without much enthusiasm, for the soul of Donald Henderson. But as she let the words run through her head, over and over: oh dear Lord, have mercy on their souls; her mind would not concentrate on the meaning. Màiri would certainly go straight to heaven without any intercession on her part and try as she might, she had no wish that Henderson should, certainly not before he had served an eternity of chastisement in purgatory.

As she repeated the words in her head, her mind turned to her own worries. She had refused to admit to herself what her body had been telling her for the past week or so, but now she had to face it.

It was not just the nausea and spells of dizziness she had noticed recently, nor the tenderness of her breasts: she had in a strange way known that she had conceived a child that last time she and Ruairidh had lain together, with such joyous abandon, on the islet the day before Henderson served his first notice of terms, such a short time ago and yet such a lifetime. Her whole body had felt different after that, though it was only now that she allowed the knowledge to come to the forefront of her mind.

What could she do?'*I would not be able to support a wife for the next year.*' Ruairidh's voice echoed in her memory. '*If you were to come to Edinburgh with me, you would have to find employment . . . .*' Employment, in a strange city? Pregnant? As reality began to sink into her consciousness, so also did a sense of utter desolation. If she were to go to Edinburgh, she would become a liability to Ruairidh, just when he was taking his final examinations. Knowing him as she did, she was convinced that he would abandon his medical studies in order to get employment and support her and their child. And she knew that if he did not qualify as the doctor he was so clearly destined to be, she would carry the guilt with her for the rest of her life.

They came in behind her and Frangan lifted Màiri's body. Tenderly, he eased it through the narrow passage and bore it in his arms to the new grave. They lowered it, in a sling of blankets and the three of them knelt down. The sun was low to the west, shedding its cool evening light over the hillside, touching their faces, all wet with tears. They prayed in silence and then Ruairidh's voice rang out with the words they had been brought up to all their lives: '*Requiém ætérnam dona eis, Dómine*. Eternal rest give unto them, O Lord,' and their voices joined in the response:' *Et lux perpétua lúceat eis*. And let perpetual light shine upon them.' The wind plucked at their hair, '*Requiéscant in pace*.' Ruairidh intoned: 'May they rest in peace' and they answered 'Amen' and blessed themselves. They stood and each took a handful of earth and threw it onto the body. Catrìona could no longer control her sobs as they filled in the grave and her weeping was a final lament.

They found another stone slab and levered it into place. Then they stood, between the two graves, while Frangan recited the *Nunc dimittis*. It was finished.

III

They decided to spend the night up there. They were in no hurry to see the devastation they knew would await them in the township, and they needed time to decide what was best to do. Sitting close together for warmth, in the last light of the sun, they tried to find the appetite to eat the stale bannocks that one of the people had carried up the hill for them, was it only yesterday?

'They will know he came looking for us,' Frangan said.

'They will never know he found us,' Ruairidh retorted. 'He was a stranger: these caves are hard to find if you don't know where to look. If the dog hadn't howled, he might never have come right up this far.'

'He was drunk,' Catrìona said. 'People will know that.'

'He could have fallen, anywhere in the hills. Knocked himself unconscious,' Ruairidh said, adding: 'but then someone would eventually find him.'

'There are plenty of deep caverns where the burns run underground, especially over to the west,' Frangan said, eagerly. 'Many is the sheep that has fallen through the turf and been swept away beneath the surface and never found . . .'

And so they made their decision: they would deny all knowledge of the disappearance of Donald Henderson. In the general upheaval and excitement of the evictions, no one would have time to make a thorough search surely . . .

'But even so,' Ruairidh said, 'whatever you had planned to do before, Frangan, I think you should go to Canada now. We cannot be certain that they won't put two and two together and start nosing around up here. There aren't that many places suitable for digging among the rocks.' He held Catrìona against his shoulder, his fingers stroking her hair. 'It need not be for ever, after all. If what they tell us is true, there are fine opportunities over there for a young man.'

Catrìona felt herself clenched into a hard knot of despair. She couldn't speak, in case she started weeping again, nor did she know what she would say when she did. Their voices came to her through a wall of misery.

'To be honest, I'm not averse to going across. As you know, I've often thought of it,' Frangan was saying. 'What is there left for us here, now? It would be a new chance for us and they say it is a good land if you are prepared to work.' They were silent for a while, and she realised they were both looking at her.

'What about Catrìona?' She closed her eyes; Ruairidh's arm was around her, firm and secure.

'I would like Catrìona to come to Edinburgh with me,' he said quietly over her head. He looked down at her, his eyebrow raised. 'Will you come, *mo gràdh?*' Without waiting for her answer, he added: 'I've already explained that unfortunately I am in no position to support her for the next year, until I have finished my training, and so she will have to find employment. But that should not be too hard. We could be married, and I might even be able to find a place for her in the hospital where I work. Then, when I'm qualified, we can set up a proper home.'

'Catrìona?' It was Frangan's voice and in it she thought she detected a note of almost childlike entreaty. She had always been the leader, for all his apparently adult ways. Now, a boy still at heart, he was more like her son than her twin. Had things been different, she would not have let that stand in the way of her decision, but it gave her a plausible excuse for what she had to do.

Twisting in her lover's arms, she looked up into his face, tears in her eyes. 'I must go with Frangan,' she said. 'I promised mother.' It was a lie, but it added weight to her apparent reason. 'We have never been separated, you see, and now, with mother dead . . . ' seeing the stunned expression of disbelief on his face, she added: 'I could return, perhaps, later, if you still . . . ' her voice faltered . . . 'if you still wanted me to.'

Frangan got to his feet. 'You must not come to Canada just for my sake,' he said. 'I can manage on my own, and if you two love each other, it would be wrong for me to keep you apart.' He turned and walked away, leaving them to talk.

'Do you love me?' Ruairidh asked her.

'You know I do.' She looked back steadily. Perhaps he would guess the real reason: if he did so, and confronted her with it, she could not lie to him. The decision would then belong to him: it would be taken from her. She willed him to see into her mind; he was a doctor, after all, surely he could tell that she was with child. His eyes searched hers, saw her tears; did they not see their entreaty? Why could he not read what was in her heart?

'You love Frangan more.' He brushed the tears from her cheeks. 'It is often so, with twins. I understand. How can I, who cannot even offer you a home at the moment, expect you to follow me, when he is going into exile so far away?'

'Oh Ruairidh *mo grádh!*' How could he not see?

She wept, unrestrainedly, clinging to him, her body heaving with her sobs. But still he didn't understand, didn't see the truth. He soothed her, till she was quiet.

'Of course you must go to Canada,' he said and she heard the bitter hurt in his voice. 'We can write to each other and, who knows, you may come home again, one day.' And then she knew that his pride was such that he could not plead with her, because he was so ashamed that he was not in a position to offer her a home at once.

Words formed in her mind; words that might give him a clue; words that might show him her condition, the sacrifice she was prepared to make for his career; words that would trap him into a course of action that would ruin his chances forever. She drew in her breath, not sure even then what she would say.

'Have you decided?' Frangan came back to them, his face anxious, trying to look unconcerned.

'She will go with you,' Ruairidh said curtly. 'It will probably be best for her, anyway. I can offer so little, cannot even be sure of a post when I do qualify.' He withdrew his arm from her shoulder, and stood up. 'I daresay there will be some fine young men, over there, and she will forget me soon enough.' It was not meant cruelly, she knew, but it cut into her bleeding heart. Yet she stayed silent and could not follow him when he walked away.

'Are you sure?' Frangan said, looking at her stricken face. 'I know you are very fond of him.' He was her twin; perhaps he would see what Ruairidh had missed. But he had never been one to look deeply into things, accepting the obvious unless some other angle was pointed out to him. Loving him as part of herself, she was nevertheless perfectly aware of his faults: charming, beguiling, handsome, fun – and selfish.

'Yes,' she said. 'I am sure. It is what I must do.'

She could not cry any more. She was bruised with grief and despair. Grief for the loss of her mother and for the terrible things that were happening around her; despair because she could not see how it was possible to go on living, without

Ruairidh. When he had gone away, the last time, to start his training, she had thought her heart was broken. Then she had learned that it was possible to recover and go on living and even to enjoy life. But her love for him then had been superficial in comparison with the profoundity of this love that had grown from her deeper knowledge of him. Frangan was part of her in the purely flesh and blood respect; Ruairidh was her heart and soul – without him, there could be no joy, ever again, no laughter, no pleasure, no beauty, no harmony. Without him, she would become an empty shell.

CHAPTER 10

I

They came down from the caves in the early morning, the three of them and the dog. Wisps of ground mist clung in the hollows: the golden eagles soared above their eyrie; rabbits skittered away as they came. They walked in silence, strung out along the path, each alone in thoughts too personal to share. Catrìona struggled with the now familiar nausea, but if she looked sick they mistook it for the tiredness they all felt and the sadness and the strain they had been under these last days.

She and Ruairidh avoided each other's eyes: neither had slept, she knew. All night she had longed for the comfort of his arms as they lay in the cold darkness; she had been too numbed even to cry any more. There had been a moment when they might have been able to talk to each other and sort out their situation. She had gone out of the cave to stand under the star-bright sky and gaze at the island spread out below, blanched in the moonlight. She could see the glint of water in the sound and the hills of the southern islands silhouetted against the night sky. Nearby, a corncrake started up its sawing noise, somewhere in the heather. And then Ruairidh came out to join her. He must have seen her get up and leave the cave. He stood beside her and took her hand and she waited for him to make it all right between them.

'I can't bear to see you suffering so much,' he whispered. 'I want you to know that I love you. I always shall. And I understand how you are feeling.' But you don't understand, her heart had cried out to him, that is the whole problem. 'You have chosen to do what you think is best,' he had continued, 'so I'm not going to try to talk you out of it. I shall think of you every day.'

She had not been able to answer, just to shake her head and cling to his hand and turn to go back into the cave, hoping he might detain her and talk the truth out of her. But he let her go and stayed outside himself for a while and then came in and lay down, apart from her. She lay awake for the rest of the night, staring into the darkness.

They had expected devastation, when they reached the township, but even so were shocked by what they found. Each building, house and byre alike, was a smoking shell, the contents stacked outside to form makeshift shelters for the inhabitants. The air was thick with smoke and charred dust. Some were loading up their carts, others lay or sat huddled among their few possessions, all hope gone. Many of the women were weeping and moaning; the children, wide eyed, thin and pale, cried with heartbreaking bewilderment; old men stood around, bemused uncertain what to do. These were the same people who had marched so proudly up the hill to the skirling of the pipes, two days before, to thumb their noses at Donald Henderson.

Catrìona looked at the home she and Frangan had grown up in. Parts of the reed thatch still smouldered on top of the walls but most was gone. The stones were blackened, the door hung open, charred but not quite destroyed. The contents of the house lay scattered outside: stools, chairs, table, meal chest, crocks and spinning wheel and what clothes and bedding they had not taken up the hill. Larger things that had been built inside the house – box-beds and dresser – had been left inside to be scorched by the burning thatch as it fell.

'Henderson himself was here to begin with,' Beathag told them, 'Drunk; but he soon left and we didn't see him again. The man in charge said we are to get to the boat as soon as we can, but what are we to do with the things we can't take?'

'So you are going?' Catrìona said.

'What else can we do? There is nothing for us here.'

'But what about the beasts? ' Beathag shrugged.

'They are all to be bought from us; their new owners can

worry about them now.' Beathag, who had always treated her animals like her children.

'But we can't just leave them untended!' Catrìona forgot her own troubles for a while as she tried to dispel the apathy that seemed to have settled over the township. 'The cows will be needing to be milked!' Beathag shrugged again. Catrìona felt some of her own vitality returning. All her life, the welfare of the beasts had taken priority over almost everything: they were their capital, after all. Her eyes swept quickly round the community, seeking support. 'The beasts will need to be milked,' she called out.

Tómas came up to her, bleary eyed, reeking, and put his arm round her shoulder. 'Don't trouble yourself, lass,' he said. 'There's some of the young ones gone to tend them now.' Lowering his voice he added: 'I'm sorry about your mother. She was a great woman.' He was the only one who remembered to show sympathy. She struggled with her ever-close tears and muttered her thanks.

'I'm glad we got her away, at any rate,' he went on. 'It would have been a terrible thing for her to have died with the knowledge of this in her last hour. It was a cruel sight to see. That Henderson, drunk as a tinker: disgusting. Enough to put a man off the stuff for life!'

For a moment she clung to his reassuring bulk and he hugged her tight. 'O Tómas, what will happen to us?'

'Hard times lie ahead, lass, right enough. But there've been hard times before and we always came through.'

'So you are staying? Not going on the boats?' He swept the idea of the boats aside with a contemptuous gesture.

'It's all right for you young people to be talking about starting a new life across the ocean, but it's different for the likes of us. What would I be doing with all them Red Indians and such. I've heard of some bad goings on over there.' In spite of herself, Catrìona chuckled.

'I don't think they have Red Indians in Canada, Tómas.'

'Maybe not, but they have bears and that's for sure, and what would I be doing if I met a bear when I was about my business?'

'Where will you go, if you stay here?' she asked.

'I shall squeeze myself in somewhere: there's still some of the old kelp workers' huts around the coast.'

'But how will you live, with no land?' He winked at her.

'I can always earn a penny or two with the *uisge-beatha*,' he murmured. 'The harder the times, the more folks need a little comfort. Don't you fuss about old Tómas. But, more important, what are you and the lad going to do? Is it true that you are forsaking your old uncle for the New World?'

She nodded, trying not to show him her misery. 'Frangan is quite keen to go,' she said. 'I must go with him: he is such a scatterbrain, he needs a woman.' Tómas looked at her for a moment and there was a shrewdness in his bloodshot eyes she had never noticed before.

'There's plenty of other lasses would be glad to take on that job,' he said. 'I thought maybe you would be going off in another direction yourself. 'I thought there was another young man equally in need of your care, and for rather longer than your brother is likely to want you.'

Close to tears she could only shake her head. 'That was just a summer game,' she said. 'Nothing more.' He was going to persist but Frangan, who had been conferring with Ruairidh, came over to them and said:

'We think we should go over to Lochboisdale in the boat and see what's what. Do you want to stay here?' Panic rose in her.

'No! Let me come too.' She didn't say, but felt, that she couldn't bear to be apart from Ruairidh for a moment, now that she was to lose him forever. Just to be near him, watching his dear face, hearing his voice, seeing the familiar grace of his movements, as if she could store it all up to sustain her through the future. The future! An eternity that stretched ahead of her like a void. Her mind still refused to examine anything beyond the present moment.

'Frangan!' Tómas's voice was authoritative: 'are you sure it is best for your sister to go with you to Canada?' Frangan shrugged.

'It was her choice. I didn't ask her to come with me. She

knows I can manage fine without her. Isn't that so, Catrìona?'
He glanced at her, impatient to get on. She nodded. His mind
was so taken up with what lay ahead that he had no perception
of what she or anyone else might be feeling. It had always
been thus with him; dashing on to the next adventure without
a backward glance. She wondered if he had already forgotten
Donald Henderson; indeed, whether he had even forgotten
Màiri . . . no, surely not! She looked at him, thinking, not
for the first time, what opposites they were in so many ways.

II

She sat in the boat, her shawl over her head and shoulders,
looking back at the pall of smoke. With a steady breeze on
their quarter and Frangan's experienced hand on the tiller
they were soon round the point and heading for the anchorage
across the bay, the tattered brown sail nicely filled. Ruairidh
sat in the stern and she knew he was watching her. When,
involuntarily, her eyes met his, she saw such unhappiness
she nearly cried out. She let herself think of the days they
had had together; the laughter, the joy, the passion, the
companionship they had shared. Was it possible that it was
to end forever? That for the rest of her life she would never
again experience that feeling of absolute harmony that she
had felt with him. And then, as she looked at him, he smiled,
and for a moment his eyebrow went up and she thought he
was trying to be philosophical; to show that he could manage
without her, was already facing a future that did not include
her. It did not occur to her that he might be trying to give her
courage and support; that he was deliberately forcing himself
to seem less wounded in order to hurt her less. She turned
and looked towards their destination.

They had the tide against them as they sailed in from the
entrance of the loch, past Calvay Island. Catrìona fixed her
eyes on the island, remembering the stories she had been
brought up with, of how the fugitive Prince Charlie had
hidden there, in the ruins of the tacksman's castle, within
sight of the French ships patrolling the Minch, looking for

him. Once, many years ago on a calm day, when she and Frangan had been sent to search for a lost ram, they had swum across the narrow sound and landed and explored the scant ruin, disappointed not to find any trace of the prince's brief sojourn. They had played one of their make-believe games, with Frangan as the prince, and herself as Neil MacEachen, his gallant follower. She looked at Frangan, to see if he, too, was remembering. He was staring ahead at the ship and she knew from the alert expression on his face that he was excited and that the only thoughts in his head were for the new beginning in a foreign land. The past was behind him. Her eyes misted over. How could she leave this place with all its memories of happier times; with every day of her life enshrined in some rock or bay or hill? Leave, and never return!

The ship lay at anchor, not far off the shore; *The Admiral:* a three-masted sailing bark, square-rigged, its brown sails furled on gaffs.

Even from a distance they could see a crowd of people on the shore and several small boats on the water. Frangan steered for the beach just north of the anchored ship. As they drew closer, they could see that a makeshift camp had been set up on the shore, with piles of luggage under shelters made from stretched blankets and tarpaulins. Groups of people sat, looking across the water at the ship. An air of lethargy hung over the scene; lethargy born of despair.

The boat ran up on to the stony beach and Ruairidh jumped ashore. He held out his hand to Catrìona and helped her climb over the gunwale. She didn't look at him as his fingers tightened on hers. The three of them walked round towards the encampment.

III

It was like a monstrous travesty of one of the gatherings that marked the cattle sales, or the annual games, Catrìona decided as they walked among the people. Fires had been lit and people sat round them, some with cooking pots. Children ran about, playing, unconscious of the drama they were part of. Thin dogs slunk from group to group, sniffing out fallen scraps. A group of officials stood conferring on the wharf, studying a sheaf of papers, pointing, counting families. A stack of meal bags lay waiting to be loaded into one of the small boats that ran back and forth to the ship.

As the trio stood looking on, a cart came over the brae from the west, pulled by a team of scraggy ponies, accompanied by a troop of policemen. It was over-laden with people and as it drew up, Catrìona realised that they were all men and that some of them were tied up. She didn't recognise any of them. Horrified, she saw marks of violence: bruises, blood, torn clothes. Their faces were sullen; one or two struggled and swore.

'Prisoners!' She exclaimed. 'But where are they from, and why so many?'

'They've brought them down from the north,' said an old man who had joined them. 'They've been rounding them up like cattle.'

'But what have they done wrong?'

'Done? Why, nothing, except to refuse to be turned off their land.'

'You mean they are being forced onto the ship like that, like criminals!'

'So it seems.' The old man shrugged and tapped his stick on the ground. 'They say there's plenty more on the way.'

'What about their families; their wives and children?'

'They are being brought down too.' He sounded almost cheerful, perhaps because he himself was not among them. ' 'Tis hard times we live in right enough,' he said. Catrìona glanced at her brother, half hoping that the enormity of such an injustice might persuade him to reconsider and stay to fight for their rights. But he was gazing towards the ship, his face alight with excitement. She turned her back and walked a little way up the brae to distance herself from what was going on, trying to suppress her anger with him for his apparent lack of sensitivity.

A man came running out of one of the huts that stood

around the head of the loch, pursued by ground officers. As she watched, they brought the man to the ground and held him there. One of the officers called out, gesturing to two men who stood by. It was plain that he was ordering one of them to come and assist. They answered him angrily, and turned away.

The wind had backed into the north-west and carried a coldness that cut through her woollen shawl and stung her cheeks. She sensed rather than saw Ruairidh making his way up to join her. Side by side, they stood, looking down on the preparations for departure.

'They say the voyage can take more than six weeks and that conditions are not comfortable on board,' he said. 'Oh Catrìona, you can't . . . ' The sickness that accompanied her most of the day now dragged at her strength. She yearned to lay her burden at his feet, but merely silenced him with her hand. She knew beyond any shadow of doubt that if she told him she was expecting his child, he would abandon his studies to care for her. They would be together for the rest of their lives: Ruairidh would have some menial employment – and when the first joy was past and as their family increased, they would look back and regret. He might even grow to hate her.

'Write to me,' she said. 'When things are different. I could come back. If you still want me . . . once I've paid off the fare, and got Frangan settled . . . '

IV

It was as if she was living in hell, tormented by sickness, misery, doubt; tempted so many times to tell Ruairidh the truth, and each time preventing herself from doing so. In the days that followed they registered for passage, settled the necessary agreements for the loan and repayment of their fares, collected up what provisions they could for the voyage, arranged for the sale of their crops and beasts. They camped out in the ruins of the township, huddled under the charred walls, stretching canvas over their heads at night. Most of their neighbours were sailing with them, except Tómas. Tómas and the *cailleach* and a few others, who had already taken their possessions off to the abandoned kelp workers' huts along the coast and had started trying to rebuild them, ready for the winter. They would try to make a few pennies at the kelp they said, though that industry had long since declined, and Tómas had a ready market for as much *uisge-beatha* as he could find grain for and his still could produce. Catrìona envied them with all her heart, though she knew that they would have a hard struggle to exist with not so much as a strip of field between them.

Ruairidh, whose lean face had grown gaunt, would have several weeks left, after they sailed, before his return to Edinburgh. The long holiday, started with such promise and such carefree happiness, hung like an anchor round his lonely shoulders. He helped families to collect up their needs and ferried goods and people, calm, reassuring, withdrawn. Intensely aware of him, all the time, Catrìona ached to comfort him, yearned for him to soften and plead with her, pined for the consolation of his arms. But he displayed for her a mock cheerfulness that she could not break through, though it did not fool her for a moment. His pride stood between them, impenetrable as the bedrock of their island home.

Catrìona put together what few possessions they had that were transportable, tied in bundles. Their homespun clothes and bedding, a few crocks, tools, a sack of meal, Màiri's crucifix, the yarn that had been intended for the loom. Assembled together, it was a pathetically modest collection with which to be starting a new life.

On the morning before the final day, two policemen rode into the township. One of them called out in English to Catrìona who was sitting by the house sorting through her small pile of clothes.

'We are looking for Frangan Macdonald, son of Aonghas and Màiri.' Her heart thumped in her chest. Trying to sound calm, she called out to Frangan who was behind the wall of the house, looking for tools. He came out and stood, legs braced, his face impudent.

'Frangan Macdonald?'

'Yes.' He tilted his head enquiringly, looking for all the world like an innocent child.

'When did you last see Mr Donald Henderson?'

'Him!' With just the right degree of disdain, Frangan let the scorn that everyone must have felt for Henderson, show. 'He was here, burning us out of our homes a few days ago.'

'Did you see him?' The man was from the mainland, with a flat, lowland accent.

'I did not. Not the last time he was here, when he did that.' He flung out an arm towards their ruined house. 'I saw him two days before, when he pulled the roof off that first one, and nearly killed Peigi Campbell, the swine.' The two policemen exchanged looks. Catrìona held her breath: had he been too strong in his obvious hatred?

'Why did you not see him when he came the last time?' The chances were that they would know the answer by now. Frangan faced them.

'Neither I, nor my sister, nor Ruairidh Campbell who lived in that house over there before it was wrecked, were here that day. We were with my mother who was dying.'

'Where?'

Did they know? Had someone been talking? Frangan looked unalarmed and managed to convey such utter contempt that the policemen shifted uncomfortably. He pointed towards the hills. Not the hills to the south, where Màiri and Henderson lay in their graves, but those to the west, where the golden eagles lived.

'There are caves up there and the eagles know us so they don't attack us,' he lied blithely.

'And why did you take your mother from her house, if she was dying?' The man clearly regretted his question as he was putting it. Frangan looked from one to the other of them. When he spoke, his voice was icy with righteous bitterness.

'We carried her away so that she could die in peace and not have to witness the barbaric acts that were carried out here. Henderson refused to allow us to keep our house until she was dead, even when we begged him and we knew that he would take great delight in making her death as uncomfortable as possible. In case you didn't know it, Mr Henderson is a bully, who enjoys making people suffer.'

The policemen departed.

'How did they know to go to you?' Catrìona was frantic with worry. Frangan shrugged, unconcerned.

'Someone will have been loose-tongued, at the inn no doubt. You can't keep those sort of secrets in a place like this.'

'There's not very much they can do, even if they do have suspicions,' Ruairidh said, later. 'Not unless they hold you back and they have nothing to convict you with at the moment.'

'They will find out, eventually, where the caves really are. They will go and look – and maybe start nosing around. It won't take long for them to ask us where we buried Mother.' Catrìona twisted her hands together, frowning with anxiety.

'They may try and climb up to the crags and with any luck will be chased off by the eagles. No local person is going to tell them anything to help them. It will be weeks, if ever, before they hear that there are no caves up there, or where they really are.' Ruairidh's reasoning calmed her. 'If you ask me, they are probably not all that distressed by the disappearance of that man. I daresay he has caused them more work and trouble than they care for. They will go on looking for him and then they will probably let the matter drop.'

V

They were to board *The Admiral* the evening before she sailed. Catrìona went over the ridge with Ruairidh, to have some moments alone with him. He held her and kissed her, not passionately but with such sadness that she wept and could not speak. They stood, embraced, for many minutes and perhaps the tears on her cheeks were not all her own. She ached with grief and wanted to take his hand and put it over her stomach and tell him that his child lay there. She shook uncontrollably and her head felt as if a tight band of metal was being screwed tighter and tighter round her brow.

When the time came Ruairidh took them across the loch for the last time. A steady downpour of rain drenched their clothes and their spirits as they came up alongside the ship. Each group of people was acting out its own private tragedy: many scenes of heartbreak, each one as poignant as the next. Women stood on the shore, waiting to be ferried out to the ship, crying out to their men who were taken out ahead of them, loaded into the holds like cattle. Men yelled and cursed, fought and were beaten by redcoats and policemen. Children screamed.

As they prepared to board the vessel, there was a commotion near the ship's stern: a scream, a splash, a man shouting. Someone had gone in over the side. People leant over the rail above them, momentarily distracted from their own woes. A man had jumped into the water and was swimming strongly for shore. A shout of encouragement from those watching from the boat was not enough to win him his freedom. He hadn't a chance. A party of redcoats were waiting for him. He was grabbed as he came ashore and dragged across the wharf to one of the little boats.

Catrìona clung to Ruairidh, unable even to say farewell, great sobs wracking her thin body. He held her fiercely. Then Frangan gently eased her away and helped her up the ladder. She stood at the rail above him, looking down, her hair flattened by the rain, shivering. She watched as Ruairidh handed up their few possessions: she was too broken to help. When the last bundle was on deck, he looked up at her: the hurt on his face was almost more than she could stand. He pushed the bow of the boat out from the lee of *The Admiral*, let the wind catch the sail and in only a few moments, wind and tide took him away from her. He turned back once and lifted his hand. Catrìona broke down then and wept for all the unsaid things in her heart. Frangan put his arm round her and held her close.

'Don't be sad,' he said. 'The new land has got much more

to offer us than this place.' He thought she was weeping for her home.

VI

An official with a list in his hand led them below to the married quarters in the lower hold. In order that they should not be separated, they had registered as Mr and Mrs Macdonald. As a single man and woman they would otherwise have been placed at opposite ends of the ship. Anyone looking at them would have known at once that they were brother and sister, but Catrìona was huddled into her shawl, the light was bad, and no one had time for close scrutiny. They found themselves in a hold lit only by smoking lamps, dim and low, reeking of human odours mingled with an indefinable stench that lurked in the woodwork, left·from a previous voyage. Wet clothes added to the sour staleness of the air and Catrìona pressed her hand to her mouth, choking and retching miserably as she fought back her nausea. There was a din of·voices, moaning, complaining, arguing.

Tiers of bunks lined the hold, barely far enough apart for people to sit upright without hitting their heads on the one above. Each was to be shared by two people. Long tables with benches, fastened to the decking, ran down the middle, already occupied by dejected looking families. Clothes and possessions hung on pegs; boxes littered the floor. Some of the families looked as if they had been established down here for years. Catrìona saw a few familiar faces: Beathag and her daughters were already disputing over who should share which berth with whom.

Because they were among the last to board *The Admiral*, there were few berths left. They found one free, at shoulder height, under an overhead beam. It required considerable agility to get up to it, but once there, they would, at least, be undisturbed by anyone climbing past them.

This wooden shelf, the length of a tall man, not more than three foot wide, was to be their home for the next weeks. Catrìona was too sick and heartbroken to care. All around, people were reacting in their own ways to the horror that lay ahead: a young man lay in a drunken stupor close to his listless wife who sat staring into space like a dummy. Three young boys chased each other round and round the tables, swinging on the upright posts that supported the bunks. A group of women in shawls and aprons stood near a water barrel, gossiping as naturally as if they had met up for a blether in one of their houses. A careworn mother with an infant at her skinny breast, tried to control a cantankerous child who coughed and cried alternately, breaking off now and then to scold her husband.

'Let's get some air before we try to sleep.' Already suffocating with claustrophobia, Catrìona pushed her way out of the hold, up a steep ladder into the quarters above and then up again, through a hatch onto the deck. The rain had stopped and darkness crept in over the water. Here and there lights flickered on the shore, reflected in the loch. They both faced towards their own hills to the south-east, each lost in thought. She could sense that the excitement and spirit of adventure that had been driving Frangan for the past days was now, at last being challenged by the tug of homesickness. But she knew also that Liùsi was among the passengers and that his carefree nature and resilience would very soon adapt to whatever lay ahead.

'I hope you are doing the right thing,' he said now, his arm across her shoulder. 'You and Ruairidh . . . he's a good man.'

'Yes.' Uncharacteristically perceptive, he sensed her reluctance to talk and didn't nag at her.

'They were talking about Henderson again, on the beach,' he told her quietly. 'There's a party of soldiers out looking for him in the hills.'

'Oh God! What if . . . '

'Don't fuss. They won't find him. And if they do, we shall be half way to the St. Lawrence.' Already he'd thrown off his anxiety, leaving her the added worry of what would happen if the ship was delayed and the body was found. Life would be so simple, she thought, if only you could put all unpleasant things behind you, forget them and think only of what lay ahead.

'Shall we try and sleep now,' she said, trying not to think of the scene below. Perhaps they would get used to it.

The stench was even worse. Flimsy partitions screened off water closets: privacy was a forgotten luxury. Unable to face the mess of greasy-looking gruel that was being served out from a vat under the command of a verminous looking deck-hand, Catrìona took her drinking cup to a barrel and scooped out water that was suspiciously murky. It tasted sour and she thought of the peaty burn water she had drunk all her life. Then she thought of the child she was carrying, Ruairidh's child, needing nourishment to sustain life. She drank some more, shuddered, and heaved herself up into their berth. She spread the blankets, made a rough nest with the bundles and lay herself down. Frangan settled beside her, touched her hand reassuringly and seemed to fall asleep at once.

She dozed fitfully and during one brief sleep she dreamt vividly of Ruairidh. It was a happy dream and in it they were walking over the moor together, laughing and free, and for a few moments after she woke up she was still caught in its happiness. And then she heard the groaning of the old woman in the berth below and caught a whiff of the sickening smell in the hold, and despair closed round her heart.

VII

Their departure was delayed while soldiers rounded up a few who had managed to escape and take refuge among the rocks on Beinn Choinnich. They were hunted like animals and brought back to *The Admiral*. As they were being embarked, a girl no older than Catrìona was dragged, screaming, out of one of the huts and thrown roughly down into a boat, a poor mad creature, half naked, her face bloated with distress.

Little as she wished to go, the delay was torture for Catrìona who pictured the soldiers in the hills, already approaching the caves and their newly dug graves.

When they were ready to sail, all the passengers were assembled on the poop deck and their names were called and checked against a list by one of the officers who stood on a raised bench. Another officer stood up then and shouted the orders for the voyage in harsh English. Some, who could not understand, looked bewildered and lost, turning to their companions for an interpretation of this foreign tongue that was from now on to be their only vehicle of communication with the outside world. One of the orders was that only the first class passengers could use the poop deck once they sailed. Steerage passengers were to confine themselves to the main deck, cluttered with lashed cargo, lifeboats and all the impedimenta of a sailing ship.

Catrìona stood, fighting her sickness, pressed on all sides by the crowd of sullen-faced, unhappy people. If this was the good Lord's way of punishing her for having loved Ruairidh, she pondered, looking around her miserably, then why were so many other people to suffer with her? Surely they had not all sinned against the commandments as she had done.

When the formalities were over and they were dismissed, she climbed down from the poop deck with Frangan and found a space from which they could watch as the sailors prepared to sail. A head wind prevented them from sailing out of the loch. A fleet of small boats were to row them out with the tide, until they were clear to take the wind on their beam. The sun shone from a cloudless sky, as hot as any August sun could be, drying out the damp from yesterday's rain, warming tired bodies, showing up the ship's old timbers and spars. The water sparkled, reflecting the hills and the blue sky. Gannets plummeted from the sky, diving for fish at the entrance to the loch. Smoke rose from a few bothies along the shore: life was going on for some people just as if nothing had happened.

On the beach, a crowd of islanders thronged the water's edge, calling and waving, and passengers leant over the rails, hands outstretched, calling back. A piper appeared, voices fell silent and over the water floated that most poignant and tragic of pibrochs . . . *cha till mi tuille* – We shall return no more.

As the men in the rowing boats strained at their oars and the ship began to move through the water, a woman's voice rang out, raw and true: *Muigh air bothag àirigh ghlinne*, Out in the bothy of the shieling of the glen . . . and a hundred voices took up the chorus of the exile's song *Tha mi sgìth 'm ònaran* . . . I am tired in solitude, I am tired and I am alone. More and more voices joined in until the whole ship had become a swelling lament. Tears poured unchecked as all the nostalgia and bitterness joined in this haunting reproach in the bright summer morning.

It was a long, hard haul, even with the tide. At the entrance to the loch they turned south to get the best advantage of the wind and current. A team of sailors swarmed up the rigging and scrambled out along the spars, precariously balanced on foot ropes to unfurl the sails. The rowing boats cast off the tow-ropes, the men called out farewells and *The Admiral* began to gather speed. As they slid round, close in to the point, Catrìona saw a figure on the rocks: it was Ruairidh, scanning the faces on deck. He saw her and, as his hand came up to salute her, an irresistible compulsion took control of her. Frangan sensed it too. With a flash of intuition that they didn't have to explain to each other, they each knew what she must do. He grabbed her hand and ran with her, towards the stern, pushing past other people, up on to the forbidden poop deck, past the startled first class passengers in their bonnets and fine dresses and shawls. They ran to the taff rail, right at the back. She took his hands, embraced him, tied her skirts between her knees and climbed over the rail. The sea was a long way down, their wake creaming far below.

'Be happy,' he said.

'God go with you,' she answered, crying, both with anguish and with joy.

'And with you,' he answered, 'hurry now.' Behind them, someone shouted in alarm. She took a deep breath – and jumped, as far out as she could.

Her fall seemed to last for ever and then she hit the water with such force that the breath was slammed out of her. The water closed over her head. Frantically she fought, kicking. She rose to the surface, gasped with relief and struck out for the shore, away from the floating hell-hole. She knew that there could be no question of it turning back in such a confined space, with rocks all round: it was committed to its course.

The current was strong, pulling her along parallel to the rocks. She swam, vigorously, her legs kicking, arms thrashing. Pausing for breath she looked back at *The Admiral*, pulling away fast now on the wind. Another minute and she wouldn't have had the courage to jump. Frangan stood balanced precariously on the taff rail so she could see him, saluting her in the way they had always used when they played their make-believe Jacobite games. It was the way the prince had bidden farewell to gallant Flora, hand upraised to the sky. She trod water, saluted back, smiling, and swam on.

Ruairidh was standing on his rock, both hands held out towards her, calling encouragement. His face was alight with joy and laughter. Whatever the outcome of this crazy deed, she knew now that she could not have lived without him. She put all her strength into reaching land. The water was icy and she felt herself tiring. She was near to Ruairidh but could not close the gap. The harder she swam, the less headway she seemed to make. She knew she would manage.

Then a searing pain gripped her, a tight clutch of agony, in her lower abdomen. She stopped and doubled up in the water, losing way. The cramp eased, she looked across at Ruairidh, about to call to him, and another pain attacked her, and another, in frightful waves of torture . . .

She couldn't even scream. Ruairidh was wading forward, reaching out, swimming towards her . . . another pain . . . she took in a mouthful of water . . .

CHAPTER 11

I

She was lying on something soft which smelt pleasantly of fresh laundry. It was too much of an effort to open her eyes; she felt langorous and content and very peaceful. Her mind seemed to be floating above her and she was aware of a curious sensation as if some part of her was slipping away. She wanted to hold on to it, whatever it was, but could not. It was as if someone was playing a tune and slowly walking away, so that the melody became fainter and fainter.

She heard sheep bleating nearby and the sharp bark of a dog. Gradually she became aware of a presence very close to her – a stirring of the air. She opened her eyes. A man was bending over her, his face vaguely familiar. She frowned:

'*Có thusa?*' The words drifted out of her mouth in a meaningless jumble, and then reformed: 'who are you?' Whatever it was that was escaping from her – the receding melody – vanished altogether, leaving a vague sense of loss. The man looked puzzled for a second, and then gave her a charming smile.

'Hullo! I'm the locum doctor here while Doctor MacKay is on holiday.'

'Doctor? But . . .?' she struggled to sit up; he restrained her.

'Lie still; don't exhaust yourself. You've been ill.' He had a gentle voice with the lilt of the West Highlands in it. 'I just want to take your temperature and then we can talk. Open, please.' She opened her mouth and he settled the thermometer under her tongue. She tried to speak.. He put his finger to his lips, shaking his head. 'Not a word,' he said. 'It's the only thermometer in the house and I can't have the end bitten off.' One of his eyebrows shot upwards, a comic trick that stirred her memory but failed to bring anything to the surface. For a moment, she was conscious of an inexplicable feeling of sadness which passed before she could nail it on to a reason. The doctor lifted her wrist and checked her pulse.

As far as she was able, lying on her back, she tried to take in her surroundings. She seemed to be in a cottagey bedroom with pretty, floral curtains and a smell of dried lavender. The whitewashed walls were hung with watercolour paintings, mostly seascapes: one beside her bed was of a beached fishing boat, surrounded by lobster creels. There was a chest of drawers painted white, with china plates on stands arranged on top and a dressing table with a skirt that matched the curtains and a triple mirror. A bunch of heather in a pottery mug stood on the windowsill. The sun streamed in through a tiny window set into walls that must have been at least four feet thick.

Her eyes came back to the doctor. She certainly didn't know him, so why this curious feeling she had seen him somewhere before? He had wavy hair, very dark, curling just above the collar of his open necked tartan shirt. His face was lean and tanned and there wasn't a spare ounce of flesh on his body. It was, she decided, a rather Puckish face, not handsome but humorous, a fact that was accentuated by the mobile eyebrow that once again shot half way up his forehead in an inverted V, as he encountered her scrutiny. He removed the thermometer, took it over to the window to read and shook it with a few expert flicks of his wrist.

'Excellent! Now you may speak,' he said. He pulled up a chair and sat by the bed, his head slightly tilted, awaiting her interrogation.

'What happened?' she said. 'I've no recollection of being ill, or of how I got here.' She tried to focus her mind and failed. 'In fact,' she added with rising agitation, 'I've no recollection of anything. Where am I? Is this your house?' He laughed.

'OK: I'll do the talking,' he said. Although he seemed entirely relaxed, she had the impression that he was watching her very carefully. 'Do you remember anything at all?' he asked. 'I mean about the time before you were ill? Who you are, for instance, and where you come from and what you are doing here?'

Her mind refused to work. There was just this present moment . . . now: she was . . . ? She shut her eyes, panic-stricken, desperately trying to force her mind into gear.

'Don't worry,' his hand was soothing on hers. 'Don't strain yourself: it's a common enough thing to happen, after all you've been through. I'm going to tell you what I know and I daresay everything will suddenly fall into place.' She opened her eyes; tears were not far away.

'You are Catriona Macdonald, your friends call you Kat. You are twenty-three. You came over from Canada recently to research into the origins of Scottish Canadians. I believe you had been awarded a scholarship of some sort. You chose to come to the Outer Isles first because you knew that your own ancestors had emigrated from here. You lodged with Flora Kate Macdonald, not far from here and began your research. That much is known from conversations you had with various people including our parish priest who was on the boat you arrived in.'

He stopped, got to his feet, went to the window and stood looking out, his back to her. It was as if he was giving her time to take in what he was telling her. She struggled to absorb what he had said so far, but his words were just sentences, with no connection to herself whatsoever. Catriona . . . Kat . . . Canada . . . Outer Isles. . . . It was as if she had no *persona* – was just a piece of blank paper on which this man, this doctor, was writing a story. She understood the story, but was not part of it. She stared at him, terrified. He turned round and continued with the tale, his eyes never leaving her face.

'You visited our parish priest and looked up in the baptism register and discovered where your ancestors had lived. The next bit is guesswork. One day you took a picnic and went out to the place, which is in the south-east foot of the island, to look for the ruins of their township. You got there, we know, because we found your bag and picnic remains among the ruins. But you didn't return in the evening. Flora Kate was worried sick, as you can imagine, and she alerted the police. By that time it was dark, so there wasn't much that could be done till the morning. But it was a fine night so no one was all that concerned, thinking merely that you had got lost and had to spend the night out in the open. When you didn't appear the next morning they sent helicopters down from the army base in Benbecula and started searching in earnest.'

Words, words, words: they pounded in her head, deafening her till she wanted to scream. They told her nothing about herself: the girl lying in this bed, listening to the story.

'They found you about a mile north of where you'd left your bag. You were lying among rocks just above the high tide mark, unconscious.' He came back to her bedside and stood looking down at her, a curious expression on his face. 'You had had a miscarriage: a foetus of about seven weeks. You had haemorrhaged badly and your condition was, to say the least of it, critical.' As he spoke, the blur in her mind suddenly began to come into focus. She was swimming . . . in pain . . . a face came closer . . . hands reached out to her . . .

'. . . Ruairidh!' she gasped. But it was the face of the doctor, with one eyebrow raised enquiringly and the hands were his hands, pressing her back on her pillows, calming her.

'Easy, now,' he said. 'Yes, I'm Ruairidh. Roderick;' his voice sounded odd. 'Rod, they call me, Rod Campbell. How did you know that, I wonder?'

It was all there, now; the shifting scenes coming together in sequence. But none of it made sense. They were just scenes, nothing more; she was the audience, not one of the actors. She was looking down on the pale girl in the bed, and she could see the other one, frantically trying to reach the shore. But who was she: Catrìona or Kat? Which was the reality? Was she experiencing a vision of the future, or had she just come from a trip back in time?

'Your memory has come back, hasn't it,' he said. She nodded weakly and turned her head away from him to hide the tears that spilled from her eyes. How could she possibly begin to explain what she didn't understand herself? How could she tell a total stranger that the seven-week foetus she had aborted had been his, that he had been her lover. For he was Ruairidh, she was certain.

There was a long silence; she was aware that he was standing over her, watching her.

'I think you ought to rest for a while,' he said eventually. 'You look exhausted. Finding your memory can be traumatic, especially when you are already weak.' She nodded again without turning her head. 'I'm going to leave you to sleep for a while. You'll feel much more yourself when you wake up.' She heard him leave the room.

Fantastic images tugged and curled in her mind, but she was outside, watching. The slim girl with the milk-white complexion, in a long, homespun worsted skirt and a coarse cotton blouse, standing barefooted on the hillside, her dark hair blowing round her neck and shoulders, a radiant smile on her face, was herself. But without a spirit: a painting of herself, with no substance, no feelings, and yet as vital and full of life as any living person. And the man, striding up the hill towards her in breeches, a leather waistcoat over his grey shirt, his lean body lithe as a cat's, his face tanned, his crow black hair curling in wild profusion: he was the doctor, Rod Campbell, and he was Ruairidh. It was Ruairidh, calling to her, hands held out, catching her as she ran down to him, lifting her in the air, laughing. She knew the strength of him, smelt the healthy male sweat, saw the gaiety in his eyes, but she felt nothing. She was not part of it. She was a spectator.

The skinny girl in jeans and a denim jacket, her long dark hair tied back from her pale face with a boot lace, who sat alone, dreaming, on a fallen tree high above a cascading waterfall in Nova Scotia, an open book on her knee, stripping a pink-gold mapel leaf in her restless fingers – that too was herself. But again, a photograph of herself, an image without feelings.

In some extraordinary way, she had become two people and in the process she had lost her own identity. As she drifted towards sleep, she wondered, in a detached way, if she would ever regain her true self with all the old passions and pains and emotions and feelings that were now mere words, belonging to replicas of herself that were as empty as chaff.

II

Some time later, she was woken by a bustling, dumpy woman, with a complexion as weathered as a farm worker's and an unruly tangle of grey hair. She put a cup and saucer on the table by the bed and said:

'The doctor said to bring you some tea and wake you at four, so that you will be able to sleep tonight. How are you feeling?' Her voice was soft, with a stronger version of the doctor's lilting island accent.

'Great! Really well rested, thank you.' It was true: she felt entirely able to cope with anything. She sat up and discovered that she was wearing one of her own cotton nightshirts. 'That tea looks inviting, just what I need.' The woman put the cup and saucer into her hands.

'I'm the doctor's housekeeper,' she supplied: 'Peggy Macdonald.' She had bright, twinkly eyes. 'Another Macdonald for you! They say you are collecting them!' Kat smiled.

'Yes. Well I was, anyway. Now I think I may have enough.' She sipped the tea. 'Delicious!' She eyed Peggy Macdonald hopefully. Perhaps she might help her to recover her identity. 'How long have I been here?'

'Just a couple of days. You were in the hospital for a week before that: very ill you were, the doctor says.' Kat wondered if she knew the nature of the illness and decided that it didn't matter. The chances were that as she had been discovered in such dramatic circumstances there would have been a great deal of information circulating on the local grapevine within a few hours.

'All that time? Wow!' The tea acted as a stimulant, filling her with energy and a desire to get up and go outside. She had wasted ten precious days. She started to extract herself from the bedclothes. Peggy intervened.

'The doctor said I wasn't to let you up till he returns,' she said. 'He's away to the hospital just now, but he shouldn't be much longer.'

'Not even to the bathroom?' Who, she wondered, had attended to her needs while she had been incapacitated. Peggy? She wanted to ask but was not sure how to phrase the question. Peggy, however, was prescient.

'Oh yes, you can go to the bathroom. You have been so doped since you came, you may not remember that I have helped you there many times.'

'Oh. No, I don't remember a thing since I got ill.'

The bathroom had the same fresh cottagey neatness as the bedroom. It gave her a slight jolt to see her own washing things on a shelf, adjacent to what must have been the doctor's shaving gear. Extraordinary questions were dancing through her mind: they tormented her, dangerous as splinters of glass. Deliberately, she avoided them. She looked in the mirror over the basin. The paleness of her face was accentuated by terrible smudges of shadow round her eyes: her mane of dark hair fell in wild disorder round her shoulders. A witch, she decided: her sense of the ridiculous bubbled to the surface. She stuck her tongue out at herself. She definitely needed a bit of moral support to get her through what seemed a completely impossible situation.

III

By the time Rod returned to the cottage, Kat was sitting up in bed reading a collection of Hugh MacDiarmid's poetry that she had found on a shelf in her room. She had wheedled out of Peggy the answers to a few of the questions that were uppermost in her mind, to help her to fix her position. She was here to convalesce, under the doctor's eye, because her bed in the hospital had been needed. The cottage belonged to Dr MacKay, a widower, ruled over by Peggy, who lived separately in her own quarters beyond the kitchen. Flora Kate Macdonald had been perfectly happy with the arrangement, not being too willing to have the responsibility of nursing a tenant who had already caused her such anxiety!

'Now that is a sight for sore eyes!' He came into her room with a brown paper bag in his hand. 'You look a lot better already.'

'That says a lot for how I must have looked before. I've had a look in the mirror. God!' She lay the book down on her lap.

'You looked what you were – very ill. Now you are on the road to recovery and it shows. Here. The best the Co-op could produce.' He dumped the bag on top of the book. She looked inside.

'Grapes. Oh, that's kind. Thank you.'

'Elderly grapes. How are you feeling?' He perched on her bed. 'A new woman, by the looks of you?'

'A witch, by the looks of me,' she retorted, offering him the bag of grapes. 'But yes, I feel just great. In fact, ready to get up. May I?'

'I don't see why not. Just for a few hours. You'll have to take it very easy for a while.' She watched his fingers hovering over the grapes. They were creative fingers, lean and sensitive. She ignored one of the glass-splinter questions in her mind.

When he left the room she got up, found her clothes, neatly folded in the chest of drawers, smelling of clean laundry. She put on a denim skirt and a sweat shirt. She seemed to have shrunk considerably and her legs felt like sucked asparagus, but apart from that, she decided, as she brushed out her hair, she looked frailer than she felt.

IV

The doctor was in a large kitchen–cum–living–room, riddling the grate of a Rayburn stove. It was a cosy room with comfortable looking armchairs and a sofa round an open fireplace at one end, and a deal table and four chairs in the cooking area. There were faded rugs and a pleasant clutter of ornaments, books, papers and plants. She looked at the paintings: they were mostly oils, by the same artist, of the jug-of-flowers-and-dish-of-oranges category: imitation Van

Gogh; bright, pleasing but amateur. A black and white collie occupied one of the armchairs.

'Say, is this your dog?' He straightened up.

'Hullo! No, Peggy's. Katie, she's called. Come and sit down.'

'No, you finish that. I need to give my legs an airing. They feel very unused.' She walked over to the window. The view was of a slope of rock-strewn turf, leading down to an inlet of the sea. Sheep grazed wherever she looked. A boat was pulled up on the beach and she could see a line of yellow bouys bobbing round the curve of the bay. 'It's beautiful!' she breathed.

'Yes. Old MacKay knew what he was doing when he bought this place.' He opened the fire door of the stove and threw in peat from a zinc bucket. 'There. Now, what about a drink. Whisky? I'm afraid there's not much else to offer you.'

'If it's allowed, yes please.'

'It is certainly allowed: best pick-me-up I've ever pre-scribed.' She prowled round the room, examining the paint-ings, touching the ornaments, reading the titles of the books on the shelves. They were mostly medical tomes, their spines faded or missing: Dr MacKay's, presumably. On a table a pile of books obviously in current use might give her more of a clue to her host's tastes: *The Collected Poems* of Edward Thomas, Turgenev's *Hunter's Notes, The Wind in the Willows*, Helen Waddell's *Beasts and Saints*. No wiser, she sat in one of the chairs and watched him pour whisky into two glasses..

Every movement he made was disturbingly familiar. And why shouldn't it be, for God's sake! The splinters pierced her mind. Eyeing his profile, she had a sudden vision of tangled limbs and heard the cries of uninhibited passion – and felt nothing; no stir of feeling towards him. It was uncanny and upsetting. How could he not have the same knowledge as she had? How could she act normally with a man about whom she knew all the most intimate details and yet felt unmoved, and to whom she was a complete stranger?

He handed her a glass and sat opposite her. 'So, how does

it feel to be back in the land of the living with all your faculties including your memory restored to you?' The light, teasing tone and the lifted eyebrow were slightly ironic. She had a brief, almost compulsive urge to ask him if he had a scar, high up on the inside of his right thigh, obtained during a nest-raiding adventure on the cliffs when he was a boy. She resisted.

'It feels pretty good, thank you,' she answered, and sipped her drink. 'And I guess it's about time I thanked you for having taken me in and for, presumably, having saved my life.' He waved her gratitude aside.

'That is my job,' he said. 'Saving lives. Do you feel strong enough to confirm my reading of what happened to you after you left Flora Kate that day?'

'Yes. Oh, yes, you were quite right. I got to the ruined village I was looking for. But I'm afraid I can't tell you what happened after that. I sat down to eat my picnic and the pains started . . . and then,' she shrugged.

'You must have wandered off trying to get help.'

'I expect so . . . .' she hesitated, gulped at her drink, took a breath, started to speak and faltered. He waited for her to go on, his face impassive. She drained the glass, set it on the table beside her chair and looked across at him. 'Listen,' she said, leaning forward, 'this is going to sound really corny I know, but I've got to tell you. I had a most extraordinary experience while I was – wherever I was. I guess you aren't going to believe this but I think I went back in time.' It sounded hysterical, neurotic, stupid. 'I went back to when that village was occupied.'

'You had a vivid dream I expect.' His voice was matter-of-fact, totally unastonished by her dramatic statement. 'It's very common. Have you ever fainted, or been unconscious before? In the waking moments, people often have incredibly real dreams, so that they come to and think they are still in the dream.'

Of course he wouldn't understand. How could she have thought he would. How could she expect anyone to understand what had happened when she didn't herself.

'It wasn't a dream,' she said quietly, speaking almost to herself. 'It happened.' She wanted to add: and you were part of it, but how could she? How could she possibly tell him about Ruairidh, and her pregnancy and that he was Ruairidh! He'd think she was propositioning him for sure!

'Tell me about it.' He smiled; he was indulging her; pacifying the excitable child; calming the overstrung patient.

'I was myself but I was there, then, in the year we . . . they . . . were cleared from their crofts. It was me, not a dream, and it all happened.' She heard herself getting wound up and tried to get a grip of herself. She saw him glance at her empty glass; obviously he thought she was suffering from a loosened tongue because of the drink she had gulped down so intemperately. 'My mother died of consumption,' she said, her voice neutral, as if she was reciting a memorised passage of prose, 'and we buried her on the hill. And there was a man called Donald Henderson, one of the factor's men. He tried to rape me and my brother killed him and we buried him up there too.'

Rod nodded complacently – it was worse than one of those nightmares when you try to shout and no sound comes out. 'It happened,' she repeated and burst into tears.

He got up, came over and sat on the arm of her chair, rubbing her shoulder, saying nothing. 'Damn! Now you'll just think you shouldn't have given me that drink and that I'm a hysterical colonial who's been reading too much Sir Walter Scott.' She scrubbed at her eyes with her knuckles and then with a handkerchief he put in her hand. 'I'm sorry.'

'Don't be. You've had a hell of a bashing; it's hardly surprising if you are a bit emotional.' Emotional! If only he knew how she yearned for some sort of emotion, rather that this lonely vacuum that occupied her heart. He gave her shoulder a final pat and went back to his chair. 'I know you do believe that whatever happened was real. Perhaps it was, in an inexplicable sort of way. Like extra-sensory perception, you know? Maybe you picked up something from a different plane; maybe it was what they call a time warp.' It was the soothing patter of a doctor with an overwrought patient.

'Yeah! Well, anyway, I apologise.' There was no point in trying to convince him and his obvious disbelief would only irritate her. She must change the subject and keep her bewildering dilemma for her private moments, until she could unravel the tangled ends. She curled her legs under her, propped her elbow on the arm of the chair and rested her chin on her hand. 'So let's talk about you.' She knew she sounded insincere, flip, but she couldn't help herself. His refusal to accept her story had put up a barrier between them. 'Where do you live when you aren't being a locum?'

'I've a practice in Edinburgh, in one of the poorest districts of the city.'

'That must be a rewarding job,' she commented.

He fingered his glass, his face more serious than she had yet seen it. 'I see things there that make me want to emulate Guy Fawkes. Britain is galloping ahead, getting richer and greedier every day, and in her own backyard there are people so deprived and wretched that they haven't even the will to live. This break I have every year saves my life and my sanity.' It was Ruairidh's bitterness, all over again; Ruairidh's compassion; Ruairidh's determination to change the world. And she was Catrìona. And they were both wooden puppets, unanimated characters acting out their parts. Steady, she admonished herself. She blinked, concentrating her attention on now: on Kat Macdonald.

'Were you born there?'

'No, I was born here.' He grinned. 'We islanders always come home.'

'Yes.' She stared into space, one finger tracing a seam on her skirt. 'Do you know, I had this weird feeling, on the boat coming over, that I was returning home even though I'd never been here before.'

'Probably that was one of the contributory reasons for your . . . shall we say . . . hallucination.'

'You can say hallucination if you like,' she retorted tartly. 'I shall continue to call it reality. But don't let's talk about that any more; it makes me cross.' He laughed, as if he was relieved to see that she was able to joke about it.

'OK. Now you tell me about you.' He stood up and got her glass. 'And I'll give you another drink to prove I don't think you were acting under the influence.'

'Nothing much to tell. I'm doing this research for a thesis on the origins of Scottish Canadians, as you know. At home I'm just another ordinary, boring female student no different from any other.'

'That sounds remarkably cynical.' She shrugged.

'It wasn't meant to be. I'm just an ordinary person, that's all.'

'No one is ordinary, or boring, when you get to know them properly. At least that is my experience.' He handed her her glass. She took it and looked at it suspiciously.

'That looks powerful.'

'It's not; the peaty water makes it darker. Just don't throw it down in one, this time.' She wondered when they would eat; she was ravenous.

'OK. So I'm unique. But uniquely dull.' Irritation made her sound childish. How could she be expected to have a rational conversation with a man whose body she had once known as intimately as her own, and yet about whom she now had no more feeling than she had for the pair of kippers in the still-life painting that hung over the bookshelf? For one thing, it seemed kind of sneaky, that she should know so much about him, when he knew nothing about her: that he always slept with his arm under his head; that he was extremely ticklish; that, to him, lovemaking was something to be enjoyed with full-bloodied passion and humour – an exquisite romp.

'Uniquely dull?' He was laughing at her again. 'What about your boy friend? Does he think you are dull too?'

'Boy friend?' She looked at him blankly. 'Oh, you mean the baby!' The baby! Whose baby? Ruairidh's? Johnny's? Confusion made her gauche. 'I don't have a boy friend,' she muttered. She couldn't be bothered to go into the saga of Johnny and all the dreary details of her broken affair with him. So: let him think she was just a tramp who slept around. What did she care. And that was probably just what he did think, from the way he was eyeing her, not that it mattered. It wasn't as if she had any feelings for him. It wasn't as if she had any feelings for anything, come to that, just sensations like hunger and thirst and tiredness.

'Peggy has left us a delicious shepherd's pie,' he said. 'She's away to her sister's. Bring your drink to the table. You mustn't stay up too long. You'll be exhausted.' No doubt she was already boring him; he was probably longing to get back to Turgenev or to watch his favourite programme on the television.

They made small talk over the shepherd's pie: his practice, her studies, his flat, her brothers. All the time, as she ate, and watched his face, she wanted to go back to that moment when her memory had returned to her and start again with him. She had got off on the wrong foot, somehow, and she had this awful feeling that she would never manage to get back in step.

'What did you think of MacDiarmid?' The question caught her by surprise.

'The poet? I think he's marvellous. I did a special paper on him when I was a kid.'

'Did you indeed! He's one of my favourites. Who else do you like?' Suddenly they stood on common ground. They threw names at each other, excitedly, 'oh, do you really like . . . ?' 'don't you prefer . . . ?' 'have you read . . . ?' She forgot her tiredness, leaning her elbows on the table, fiddling with her knife, while he sat back, his food half-eaten, extolling the virtues of some obscure poet she'd never heard of.

When he finally shooed her off to her room, she was clutching an armful of books, with the instruction that she was not to sit up reading all night and she was to stay in bed until Peggy brought her her breakfast.

'I shall be in the surgery all morning,' he told her. 'But I'm free in the afternoon unless there is a drama.'

'Like someone being brought in off the rocks in a helicopter?'

'Heaven forbid! I can only cope with one visitation from the past at a time.' She refused to be drawn.

'Perhaps one day I may be able to prove my case,' she said lightly. 'Thank you for everything.'

'Sleep well,' he said. 'Call if you need anything.'

She lay in her bed and listened to him clearing up in the kitchen, putting out the dog, making up the fire.

. . . Ruairidh had had a particular way of damping down the fire for the night: *smàladh an teine* they called it – smooring the fire. Covering the glowing peats with ash to keep them alight till morning. Her mother had had a special prayer she said, when she smoored her fire. *Smàlaidh mise nochd an teine*, I shall smoor the fire tonight, as Mary would smoor the fire. . . .

Her mother . . . coughing up her lungs in a cave on the hill . . . buried in the twilight . . . Catrìona's face was wet with tears . . .

. . . Kat stared dry-eyed out of the tiny window, her heart as empty as a husk.

CHAPTER 12

I

Tough as a healthy young animal, pampered by Peggy, left almost entirely to her own devices by Rod, Kat threw off the effects of her illness with robust ease. Rod had imformed her he didn't hold with molly-coddling and when Peggy fussed he told her to let nature take its course. Within a week she was away with her knapsack again, searching and exploring, photographing, scribbling, talking to anyone she met.

It was a queer limbo she was living in, sharing a house with a man she could remember as a lover and now knew as a totally impersonal host, polite but aloof, whose undeniably charismatic personality touched her not at all. The vivid memories that tormented her whenever she was with him, made no impression on her. She felt that there was some key, somewhere, waiting to be turned, that would unlock whatever it was that held her true identity captive and imprisoned her emotions.

Meanwhile, there was so much to be done, to make up for the time she had lost.

II

'Can I give you a lift?' A rusty, corrugated van stopped beside her on the single track road. A face, with jowels that were bristly with yesterday's beard and a nose that was maroon from a lifetime of weather and whisky, peered at her from a window frame green with moss.

'I'm going to Daliburgh.'

'Hop in.' He leant across and opened the door and she clambered over a coil of rope and squeezed onto the passenger seat beside an old woman with a smile that was all gums.

'Thank you,' she said. 'It's further than I thought.'

'Why walk when you can ride,' he said magnanimously. 'You'll be the Canadian lassie, over to find her ancestors.' It was a statement, not a query and totally lacking in any irony.

'Yes, that's right. It must be funny for you who have always lived here, when people like me come over trying to find our roots.'

'Not at all. It was only by the grace of God that my own family stayed and yours went away. And the reason for that was that they didn't have any land at all, so no one could turn them off it!' He roared with laughter and put a hand like a sledgehammer on the horn as a sheep ambled across the road. 'Mark you, I often wish my own people had gone away to the new land. There was many a fortune to be made, I'm told, and you see some of them coming back now, all shiny motor cars and yachts with fancy names. They have some peculiar notions, right enough. We had one gentleman last summer who was asking the factor if he could buy the house his ancestors were born in and take it back to America in pieces.' He chuckled. 'He had a mind to rebuild it in his back garden! I told him he could have my house instead, right enough, if he would exchange it for his own in the States. He said he needed his own to live in and that the bothy was just to look at!'

'Well, I'm afraid my family didn't make any sort of a fortune,' she confessed. 'Far from it. To begin with, they had a terrible struggle, just existing and then they settled down and made about the same as anyone else.' They rumbled past a reedy lochan with a rowing boat pulled up on the edge: plovers hovered over the swampy ground; a few shaggy, long-haired cattle grazed a patch of turf.

'De t' ainm a th' ort?' The old woman, little more of her than a bundle of bones in wrappings of wool and quilted nylon, had a remarkably shrill voice. Kat felt that shifting of consciousness which was becoming increasingly familiar since her illness, a bewildering slither of control over herself.

'Catrìona.'

'You have the Gaelic!' The man sounded delighted.

'No!' The van lurched into a passing place just in time

to allow room for a lumbering lorry loaded with dripping seaweed. 'No, I just recognise a few simple sentences!' How else could she explain!

The old woman seemed satisfied. She put a bony hand on Kat's knee and muttered something incomprehensible.

'Ach, don't heed her,' boomed the driver. 'She's just a *cailleach.*' For a second, she had a picture of an old woman, toiling down the hill with a creel of peats on her back and she knew that she must not look her in the eye in case she was turned into a slug, or worse. She stared out of the window, concentrating her will on this moment, now. Kat Macdonald, taking a lift in a van with a man and an old woman. Now.

'Was it the shop you were wanting?'

'No, thank you. I was going across to the church to see the priest. Father Campbell.'

'Well, you're lucky. He's not often at the presbytery at this time of day, but he is this day on account of his car's gone off to be done.' An overpowering smell of fish wafted up from the back of the van.

'Where do you live?' Kat asked.

'Just along the road from where you're staying yourself. We was out on the hillside looking for you when you disappeared.'

'Oh! That was kind of you.' How many people had been involved? How many had been present when she was discovered? 'I'm afraid I was a nuisance.'

'Not at all. It took us away from the hay which is a tedious business to be sure. I'll put you down here. The church is five minutes along the road there.'

'*Gun robh math agad,*' 'Thank you very much.' She stood in the road, bewildered, not sure what she had said. The old woman leaned towards her and smiled her toothless smile.

'*Slàn leat,*' she screeched. 'Goodbye.'

With a blare of the horn, the van moved off, leaving her standing at a crossroads beside a loch covered in water lilies. To her right, she knew, lay Lochboisdale. Lochboisdale, where the transport boats lay, with their overcrowded, stinking holds . . . no! Lochboisdale was the ferry terminal, where the the roll-on roll-off steamer docked and disgorged its passengers onto the pier among the container lorries and cranes, below the hotel.

Who was she? Would the wise old priest be able to help her? Would he believe her story? On the whole, priests were wary of the supernatural, as far as she could remember, falling over themselves to disprove any claims of visions or miracles by their parishioners. Look at the fuss they made over poor little Bernadette, and over those children in Fatima. Not that she was claiming to have seen the Virgin Mary, just a complete slice out of the past . . . that was all.

III

She came to the priest's house behind the church, that austere, grey building, as sturdy and indomitable as the faith it contained. The same nun came to the door and stood aside to let her in. She was smiling, less forbidding than she had been the last time.

'Come away into the parlour, I was just going to make Father his coffee; will I make some for you too?'

'Thank you.'

'He'll be with you directly.'

She sat down, remembering her previous visit. How she had gone away, that time, so excited with those names and dates that had offered such promise and which were now so painfully familiar. She remembered her discovery that her ancestor Catrìona had shared a birthday with herself. This information now seemed profoundly significant.

'Miss Macdonald! I'm delighted to see you again.' The old priest came into the room, smiling and holding out his hand. 'Are you perfectly recovered from your misadventure. We prayed for you.'

'Oh!' Kat blinked and took his hand. 'Thank you.' Presumably he had been aware of the exact nature of her illness. He gave her hand a little pat and pointed her towards an armchair.

'Don't look so surprised.'

'But my . . . misadventure, as you call it, . . . was hardly one I would have expected to be prayed about.'

'Child! What did they ever teach you in your catechism classes? We are not here to judge, and we are all subject to the frailties of human nature. Now, what can I do for you?'

A light tap on the door heralded the entrance of the nun with a tray. Kat took a cup and a home-made biscuit. The nun put the other cup beside Father Campbell and went out.

The coffee was made with milk and a lot of sugar. The biscuit was made of oats and treacle and was substantial. The priest sat waiting.

'Father, I . . . I've got the most ridiculous story to tell you. I expect you will probably say what the doctor says – that I've had a very vivid dream. But it wasn't a dream and until I can prove it in some way I . . . well, I think I'm deranged.'

'Tell me.' His gentle voice gave her encouragement.

She told him the whole story. About Johnny and her need to get away and her realisation that she was pregnant almost as soon as she arrived on the island. She described that walk out to Rubha na h-Ordaig, and the sudden attack of pain. And then she told him all that happened during her transmigration period, up to the moment she had been swimming ashore to join Ruairidh. All the time she was speaking, he sat perfectly still, watching her face intently and it was impossible to tell what he was thinking.

'My last memory is of pain, and of Ruairidh trying to reach me.' She stopped and sipped the coffee, now tepid with a skin on top which she eased aside, surreptitiously, with her finger.

'And what was the next thing you remember.' It was the first time he had spoken; she realised that this was the bit she had been shying away from.

'I came to my senses in bed in Rod Campbell's house. Or rather, in Dr MacKay's house.' She stopped.

'And . . . ?'

'Rod – Father, Rod is Ruairidh!' She stared at him, waiting

for some sort of ridicule, or disbelief, or sarcasm. None came. The shrewd blue eyes stared back at her over the beaky nose and he nodded.

'Yes, I can see we have a problem on our hands.' We: he had taken up her cause. She breathed out a long sigh of relief. From listener, he changed to inquisitor, his questions brisk and delivered in an impersonal way that made it easier for her to supply the incredible answers. 'If Rod Campbell is Ruairidh Campbell: who are you?'

'That's the trouble, Father, I don't know. I'm Kat Macdonald in everything, except that . . . ' she leaned forward, . . . 'this sounds so crazy, Father, but every now and then I understand and speak Gaelic, and every now and then I have flashbacks to that time before, and feel just as much part of it as I was when I was there . . . '

'*De'n aois a tha thu?*' He threw it at her suddenly, his voice sharp. She frowned and shook her head.

'No, that means nothing at all to me.'

'I asked you how old you were. An easy one, had you unconsciously taken in a few Gaelic phrases as you went about doing your research. Phrases that might come to the surface now and then without you thinking about it.'

'On my way here, I was given a lift and the old lady in the van asked me my name, in Gaelic. I understood her and answered, although now I haven't any idea how to say: what is your name.'

'*C'ainm a th' ort?*' She shrugged.

'Is that it? Honestly, Father, it means nothing to me at all. And I was able to thank them for my lift in Gaelic.' She put the cup and saucer on the table and fiddled with the biscuit, not wanting to fill her mouth with its rough dryness while they were talking and yet afraid to offend the nun by not eating it.

'Tell me, how is it, between yourself and the doctor? Have you told him any of this?'

'This is really why I've come to you Father: because I seem to have lost some part of myself completely.' She had thought it would be embarrassing, but his detached, impersonal manner made her feel at ease. No doubt his years of experience on the other side of the grille in the confessional had made him a good listener. 'Rod is Ruairidh, of that I am absolutely certain, but, whoever I am, I have no feelings about him whatsoever. I can remember every sensation that existed between Catrìona and Ruairidh.' She felt herself blushing, but went on. 'I know exactly *how* Catrìona felt, but it is only as a spectator. It is as if I have read a description that stirred my imagination; but it isn't my feeling . . . it's sort of . . . received awareness. Oh, God! I don't know. I'm so confused.'

'Of course you are confused.' He examined his finger nails, thinking. 'You mean, Kat Macdonald has no feelings at all for Rod Campbell?'

'As a man, no. Absolutely none. Oh, sure, I like him. He is very charming and kind and amusing and interesting. But only in the way that a character in a film is – you know, secondhand. And yet, I can't help looking at him and remembering how it was between Catrìona and Ruairidh. I keep thinking . . . thinking, that was him and me, Father!'

'Certainly things do seem to be complicated, child. What are we going to do with you?' She waited, as if he could solve the whole thing as easily as he could administer absolution. 'What have you told him? Anything?'

'I tried to tell him what had happened to me in that time, but he said it had just been a vivid dream – very common, he said. I didn't tell him that he had had any part of it. How could I?'

'How indeed! So, what is his attitude towards you? You are a beautiful young lady, sharing his house. Does he not show signs of becoming fond of you?'

'No. I don't really see how he could without some sort of response from me. It takes two to form a relationship: I'm just a zombie!' She got up restlessly and paced the room, gripping her hands together, 'Father what can I do? I've lost a part of myself and I really don't know who I am.' She straightened a pile of books on a table, absent mindedly tracing the title with her finger: *Sign of Contradiction*, it was called – very apt. 'I'm trapped in some sort of limbo between two existences and I can't get out and I don't even know which way I'm supposed to go: forwards to the twentieth century or backwards to the nineteenth.' She swung round, her fists clenched. 'Whose baby was it, Father? Johnny's, or Ruairidh's?'

The old man didn't answer her at once. He combed his white hair with the fingers of one hand, his eyes closed. She thought he might be praying. Then he said:

'We are both out of our depth and for the moment, I don't know what I can do to help you. The story you have told me is so completely outside my experience that I must think about it, and pray.' He didn't, she noticed, give her a homily on how she should pray too, nor indeed on how she should perhaps consider her lapsed faith. He had taken her problem on to his shoulders and looked for no return from her.

'I am certain that you will come out of this without any ill effect,' he went on. 'But I cannot see how or when. The workings of the mind are beyond our comprehension.' He smiled at her. 'I am not preaching to you, merely stating a fact, when I say that as long as we have faith, the good Lord will take care of us.' She lowered her eyes, uneasily, wondering if she should show some sort of piety and then knowing that he would spot insincerity a mile off. She gave a quick nod. He stood up.

'Go out and live your life as if nothing had happened,' he advised. 'For the moment it is all you can do. Go on with your research: who knows – you may unearth some clue that will give you back your identity.' He went over to one of the bookshelves, ran his hand along a row of books, pulling out several. 'Here, borrow these. Some of them are dry as dust, but they will give you some new slants on the clearing of the land.' He put them into her hands. 'Come and see me any time, and don't let this weigh on your mind too much. Try to . . . well, not forget, for that would be impossible . . . but try to fill your mind with your work, so that you aren't brooding too much. Solutions very often come to us when we are least expecting to find them.'

'Thank you Father.' She glanced down at the books. 'I'll look after them and return them to you. And thank you for not telling me I'm a hysterical colonial with a head full of fancy notions.' He chuckled.

'I'd not call you hysterical. On the contrary, I believe you are someone with a mind that goes deeper into things than most people. Away with you now, and get that sun into your bones. We don't often have such unbroken good weather here.' He ushered her into the entrance hall. 'God bless you now.'

He stood at the door of the presbytery, watching her as she walked away down the road, and when she turned at the corner, he was still there, one hand raised. She waved.

IV

She had at last managed to stop Peggy bringing her breakfast in bed and today was up before her host, eating home baked bread and honey and drinking Peggy's strong tea, when he appeared.

'How would a day on the water appeal to you?' he said, helping himself to porridge from a black pot on the stove. 'I have the use of Dr MacKay's boat and I rather like the idea of fishing.'

'Some mackerel would be nice,' observed Peggy, from the sink.

'Don't you have a surgery today?' Kat looked up from the book she had been reading, propped against the honey jar.

'No, emergencies only on Saturdays and it's far too nice a day for anyone to need a doctor.' He sat down at the table and reached for the tea pot. 'Anyway, I carry a pager. What about you Peggy? Would you come too?'

'Certainly not, thank you doctor. The sea turns my stomach quicker than thunder turns the milk.' She put toast on the table. 'And it might do the same for Catriona, I'm thinking, her being in convalescence.'

'I'm not too good in cabins, in a rough sea, like coming over in the steamer,' Kat admitted. 'But I'm fine in the open air. Anyway, it won't be rough on a day like this surely. I love sea fishing, and honestly, Peggy, I'm not convalescent any more. I feel as strong as an ox.' Peggy pursed her lips and looked at Rod.

'It'll do her good to get some sea air,' he said. 'Could you be a saint, Peggy, and fix us up with a picnic?' Foiled of her role as guardian nurse, Peggy threw herself busily into that of provider. She assembled a quantity of ingredients on the table and threw together a picnic substantial enough to feed a boatload of hungry men. Cheese baps, slices of yesterday's mutton, cake, biscuits, apples, oatcakes. Kat watched, as she finished her tea.

'Hey! I shall get as fat as a pig,' she said, as some scones were added to the pile. As she spoke, she remembered the last picnic she had had, or started to have – Flora Kate's. She pushed the thought aside and read a sentence from her book to fix her mind elsewhere.

'Bring plenty of sweaters,' Rod said. 'It can be bloody cold on the water.'

'Not on a day like this, surely?'

'Don't argue, woman.' He was preoccupied, collecting up what was needed into a cardboard carton. Fishing lines wound round wooden frames; hooks, weights, tools. 'Do you know where the mackerel are feeding, Peggy?' he asked, lifting a plastic map case with a chart inside from a drawer in the table.

'Out where they always are, by the MacKenzie rock.' He nodded. Kat felt useless, a child being given a treat by two adults. She started to clear the breakfast things off the table but Peggy elbowed her away from the sink.

'Away and get yourself ready, I can do the dishes after you've gone.'

'If you want to make yourself useful, you'll find a fish box round the side of the house,' Rod said. It was as if she was in the way. Almost sulkily, she fetched two sweaters and went outside into the sunshine. The box was heavy, even empty, and awkward to carry. She lugged it round to the front door and sat on it, looking down at the beach and the boat, apprehensive about having to spend a whole day alone with Rod. Since she had arrived she had hardly seen him except at supper time if he was not out on an urgent case, and they often ate whatever Peggy had left, in silence, each reading a book. And she had been in the habit of going straight to bed after supper, not so much from tiredness but in order to avoid being with him. They had had no proper conversation since that first evening when they had discovered a common taste for reading.

A pair of oyster-catchers flew past, their raucous cries filling the air. The old collie, Katie, came round the corner and flopped down at her feet. The sky was postcard blue and there was not a breath of wind.

It was a day to be happy in, not to brood and worry and let niggling questions torment her mind. She took a deep breath and resolved to do her best to enjoy herself and to be an amusing companion to her long-suffering host.

'There you are: good!' He erupted from the house, carrying a canvas bag and the fishing gear. 'Let's go.' Peggy appeared in the doorway.

'See you stay well wrapped up,' she said. 'Doctor, she can't carry that box on her own.'

'Of course I can,' she said, suddenly irritated by being so fussed over and then instantly ashamed. 'Thanks, Peggy. I'm fine.' She picked it up. 'See, strong as an ox!' She followed Rod down the hill to the beach, determined not to rest the box on a rock on the way. When she reached the boat she was panting, her arms ached and she had a stitch. He glanced at her.

'I hope you haven't done yourself a mischief?' he said. 'You should have let Peggy help you.'

The boat was on an ingenious system of ropes which enabled it to be pulled in to the stone jetty for loading, or out towards a mooring bouy with a ring in the top through which the bow rope ran. Rod untied a knot and pulled it in, stern first, steadying it against the seaweed-cushioned pier. Kat climbed in and took the stuff he handed down to her. It was an open, clinker built boat, about fifteen foot, sturdy and well maintained. She held on to the pier while he fiddled with the engine and then, on his instruction, pushed off and they were away.

She sat back and watched the land recede. The water was very clear; she could see a forest of weed, like another kingdom deep down; now and then a huge jelly fish floated past. The sun was hot on her face: she rolled up her sleeves and trailed a hand in the water. The engine puttered, leaving a trail of smoke over their wash. At first it was glass-calm, with barely a ripple. Then they rounded the point and ran into a swell: not waves but long, slow undulations that gave a pleasant roll to the boat.

'See those gannets?' Rod shouted, over the engine, pointing ahead of them. She followed his arm upwards and saw them, a pair of great white birds, high above. One came gliding down over the water in a graceful curve. 'Look, it's going to dive,' Rod said. She watched. It climbed up and up, hung for a moment and then plummeted like a streamlined rocket, into the sea.

'Wow! Could that really see a fish from right up there?' He shrugged.

'Seems impossible, but that's what they do.'

'Will we see it come up with whatever it caught?'

'It's too far away, but if we were closer, yes, probably.'

'So now we know where the fish are.'

'That's right.' When they were close to the large red buoy that marked the MacKenzie rock, he glanced at the fishing gear and said: 'Have you done this before?' She nodded. 'Would you like to get a line ready.'

She disentangled one of the lines, unravelled a trace of eight vicious-looking hooks and clipped a lead weight on to the end. She sat holding either end of the trace in her hands, careful to keep the hooks dangling free between. He was watching two points ashore, one on his right and one over his shoulder.

'When the hotel is between those two rocks,' he said, 'we'll start fishing.' He took a final bearing, cut the engine and said: 'Now. Line over.'

She held the hooks over the side and dropped them neatly

into the water, watching the weight spiral away downwards till it was out of sight.

'I can see you're an old hand,' Rod said, his fingers busy with a second line. Almost immediately, she felt a jerk, and another, and all at once her line was alive with movement. She gave it a sharp tug and began to pull it in, hand over hand, laying the wet line into a coil at her feet. She stared into the water as she pulled, she could see them, several of them, silvery shapes swimming round the line. The first one broke the surface, dancing on the end of its hook, a fine, big mackerel, its metallic, blue-green scales shining in the sun. Rod, already pulling in his own line, grinned across at her. He was as excited as a school boy.

'We're in among 'em' he said. 'Can you manage?'

'Sure.' She put her foot on the gunwhale, anchoring the rest of the line, still jumping with fish, gripped the first one and yanked it off the hook and into the box. Then she took up the next length of line and repeated the operation. Rod was now busy with his own fish.

'Five, good big ones, my God!' she gasped.

'Get your line back in woman,' he said, 'don't blether.' It was said affectionately, as if they were accomplices, filling her with a feeling of companionship she had not experienced with him before.

They had time for three hauls before the boat drifted past the feeding ground. The next cast produced no fish.

'Right, lines in;' Rod ordered. 'We'll do that sweep again.' With the lines coiled loosely inboard, he started the engine and took the boat back, watching the hotel and the two rocks. In the box, a couple of dozen fish flopped and gasped and lay still. A few gulls kept station with them, including a fulmar, lozenge-shaped and beady eyed, who flew just behind them, watching their movements.

They made the same run, over and over, until the fish-box was full. The sun was high in the sky; Kat's hands were slimy with fish and stung from the glutinous tendrils of jelly fish, that had got entangled in the line; the legs of her jeans were wet from dripping sea-water.

'That'll do,' Rod said. 'There's enough fish there to feed the whole glen tonight.' He looked relaxed and healthy as he leaned over the side and washed his hands in the sea. Wiping them on a rag, he looked across at her. 'How would you like to land and make a fire and have mackerel for lunch. They are never so delicious as when they are fresh out of the water.'

'But what about Peggy's picnic! She'll be mortally offended if we don't eat it all.'

'She won't know. What we can't eat we can philanthropically feed to the gulls!'

'That's a wicked waste.'

'Nonsense, gulls must eat!' He glanced down at the chart on the seat. 'Let's see – hmm . . . ' he looked up. 'Do you think it would be bad for you to go back to Rubha na h-Ordaig?' His eyebrow was raised. 'It might help you to throw off your – vision.' She hesitated. It would seem petty to say she would prefer not to risk another visit to the place that had had such a profound effect on her, particularly as he so clearly looked on it all as a dream and as such, best exorcised by a down-to-earth approach. She shrugged, trying to look casual.

'Sure, let's go. After all, I didn't get much of a chance to explore it, last time.'

'Except in your imagination.' She refused to be drawn. He started the engine again and headed the boat towards the land. The sea was navy blue, under the lee of the rock cliff and the swell was stronger as they rounded the point. Kat stared at the shore, trying, in spite of herself, to reconstruct what had happened. But all she saw was unfamiliar rocky coast, rising steeply to turf.

Then, as she gazed, her mind began to slip away again. I am Kat Macdonald, she repeated to herself, digging her nails into her palms, concentrating on her knowledge of herself.

'We can't go into the loch, the tide'll be going out soon and we'd get stuck in there,' Rod called, over the noise of the engine. 'We can beach the boat, further on, and walk over the ridge. OK?' She nodded, tense, her teeth clenched in desperation. I am Kat Macdonald: I am a Canadian: I am a student. I belong to the twentieth century. I travel in aeroplanes. Fiercely, she chanted her silent litany. This was crazy; she ought not to be here; Rod ought to see how dangerous it was for her. She glared at him, furious, but he didn't seem to notice.

The boat ran up on the stony sand. Rod jumped ashore and looped a rope round a rock. He put his shoulder against the bow, testing how easily he could push it down the beach when the tide went out.

'We'll have to keep an eye on it,' he said. 'Tide's just about on the turn now.'

'Where shall we make the fire?' she asked, reluctant to go away from the boat, her link with the present, towards where she remembered the ruined township to lie.

'Here, don't you think. But let's first go and explore the ruins.'

Every part of her cried: NO! But still she followed him, up over the ridge. The loch lay below them, with its backdrop of purple-blue hills, linked to the sea on the right by the long narrow passage between sheer cliffs, cut off at low tide by a wall of rock across the entrance. And opposite, half left, at the head of the loch . . . she felt that shifting of reason taking over . . . the softening of reality . . . the blurring of focus . . . the slipping away . . .

CHAPTER 13

. . . it was over . . . finished. She lay back on the improvised bed of heather and bracken, light-headed with exhaustion, weakened by loss, but no longer in pain. Beyond, curls of smoke still rose from the smouldering ruins of the houses and an acrid stench of burnt thatch lingered on the air.

There was no one to be seen, no person, no animals. Those who had not sailed had trundled their few belongings to some other place: to the old shielings and the abandoned kelp-workers' huts. There was just herself: herself and Ruairidh.

He came to her now, his face taut with worry. 'Why did you not tell me you were with child?' he said, bending over to smooth her hair from her brow.

'If you had known, what would you have done?' Her voice was a thin, distant whisper. She felt completely peaceful.

'I should have taken you back to Edinburgh with me, *mo gràdh*.' She smiled.

'That is why I didn't tell you; I knew that I wouldn't be able to earn my living. To support me and a child, you would have had to give up your training before you sat your final examinations. I could not have done that to you.' His hand gripped hers.

'O Catrìona, if you only knew what torture I went through, thinking your love had been just a passing thing. If I had only known why . . . '

'. . . you would have stopped me going and ruined your chances for the future.'

'And what sort of future do you suppose I would have had without you? Even if I had become the greatest surgeon in the country, it would have counted for nothing, without you.'

A glimmer of mischief lit her face. 'Well, now you have

the chance to become the greatest surgeon in the country and to have me beside you!'

The tension in him evaporated; he laid his cheek against hers. 'You will never know how happy you have made me, by coming back. Now, all things are possible. I love you.'

'And I love you.' Waves of sleep lapped over her. 'Soon I shall be strong again' she murmured. 'Strong enough to earn my living while you take your examinations.' As she drifted off, she was conscious only of the grip of his hand as he watched over her and a sensation of exquisite joy.

Later, in the darkness, she awoke. She was aware of his sleeping form beside her, and then of a terrible, warm, draining, flooding loss that she was powerless to staunch . . . she was too tired to wake him . . . too weak even to say his name . . .

II

'Kat!' She was slipping away . . . letting go . . . drifting . . . 'Kat!' a voice was trying to tug her back . . . she didn't want to come . . . 'Kat! She felt herself being jerked into consciousness. . . .

She was sitting on something hard, her head held down between her knees by a firm hand. 'Kat, are you all right?' She struggled and the pressure on the back of her neck eased at once. Carefully she lifted her head and peered around; Rod's anxious face swam before her eyes. Waves of dizzy nausea threatened to overpower her; she lowered her head into her hands. She still felt as if a part of her was trying to drift off into some other, far distant place but now she resisted, not wanting to go, sensing a threat of danger if she let go. Gradually her senses steadied, crystallised, brought her firmly back to now: she was aware only of the faint echo of something she could not place. And then that, too, faded and was lost.

'God! I feel awful! What happened?' Her head was a vortex.

'You fainted.' Rod's voice was close beside her, his hand on her shoulder. 'Kat, I'm sorry. I should never have brought you back here. How could I have been so stupid! I deserve to be struck off the register.' He sounded abject, and so he might she thought with a sudden revival of spirit.

'Look; can I lie flat? My head feels very peculiar.' His face was a blur; she screwed up her eyes to bring it into focus. 'Hey, don't look so worried. I've survived worse than this.' He supported her as she slid off the rock and lay down on the springy heather. She closed her eyes and lay perfectly still. The dizziness settled. 'That's better.' She waited, forcing herself to relax until the nausea had passed. Then she sneaked a look at him.

He was staring down at her with an extraordinary expression on his face, dazed and incredulous. 'Rod? What are you looking at me like that for?' She tried to jerk him out of his trance. 'You look as if you've seen a ghost for heaven's sake.' She snapped her fingers in front of his eyes. 'Hey, Rod! Wake up! I'm the one who sees ghosts, remember, not you!' He shivered, blinked, and shook his head violently, throwing off whatever it was that had transfixed him.

'Sorry. I . . . ' he stared down at her. A flash of intuition left her with the certainty that he had had some sort of experience while she had been unconscious. What had happened? She realised then that she herself felt considerably more orientated than she had for days. She reached out and prodded his arm.

'Listen! I guess you suddenly don't think I'm such a dreamer as you previously thought. Right?' Slowly, his eyes on hers, he nodded. 'OK, let's take it very slowly.' She was aware of a feeling of strong power; it was up to her to steer the course for the time being. He was newly into this extraordinary situation, this limbo of identity, if indeed he was now in the same state as herself. How much had he experienced, anyway, in that brief moment? Did he now know as much as she . . . ? And what did she know, anyway? She tried to recall what had happened to her during the time she had been in a faint, but that part of her mind was out of focus.

'Kat, there is one thing I've got to ask you.' He looked away towards the ruined township and then back to her. 'Was I . . . when you were ill and you had that . . . that

dream, vision, call it what you like, . . . was I a part of it?'
His forehead was creased with bewilderment.

'Yes.' She couldn't meet his eyes. 'Look, Rod, there's a
hell of a lot of talking we have to do,' she said, 'but not now.'
Again he shook his head. He looked so bemused that she felt
she had to reduce the situation to a semblance of normality,
until they could somehow untangle it.

'I guess I fainted, because this place has a bizarre effect on
me, and because we had a heavy time, fishing, and because
I lugged that stupid box just to show how big and strong I
am, and because I haven't yet quite recovered from having
been ill. That's all. Whatever happened to you, can keep
until later. OK? Right now, I think we need to build that
fire and cook those fish and forget about everything except
the present.'

She felt energy surging through her. All the effects of
her faintness had gone. For the first time since her fateful
picnic here, all those days ago, she felt wholly herself. Kat
Macdonald. She leapt to her feet and started to collect wood
for the fire. She snapped off silver twigs of dead heather and
made a pile of them against a rock. Rod didn't move. He sat
watching her, his face inscrutable. There was an abundance
of driftwood along the beach, branches, planks, a broken
fish box, a chair leg. She built up a fire, using a twist of
paper from the picnic bag. All the time, he watched her,
saying nothing.

'Girl scout, that's me,' she said brightly, trying to snap
him out of his reverie. 'Of course we never allow paper, at
home, but then I daresay these twigs are fairly damp.' She
sat back on her heels. 'There! How's that. All we need now
is a match.' She looked up at him. Suddenly, his face broke
into a grin. He, too, was himself again.

'You don't mean to tell me you've gone to all that trouble,
and you haven't got a match?' he said. Ruefully, she shook her
head. 'Don't girl scouts learn how to make fire by rubbing
sticks together, or magnifying the sun's rays through glass,
or whatever it was Robinson Crusoe did?'

'Not this girl scout. Anyway, whose idea was it to have a

fire in the first place? Not mine and that's for sure. Come on doctor, I bet you've got matches hidden about your person.' He reached into the sail bag and produced Peggy's picnic.

'If Peggy hasn't put in a box of matches, I'm prepared to pay a forfeit,' he said. 'That woman is superhuman.'

Sure enough, there was a box, inside a tin which also contained a firelighter. 'Peggy doesn't believe in girl scouts,' he said, tossing the box across to her.

She lit the paper and watched as he selected two mackerel from the boat and laid them on a rock by the edge of the sea. He took a penknife from his pocket, opened it, tested the blade with his thumb, and gutted the fish quickly and neatly.

'I suppose all doctors are pretty good at disembowling things,' she observed. He gave a shout of laughter.

'I'm not sure that the great Mr Peterson who instructed me in the art of dissection, would have been all that happy with the comparison,' he retorted, washing the fish in the water and shaking them dry.

'We don't have a pan,' she said.

'Some girl scout, you.' He stirred the fire and slid a flattish rock into the heart of it. 'When the flames die down a bit, put them on that and they'll cook in a trice.'

They sat near the fire, the sun hot on their faces, the gentle surge of the sea in the background. High overhead a transatlantic jet drew a thin vapour trail across the sky. They avoided any reference to what had happened. Rod delved into the picnic bag and produced two cans of lager. He held one out to her and as she took it from him, their fingers met. He withdrew his hand so sharply she almost dropped the can. For a second, as their eyes met, she saw his eyebrow twitch in an almost imperceptible look of enquiry. Ignoring it, she tugged at the ring on the can, opened it and tipped it to her mouth.

'Delicious!' She leaned back against a rock. 'Who could ever want to live anywhere else?' She kept her tone deliberately neutral.

'Idyllic on a day like this, I grant you, but you might

feel differently if you lived here all the year round,' he said, feeding wood on to the fire. 'In the winter, when days are short, it can be damp and cold and wild.'

'Which part of the island were you born in?'

'Up in the north. My father was an architect working for the army in Benbecula.'

'Is it as beautiful, up there?'

'Not so beautiful as this bit.' He dropped the two fish on to the rock in the fire and adjusted them with a stick.

'Was that where your ancestors came from?' She regretted the words as she spoke them; neither of them were ready for analysis yet. He faced her across the fire.

'No. My ancestors came from here, same as yours, as you know perfectly well.'

Trying to sound normal, she said, 'Do you know what happened to them?' He didn't answer, just gave a slight shrug and busied himself with the fish.

Once again the present began to shift, reality softening at the edges, splinters of glass distorting her reason. She clung on to 'Now', biting the inside of her lips. She was, on the brink of discovery: she was sure that she was close to the key that might release her from her emotionless void and she was equally sure that if she took a false step she might finish up on the wrong side of sanity. These changes that had been tormenting her were becoming more and more frequent, more and more confusing. Even now, looking at Rod bent over the fire, turning the mackerel on the stone, she saw Ruairidh, the flames lighting his lean face, his shock of black hair stirring in the breeze, his hands deft with the two sticks . . . .

'I am Kat Macdonald, I am Canadian, I am alive. This is Now!'

'What?' Rod's eyebrow was raised: she must have spoken aloud. 'What did you say?'

'Nothing, sorry: just chuntering to myself.' She must keep a grip on herself. Strange wisps of unreality hovered in her mind. But still she couldn't drag herself away from her obsession.

'Rod: do you know of anyone on the island who I can talk to, who might be able to tell me something about my ancestors?' She stopped him, as he started to speak. 'I know I'm becoming a dead bore, but, well . . . if I don't get it sorted out in my mind soon, I think I shall blow a fuse.' She held his eyes with her own. 'I think you know what I mean, now?' His eyes never left her face as he nodded. 'I think we should not try to discuss . . . well . . . to talk about the past, until we can talk to someone outside it all.' It sounded so jumbled, but she knew he knew what she meant and that he agreed.

'The Bard,' he said. 'John MacFie. He might be able to tell you. He's ninety odd and his father was alive in those times.'

'Bard? I thought..?'

'They call him the Bard. He writes Gaelic poetry, has had lots published. Almost a seer, is John.'

'Please. Will you take me to him?'

III

John MacFie, the Bard, lived in one of the few surviving thatched houses, set back off the road in a fold of the hill. It was more sophisticated than a black house, in that it had rooms with ceilings and a chimney at one end, but its outside appearance was much the same, with the rounded corners and the reed–thatch without gable ends, anchored with stones tied to rope. Even Kat had to stoop to go in through the door, set in the thick wall.

The Bard, in spite of his age, was upright and lucid, with all his senses intact. He had an aristocratic face, beaky with a long chin, and faded, far away eyes.

'Come in and welcome,' he greeted them, ushering them into the kitchen where the floor was a strip of linoleum over the rough earth, so that here and there pebbles had broken the surface. A dresser was stacked with functional kitchenware, the table was strewn with papers and books, a dog lay in front of the Rayburn whose door was open.

Kat was offered the only chair. Rod sat on the bench under the window, and the Bard, having moved a kettle on to the stove, took up his stance propped against the front of it. His voice had the same gentle cadence as all the island voices.

'Indeed, my father was alive then, but he was just a bairn, too young to remember. His father it was, who used to tell us the stories of how they lived, then; he lived to be nearly a hundred and he never lost his memory or his reason.'

'What happened to the people who didn't emigrate?' Kat asked.

'There was various things for them to do, but it was hard times for some of them, with their land taken from them. Many people suffered hunger and poverty.' He had a sonorous voice and a gift for oratory; it was like listening to a composed sermon. 'There was road building – destitution roads they called them because they were built to give employment, and there was the fishing. They were sending shiploads of salted fish as far as Odessa, on the Black sea, I believe.' The Bard's smile was full of dry humour. 'You'd think they had enough salt fish of their own, there!' He lifted the lid from the kettle and peered inside.'The kelp was pretty nearly a dead thing by then of course, that was most of the trouble.' He looked at his audience to discover if they knew what he was talking about. 'You will know that when the kelp was a thriving industry, the proprietors encouraged people to come to the islands to provide cheap labour, and because the work was so hard, no one had time to see to their land apart from growing potatoes and keeping a few beasts. And so, when the kelp market collapsed, there were too many people on poor and inadequate land.'

'Why did the kelp market fail?' Kat had not intended to encourage a history lesson, wanting to lead the old man back to more specific memories, but his rich voice was a pleasure to listen to and he spoke from his heart, so that what he said shook off the dust of history books and came alive.

'After the Napoleonic Wars, they lifted import duties and other countries were able to provide raw materials cheaper than kelp. It was the Spanish, I believe, who were mainly to blame. Fortunes were lost, that is for sure.' He sounded delighted.

'So your family didn't emigrate?'

'There was no need. My grandfather was an educated man, having taken instruction with the laird's children. He in his turn was able to teach, for which he was paid a little, and he acted as scribe for those who could not write. In those times, when many had already gone away, folk liked to keep in touch with their exiled families and many letters were sent backwards and forwards across the ocean.'

'Would your grandfather have remembered people like my ancestors who went to Canada on *The Admiral*, in 1851?'

'Certainly he would have known them, if they came from this part of the island.'

'I believe they came from a township out by . . . by Rubha na h-Ordaig.' Her voice faltered, so important, now, was her quest. She sensed the tension in Rod, who had not moved or spoken since they had settled in the kitchen; who had been distracted ever since she had fainted and who now watched her with fascinated, bewildered eyes. 'All I know is that one of them was called Frangan Macdonald.'

'There was plenty of them,' he said. 'Macdonalds, I mean. In the old days, it was Macdonalds who ruled the island and all the clan were related to the chief or took his name.'

'Yes, I know. But this Frangan Macdonald had a twin sister, Catrìona, which could make it easier to identify him.'

'Frangan and Catrìona Macdonald? Yes.' She held her breath, willing him to remember. He searched his mind, rubbing his forehead with fingers bent with arthritis. 'Yes, there is something there. Wait, while I think.' As if to fuel his memory, he took a dented aluminium teapot from the dresser, spooned a generous helping of tea into it and filled it with water from the kettle. He stirred the contents vigorously, muttering the two names over and over to himself. His guests sat, motionless, silent, tense, watching his every move. He poured the tea into mugs, added milk from a tin and sugar from a bag and handed one to each of them. Then he took up his own and resumed his stance in front of the Rayburn.

'Yes, there was a story about those two,' he said. 'It is coming back to me. They went on the ship, both of them, quite young, they were. I think their mother had died. There was some story about one of the factor's agents going missing and maybe Frangan Macdonald had had a hand in it, something of the kind. Anyway, they sailed.'

'Both of them?'

'I believe so. Yes, now I remember the story. Frangan came back, at the turn of the century, when I was too young to remember. That's right. He came back to look for his sister. It came out that when the ship sailed, Catrìona had jumped into the sea and swum ashore. The ship sailed on without her.'

'What happened to her?' Kat's voice was barely audible, her heart seemed to have stopped beating as she waited for his answer.

'Well that is the strange thing. I don't know. Things were very confused at that time, with the people going and the people left behind. Everyone was looking after themselves and not too concerned with what other folk were doing. All I can tell you is that there was talk of a lover, and a bairn. That's all. If I said any more, it would be conjecture. But I can tell you this. Frangan didn't find his sister, nor could anyone tell him what had happened to her. Either they did not know, or they did not choose to tell. Whatever the reason, he discovered nothing. He went back over the sea and was never heard of again.'

A peat shifted in the fire, sending up sparks. The dog stood up, stretched and lay down again.

Rod spoke and Kat was very conscious of his eyes on her face.

'John, did you ever hear tell of my ancestors at that time?'

'Campbells? There was plenty of them, too. Your own family left the island right enough, but I don't think they went to Canada. I believe one of them was a doctor, like yourself.' He gulped down his tea. 'It was your own father who came back to live here.'

'Yes.'

'Do you think there is anyone who might know what happened?' Kat pleaded, seeing her last chance slipping away. 'To Catrìona, I mean.'

'If Frangan couldn't discover, all those years ago, I'm thinking you aren't likely to do so now.' The shrewd old eyes bored into hers. He spoke again, in Gaelic. The words meant nothing to Kat: a jumble of foreign sounds, no more.

'What does that mean?' she asked. He jerked his head at Rod, who answered for him.

'It means, that the past is the past, over and finished, and it is up to each of us to go forward, and pursue our destiny.'

Desolation settled over Kat; the Bard had failed to give her the key to her prison. She was still locked in her limbo, a person without a soul. And now, with her last hope gone, she faced a future in which she would never find her identity, never know human emotion again; eternity in a void.

IV

Outside in the sunshine, it was as if the Bard had woven a spell round them; as if they were both being driven by some external force that had taken control of them. Without looking at each other, without speaking, they began to walk, not back towards the house, but away down to where the road ended and the track out to Rubha na h-Ordaig began. Like two spectres, they strode on, taking the route Kat had followed, that first time. The heather was in full flower, now, and the golden eagles were still there, circling high over their eyrie. Up over the ridge they went, down into the valley, through the peaty bog, over the rough, stony track. Past the lochans, along the burn and over the stepping stones.

They were two shadows, without substance, now climbing up into the hills towards the caves. Not one word had either of them spoken since they had said goodbye to the Bard. Linnets, skylarks, wheatears, darted out from under their feet. Sheep ran from them, rabbits popped into holes, grouse exploded, whirring, and flew out of range. They were no more animated than people on a picture postcard, nor the scene more real: the blue sky, the purple heather, the lichen on the rocks and the two figures in jeans and tartan shirts, hiking up the path.

They stopped in front of the cave, and faced each other. He reached out and took her hand, his face blank, his touch ethereal. Hand in hand, two human bodies without souls, emotionless, they walked round from the cave to the south-facing plateau.

Very slowly, as if they were moving under water, they came to their knees before one of the flattish rocks embedded in the turf. He took a penknife from his pocket and scraped lichen from the stone surface, carefully, wiping away the loose, silvery flakes. She took up a heather twig and rubbed. Gradually, words could be seen. Gaelic words, followed by a name, Donald Henderson, August 1851. In silence, they turned to the second stone and cleared it, too, of its shroud of lichen. Màiri Macdonald, they read, August 1851.

She turned away; she was weeping but she felt nothing. Tears of despair, without comprehension. Alone, he moved past her, beyond the two stones to where a third one lay, almost covered in moss, at an angle to the others. Alone, he cleared it and read the inscription. She stood, watching, hesitating. He reached out a hand towards her.

She walked across and bent to read the engraved words. She was conscious only of an icy coldness that pervaded her. Catrìona Macdonald, she read. August, 1851. She was shaking uncontrollably, her tears falling without check, a whirling tornado of splintered glass torturing her mind. She felt a loneliness so intense that it threatened to overwhelm her.

Rod lifted his head; his voice rang out over the hillside.

'*Requiém ætérnam dona eis, Dómine.* Rest eternal grant unto them Lord.' Her voice joined his: '*Et lux perpétua lúceat eis. Requiéscant in pace, Amen* And let perpetual light shine upon them. And may they rest in peace.'

For a moment she suffered an agony so searing that she felt she was being literally ripped apart. She heard herself scream, an unearthly, primal cry that echoed round the crags and dissolved into the atmosphere.

And then she was in his arms, clinging to him, and he was soothing her, calming her, murmuring into her hair and she didn't know why she was weeping because waves of relief billowed and surged in her heart.

V

'I still don't really understand.' Kat lay beside him on the summit above the cave, the whole island spread out below them. She was propped on an elbow, teasing his profile with her finger. 'All this love that has been locked up; I knew it was there, should be there, but I couldn't feel anything. I could remember, all the time, what I had felt for you – the intensity of it – but I couldn't bring it back.'

'Did you try? I thought you were rather a cold fish to begin with.' He grabbed her hand as she tweaked his nose.

'I didn't exactly try, but it bothered me that I could remember . . . well, all sorts of rather . . . er . . . disturbing details about how it had been in those days . . . and yet I remained completely detached.'

'Tell me some of the disturbing details.'

'Certainly not!'

'Pity. I don't want to get it wrong, second time round.'

'Who says there will be a second time round! Tell me something, Roderick Campbell: do you by any chance have a scar, high up on the inside of your thigh?'

'I do, Catrìona Macdonald and I shan't be surprised if you tell me your fingers are all too familiar with it!'

She looked into his eyes. 'What did you see, when I fainted?'

'Hard to explain, except that you will understand because of what was happening to you. As you conked out I had this vivid awareness of the whole story of our shared past. It was like a sort of blinding flash of enlightenment. It was so quick that I can't really describe what I saw. But all I can say is that in that brief moment I knew everything that had happened. And like you, I didn't know who I really was.'

'That was the most frightening part, the fear that one

might never be one whole person again.' She stared out over the sound, watching a fishing boat. 'Poor Catrìona: I suppose in some strange way she never quite broke free . . . until you liberated her just now . . . so when I came back looking for her . . . oh, I don't understand!'

'Perhaps we shall never completely understand. It doesn't matter now, does it?' He looked up at her, his eyes alight with love and laughter, and the closeness of him sent shocks of feeling through her body.

She laid her head on his chest, hugging him, choked with an exquisite, unfamiliar emotion she greeted raptuously, as love.

'Darling Rod. No, of course it doesn't matter any more.' She let her lips move lightly across his face to the corner of his mouth. 'Even so,' she murmured, 'I can't help wondering . . . can you?'

A skylark soared overhead and in the distance, a dog barked. The air was fragrant with the scent of wild thyme and clover.

Hours passed.

'Rod,' she said.

'Mmm.' He was drowsy in her arms.

'Just one thing more.'

'Mmm.'

'Your ancestor, Ruairidh. What happened to him?' Rod opened one eye and grinned at her, the eyebrow shooting upwards.

'He went back to Edinburgh, passed all his examinations and became one of the top surgeons of his day.'

'Did he ever get married?' She saw his glint of amusement and made a face at him. 'Not that it matters, of course . . . '

'No, *mo gràdh*, it does not matter.' He fingered a strand of her hair and tucked it behind her ear. Her silence forced him to go on.'He mourned his Catrìona for the rest of his life, but he was lonely and he needed someone to keep house for him and sit at the head of his table when he entertained.' She waited, now wanting only the knowledge of Ruairidh's happiness. 'When he was in his forties, he married the widow of a close friend. She was kind and comfortable and rather plump, if family history and pictures are to be believed.' Kat knew he was laughing at her but still she persisted.

'Did they . . . were there any children?'

'One son – my grandfather. They called him Rory.' He leant over her, his face close to hers. 'And that is where we shall leave them. As the Bard said: the past is the past, over and finished and it is up to each of us to go forward and pursue our destiny.' He murmured, against her lips, 'and I propose to pursue my destiny, with your co-operation, to a very satisfactory, happy, permanent conclusion.'